PE

The Family Secret

Fiona Palmer lives in the tiny rural town of Pingaring in Western Australia, three and a half hours south-east of Perth. She discovered Danielle Steel at the age of eleven, and has now written her own brand of rural romance. She has attended romance writers' groups and received an Australian Society of Authors mentorship for her first novel, *The Family Farm*. She has extensive farming experience, does the local mail run, and was a speedway-racing driver for seven years. She spends her days writing, working as a farmhand, helping out in the community and looking after her two children.

fionapalmer.com

PRAISE FOR FIONA PALMER

'A delightful piece of rural romance.'
BALLARAT COURIER

'A rollicking romance that will have readers cheering
on the heroine . . . Evokes the light, people, atmosphere
and attitudes of a small country town.'
WEEKLY TIMES

'A moving story that reveals the beauty of the bush and
the resilience of rural communities during times of hardship.'
QUEENSLAND COUNTRY LIFE

'A good old-fashioned love story.'
SUNDAY MAIL BRISBANE

'Palmer's characterisation of the town's many colourful
identities is delightful and will bring a smile to those who
have experienced country life.'
WEST AUSTRALIAN

'A heartwarming romance about finding true love and
following your dreams.'
FEMAIL.COM.AU

'Distinctly Australian . . . heartwarming and enjoyable . . .
a well-written and engaging read.'
BOOK'D OUT

'A great addition to your shelf if you love strong
characters and beautiful Aussie landscapes.'
THE AUSTRALIAN BOOKSHELF

FIONA PALMER

The Family Secret

PENGUIN BOOKS

PENGUIN BOOKS

UK | USA | Canada | Ireland | Australia
India | New Zealand | South Africa | China

Penguin Books is part of the Penguin Random House group of companies
whose addresses can be found at global.penguinrandomhouse.com.

Penguin
Random House
Australia

First published by Penguin Random House Australia Pty Ltd, 2016
This edition published by Penguin Random House Australia Pty Ltd, 2017

1 3 5 7 9 10 8 6 4 2

Text copyright © Fiona Palmer 2016.

Cover design by Laura Thomas © Penguin Random House Australia Pty Ltd
Text design by Samantha Jayaweera © Penguin Random House Australia Pty Ltd
Cover photographs: Woman: Mark Webster/Getty Images; Man: PeopleImages/Getty
Images; Landscape: konradlew/Getty Images; Sky: Indigo Storm Photography
Internal photograph: Mimosa: Diana Taliun/Shutterstock
Typeset in Sabon by Samantha Jayaweera, Penguin Random House Australia Pty Ltd
Colour separation by Splitting Image Colour Studio, Clayton, Victoria
Printed and bound in Australia by Griffin Press, an accredited ISO AS/NZS
14001 Environmental Management Systems printer.

National Library of Australia Cataloguing-in-Publication data is available.

Palmer, Fiona, author
The family secret/Fiona Palmer
9780143787099 (paperback)

Romance fiction
Families–Fiction

penguin.com.au

MIX
Paper from
responsible sources
FSC® C009448

To Ned and Bob, plus all the other Vets
who spent time in Vietnam

In memory of Joyce Palmer

Chapter 1

'BLOODY rain. It's harvest, for crying out loud.' Kim cursed as she peered through her windscreen into the darkness. The wipers whipped on the fastest setting but struggled to keep up with the deluge. The crazy storm had set the radio crackling, and the sound grated on Kim's tightly bound nerves. She snapped off the radio and looked up just as a body of water appeared on the gravel road ahead. 'Crap!'

Kim wasn't going very fast but the floodway was not something she wanted to rush into at any speed. She stopped just at the edge of the lapping water, the idling motor hardly audible over the rain on the roof of her ute. She checked the water level against the bushes at the sides of the road, and deemed it just low enough to pass through. Slowly she entered the floodway.

It had started raining this morning, which of course made it the perfect time to drive 80 kilometres to pick up a belt for her header. Normally parts would come by post, but somehow it had ended up being sent with another farmer's order. In the bush it was sometimes quicker just to drive and pick it up yourself rather than wait for it to be reposted.

Kim sighed as she crept across the washed-out road, the ute lurching on unseen potholes. She hadn't taken this back road home in years. She'd hoped to save time, but now she remembered, of course, that it was prone to flooding. So much for a shortcut.

The area was surrounded by salt lakes. Neighbouring towns weren't called Lake Grace and Lake Biddy for no reason. When heavy rain came, especially when the ground was rock hard, the water would flow along the gullies and over roads in no time – but no one had expected this much rain to drop so suddenly in summer. Three more days and the harvest would have been finished.

Kim wanted to see how far the water had risen up the side of her ute, but darkness surrounded her. Before too long she made it to the other side without any water inside the cab, but from what she could tell, the floodwaters were still rising. Any later and she wouldn't have made it through.

Eager to get home, she drove on, the headlights making the trees' leaves glisten and the dark trunks shimmer. It really was a pretty sight, especially during such a long, hot harvest. But Kim would have appreciated it ten times more if it had happened just a few days later, with enough time to get the crop off. Now they'd be set back at least a week – not to mention the possibility of sprouting and staining on their grain. To top it off, her brother Matt had sent her a text earlier telling her they'd had hail. His message had been more swear words than anything else.

A murky, watery mass appeared before her – another floodway.

Kim stopped at the edge and mumbled a curse. This one looked deeper and was running faster than the last. Getting out of the vehicle, Kim made her way to the water's edge. The ute lights drilled holes into the night, allowing her to see the full force of the flow.

'Damn it.' Her options were to try to cross, to go back through the other floodway again or to stay here for the night. None sounded much fun. She'd been lucky to get through the first floodway as it was. By morning the water should ease off and the road would be passable – it was just a matter of waiting it out. As her shirt started to soak through, she bent down to pick up a stick to throw in frustration. But while she did so she heard a dreaded sound – *plop!* – as her mobile phone slipped from her top pocket into the water.

'Oh, shit! Dave.' Kim fished her phone out of the water and tried to dry it on the underside of her blue checked flannel shirt as she went back to the ute.

Her phone, a Telstra Dave, had been cursed since the day she got it. Sure, Telstra Dave came with waterproof Gorilla Glass, but that meant zilch since Kim had dropped the phone three weeks ago, shattering the screen. Some sticky tape held most of the glass in place, but waterproof it wasn't. Kim sat in the ute, slammed the door shut and turned on the dim interior light. Some chunks of the screen were now missing and moisture dripped from the cracks. The screen was blank. 'Bloody hell.' Kim threw it to the passenger side and hit the steering wheel with her hand. Today was not her day. Now she couldn't even call her brother and let him know what was happening.

Kim tilted her head back and groaned. What to do? She knew she was probably next to Tom Murphy's land and thought about walking to his house, but the stories of Tom's creepy worker soon put her off that idea. Plus it was pitch dark and she didn't know which direction to head. She'd rather stay in her ute all night, wet, than run into Crazy Harry on a night like this.

Ten minutes later, still cursing the rain and Dave, she noticed headlights bouncing their way towards her. They weren't on the road though – the lights were coming from her right, in a nearby paddock. Was it Tom out checking that his stock hadn't been washed away? The lights drew closer until a ute pulled up on the other side of the fence line. Kim got out and shielded her eyes from the glare. The rain was easing off.

'G'day,' yelled out a friendly voice. A tall stocky man walked towards the fence, a wide-brimmed hat protecting his head.

Kim ventured forwards. 'Hi.' She tried to see if this was Tom Murphy, whom she'd met on a few occasions in Lake Grace when collecting chemical and other farming supplies, but she struggled to make a match in the dark.

'You'll be stuck now,' the man said, stating the obvious, his hands resting on his hips. 'For a good while too. Did you want to come back to the house and get out of the wet? This won't be passable until early morning. You're welcome to camp the night.'

'Is there no other way out? Any access through the farm?'

'Sorry, lass, there isn't. I know this place like the back of my hand, and when she floods, there ain't nothin' you can do about it. There's a hot stew on the fireplace, if you're hungry?'

It had to be Tom. His wife's cooking was legendary. After all, she was the president of the local CWA. Kim's belly rumbled at the mere thought of food. It was almost loud enough to match the low thunder.

'Sure, that sounds great, thanks.' Kim couldn't find any excuse not to. Besides, she could ask to use his phone to call Matt. She headed towards the man and climbed over the fence. 'Thanks so much for your kindness,' she said. 'I'm Kim.'

She held out her hand as a flash of lightning erupted across the sky, illuminating the man in front of her. Her heart raced as she saw a scar twisted across his face, and a feeling of dread shuddered through her. This was not Tom Murphy. And if it wasn't Tom, then the only other person it could be was his worker, and that meant . . .

Kim swallowed hard as his hand slid into hers and shook it. No, it couldn't be Hermit Harry – or Crazy Harry, as some liked to call him. He was almost folklore – whispered about at bonfires or by the torchlight at sleepovers to scare everyone. No one had seen Hermit Harry – not in town, not at church, not anywhere – but they'd seen his ute driving around Tom Murphy's farm. When she was growing up, the older kids had claimed he was burying dead bodies. There were kids who liked to sneak up on his house at night as a dare, to try to catch a glimpse of him, but the shotgun fired over their heads had put an end to that. Someone must have got a good look, though, as Kim had heard the nickname 'Scarface' used to describe him. She could only imagine how scary it must have been for a kid to encounter this man at night. Hell, she was terrified now and she was twenty-seven!

'Call me Harry,' he said.

Bloody hell. Kim's knees trembled as she tried to keep her breathing normal.

'Come on. Jump in and get out of the wet.'

Kim watched him move to his ute but her feet remained planted to the spot. Her mind raced with ways to back out of the invitation. Maybe she should say her brother was on his way, and that she'd better stay put. Then she realised she was letting the stories of her youth get to her. If he really was that terrifying, why would Tom Murphy have employed him all these years? Maybe Hermit Harry was just that: a hermit who didn't like to go off farm? He might have scared away kids with his shotgun, but no one had ever been shot.

Giving Harry the benefit of the doubt, Kim walked towards his ute and tried not to think about her possible impending death and muddy gravesite.

Chapter 2

'YOU'RE lucky I found you,' said Harry as Kim climbed into his ute. 'I was just doing a quick check on the sheep and happened to see your lights.'

Right now Kim was wondering just how lucky she was. *Unlucky* seemed to be more appropriate. She could blame her phone, or the farmer who had her spare part, or even the postal mob for sending it to him in the first place – or she could blame the heavens for the bloody rain, which had set this whole sequence of events in motion. She should have stayed home. But now she was sitting in Hermit Harry's ute.

'Thank you,' she said. A silence fell that Kim was keen to fill. 'Were the sheep okay?'

'Yeah, they were all up on the high ground. They'll be fine there. I just like to double-check. So where're you from, Kim?'

Oh no. Was he trying to find out if she had family waiting for her? 'Um, I'm from Lake Biddy way. I work the family farm with my brother, Matt Richards.'

'Ah, yep. I recall a David Richards. Tom bought his seeder bar a few years back. Is that your family?'

Kim nodded. 'Yep, that's my dad.'

They drove through the darkness, Harry steering with precise knowledge of the land. He'd slow down for bumps that Kim couldn't see, but she'd feel the ute lurch a moment later.

'Did you finish the harvest before the rain?' he asked.

'No, and we only had a few days to go.'

'Bloody typical. Mother Nature loves to remind us who's in charge.'

Kim almost smiled. He certainly had that right. For a hermit, Harry was friendly enough. Mind you, Kim had no prior experience of hermits. This was all new territory.

Soon Kim could see a light, and a small house loomed into sight. It had a tin roof and a large shrubby garden blocking any real view of the dwelling.

Harry parked in a lean-to off to the side of the house. The verandah light was on, and another sensor one flashed on when they pulled up. She saw two kelpie dogs by the door, wagging their tails.

'Don't mind the girls. They're friendly. The black and tan is Molly and the red one is Bindi.'

As Kim got out both dogs barked at the visitor, but on noticing Harry they forgot Kim and rushed up to him.

'See, I wasn't gone long,' he said, patting them. 'This is Kim.'

Kim had never been introduced to dogs before but both wandered over to her and had a sniff up and down her jeans. 'Bet you can smell a lot of animals on there.' Kim smiled. 'I have two pet sheep, a kangaroo and a kelpie called Jo.'

'And I thought I had a few pets,' said Harry with a chuckle. 'Come on. Let's get inside.' He walked to the door and kicked off his boots.

The verandah was covered with pot plants and had been swept clean. Kim thought hermits lived in derelict homes, not real houses with well-tended gardens and pot plants that needed regular attention. She could feel her guard starting to drop.

She took off her own boots and followed Harry inside. His hat came off the moment he walked in the door, exposing thin greying hair. The lights were on and the house was warm. A delicious aroma filled the air. Inside his house was tidy – probably cleaner than her own house, Kim thought. The furniture was old but well cared for, and rugs covered the jarrah floorboards. The only obviously new thing was the TV. She'd half expected some square, heavy, old-fashioned TV, or none at all. Maybe Harry sat in the blue chair with the worn arms watching *House Husbands* like the rest of Australia? Or maybe *Game of Thrones* was more to his taste? Actually, going by Harry's house, Kim guessed *Better Homes and Gardens* would be more his style.

On the wall sat a large black IKEA bookshelf with rows and rows of books. She would have loved to have seen what he liked reading. Romance? Or thrillers? But it was the sight of two more dogs on the couch that caught her attention as they observed her with interest.

'Ah, the old girl is Pepper. I've had her for a long time so she gets the special treatment. The other one is Jess – she's terrified of storms, which is the only time she gets to come inside. Make yourself at home,' he said, before heading off into the kitchen.

Kim could see Jess, the younger dog, was shaking, the tan patches above her eyes almost quivering too. Kim stepped over and rubbed her ears. 'It's okay, Jess.' The older dog with the same tan patches crawled across the couch towards them, hoping for some love as well. Kim obliged and gave her a scratch on the neck.

'Jess is one of Pepper's babies,' said Harry as he came back in. 'I kept Jess 'cos she was the spittin' image of Pepper.' He nervously held out a bundle of linen. 'There's a towel in case you want a shower or just to dry off,' he said. 'And some clean sheets for your room.'

Kim took them and followed him down a passage. He stopped by a door.

'You can camp here for the night. It's only been used on the odd occasion, say if we have a good year and Tom gets in a Pommy worker to help out. Other than that it stays empty, so I'm sorry about the dust and spiders. I don't usually venture in here.'

Harry's hands fidgeted by his sides and his eyes twitched nervously. In the light of the passage Kim had time to really study him. Besides the scar, his face was tanned and lined with wrinkles, like most men of the land who worked long hours in the sun. Yet his brown eyes appeared kind, not worthy of fear. If anything, *he* seemed fearful. Probably because he wasn't used to having new people around. She thought he was doing all right, considering. He must get enough interaction with Tom to keep up his social skills.

'Thank you,' she said. 'It's greatly appreciated.'

'Yes, no worries. Right. Um, bathroom is at the end of the hallway, toilet is outside at the end of the verandah in the washhouse. I'll go and check on dinner. Should be ready in ten.'

He turned and headed back to the kitchen before she could utter another word.

Kim opened the door and walked into the spare room. It was simply furnished, with a single bed. The floorboards were worn and the walls painted in flaking cream paint, while the patterned curtains looked like they'd dissolve if they were ever washed. The old spring mattress had a few stains, but the sheets in her arms were clean. Quickly she dried her hair with the towel and then made the bed. Her shirt was still damp but would dry quickly in the warm house. There was no way Kim was going to have a shower here.

Knuckles rapped against her door. She turned to find Harry there holding a pile of blankets.

'You might need these.'

He didn't step into the room so Kim went and took the blankets, placing them on the end of the bed. 'Thanks. Hey, Harry, do you have a phone I can use to call my brother, to let him know I'm okay?'

'Yes, sure. This way.'

He led her to another room, much the same size as the one she'd left, fitted out as an office with a simple desk, an old filing cabinet, some photos on the wall and an ancient computer. The brown patterned carpet looked like it hadn't been changed since the house was built.

'Phone's just there,' he said, pointing to the old handset sitting on the desk. She had the same one at home tucked in a cupboard for when the power went out and her portable ones didn't work.

'Cheers, Harry.'

He left her, and as she sat down Kim wondered who Harry called on this phone. Did he have family? Did they ever visit him? Or was this just to talk to Tom?

Picking up the receiver, she pressed it against her ear and dialled her brother's number.

'Y'ello,' came his deep voice.

Kim had been half expecting Lauren to answer, but she was probably busy making tea or getting the kids into the shower or even bed. It was nearly eight-thirty.

'Hey, bro. It's me.'

'Hey, sis. All sorted with the part? Wanna bring it up?'

'Actually, I'm not home yet,' she said.

'What? What are you doing?'

'I got stuck between the floodways out near Tom Murphy's place.'

'Ah, shit. Want me to come and get you?'

'No, I'm okay. Someone came and picked me up.' Kim wasn't sure if she should mention who. She didn't want him to worry.

'Tom? Is he bringing you home or you camping the night? I can come get you if you need.'

Matt was a good brother. He wasn't just her brother, he was her partner in the family farm, and he respected her completely. The feeling was mutual – she held her brother up on a gold pedestal. They'd been close growing up, and not once had he baulked at sharing the farm with her once their parents retired. In his eyes, it had been fifty-fifty right from the get-go. She was lucky her parents had felt the same and were so supportive of her desire to be a farmer, which wasn't always the case for their generation.

'No, we're landlocked at the moment. Can't get in or out. I'm staying with Harry for the night. He'll take me back to the ute in the morning once the water's dropped. I just wanted to let you know before you sent out a search party. I couldn't text 'cos I dropped Dave in the water.'

'Bloody Dave. I told you he'd be trouble.' Matt always teased her about Dave, which was the second one she'd owned after she'd accidentally run over her previous phone. 'Hope you never treat your men like you do your phones, sis,' he'd once told her.

'Hang on – did you just say you were staying with Harry? Who's Harry?'

Kim couldn't find a way to answer him.

'Kim? Shit, is that Hermit Harry? Tom's worker Harry?'

'Yes, that's the one.'

'Oh my god,' said Matt loudly.

Then Kim heard her sister-in-law Loz in the background. 'What?'

'Kim's staying the night with Crazy Harry. You know, I told you about Scarface Harry,' said Matt to his wife.

'No way! Hermit Harry? Tell her to run now,' said Lauren.

'Matt, Matt!' Kim almost shouted to get his attention. 'It's all right. I'll be fine. Please don't worry.' Kim wanted to tell him more – about Harry's house, his friendly dogs, about the food on the stove – but she didn't dare in case Harry could hear the conversation.

'So, sis, what's he like? Does he really have a scar? Are you scared? Can you get a photo of him?'

Typical Matt. 'He seems lovely, actually. Yes, he does. No, I'm fine. And Dave took a dive into the water, remember,' she replied. 'Now, I'd better go. I'll be home in the morning, I hope.'

'If you're not back by lunch, I'm coming over there with the shotgun. Okay?'

Kim wasn't sure if he was serious or not. 'Yep. Don't worry. See ya tomorrow.'

'I hope so. I wanna hear all about it. No one has been into Harry's den,' he said with awe.

Kim laughed. 'Goodnight.' Then she hung up and headed to the kitchen to find Harry.

He stood at the bench where a slow cooker sat, stirring what was inside. The aroma was overpoweringly good.

'Anything I can do?' she asked.

'Sure. Help yourself to a plate, and load 'er up – there's bread on the table too,' he said, gesturing to the pine table in the middle of the kitchen.

Harry had obviously made improvements to the house over the years. Like the pale-blue benchtop; the cupboards looked as if they'd been painted at some point too. The kitchen sported cream wallpaper with a blue floral pattern on it, and the floorboards had been sanded and sealed. Kim had noticed that the ceiling in the main room had been replaced, yet the plaster in her room sagged with age.

She picked up a plate and joined Harry. 'It smells good. I think you might be a better cook than me, Harry,' she said.

'I don't know about that, lass. I've had many disasters over the years and got to this point through much trial and error.'

Kim laughed. 'Well, I know what that's like. I'm still going through that stage.'

They filled their plates and sat at the table, Harry at the end, Kim to the side.

It was good stew. Kim looked at the lumps of meat on her plate and suddenly wondered whether it was rabbit or roo. Maybe Harry was living self-sufficiently here, with his own vegie garden and an endless supply of rabbit. Her stomach churned. No, maybe she wouldn't ask. It was better to be none the wiser sometimes.

They chatted about farm work as they ate. Harry was really talkative, and Kim wondered whether he was lonely. When was the last time he'd chatted to anyone besides Tom or his occasional extra workers?

'This stew is amazing, Harry,' she said, before scooping up another mouthful. It was hard to talk when all she wanted to do was keep eating.

The more they talked, the more Kim got the feeling that Harry was impressed with her knowledge of farming. He kept shaking his head as if in disbelief. Living a hermit life, would he know that girls were now out working farms too? He'd assumed she was married to a farmer and quickly apologised when she set him straight.

'Sorry, Kim. I don't really get out much.'

Kim didn't know how to respond to that. She found her focus trained on his scar. She couldn't help it, and he caught her staring.

'Sorry, I didn't mean to stare. It's a ripper,' she said.

'Yes, that it is. I was in Vietnam when I was younger than you,' he said.

'You fought in the war? Was it awful?'

'You could say that,' he said, before getting up and reaching for her empty plate. 'I lost my best mate in that bloody war.' He was staring off into space for a moment before he glanced back to her. 'Sorry, Kim, I don't do personal conversation. One of the reasons I moved out here.'

All Kim's burning questions about his private life – if he'd been married or had kids, where he'd grown up – died away with his words. She could tell that she'd hit a nerve, and, keen not to create a bad vibe, she jumped up and offered to do the dishes. In the end they did them together.

Harry walked her to her room later that night, which she found a little unnerving. What if he preyed on his victims when they were asleep? What if he'd drugged her dinner? Then Kim almost laughed out loud at her wayward thoughts. Harry seemed anything but dangerous.

'Now, please lock the door. There's a bolt up the top.'

Kim screwed up her face as she tried to fathom the meaning behind his words. Was this just so she would feel safer?

'Oh, okay. Night, Harry. Thanks for your hospitality.'

'My pleasure.'

Kim shut the door to her room and looked up at the bolt.

'Don't forget the lock,' he said from the other side of her door.

Kim reached up and slid the bolt into place with a loud click, and it was only then that she heard Harry's footsteps echo along the passageway back to the lounge room.

Well, that was strange, Kim thought. At least she knew she was safe. Matt would try to tell her that Harry probably turned into a werewolf at night, or a giant bunyip that devoured girls.

Shaking her head, she finished making her bed. In the process she accidentally kicked a box underneath it, which caused the top to open. Kim was curious. She bent down to look at the old trunk and lifted the dusty half-opened lid. There were some clothes in there – something that looked quilted, a knitted baby's bonnet – a large collection of letters bound with string and some photos resting on top. Kim picked them up and studied the photo of two young men in khaki green. Straight away she guessed it had been taken in Vietnam because of the jungle background. Turning it over, written on the back in pencil were two names. *John and Harry.*

Kim looked at the two fresh-faced men with their arms around each other. Both had big smiles. Kim wondered which one was Harry. Neither had a scar, plus they were so young-looking and wearing baggy hats. There was another photo of an older couple by a house, and one of a beautiful girl in a pretty blue dress. On the back of both of them was written *Lake Grace 1969.* She wondered what other things this trunk contained, but felt she'd violated Harry's privacy enough.

Putting the photos back carefully and closing the lid on the trunk, she turned off the light, took off her clothes and crawled into bed. Then she got back out and slipped her shirt back on.

Just in case something happened. The voice in the back of her mind kept her wary. Good men were known to hold deep, dark secrets. Murderers walked the streets with their families. It was a horrible world that they lived in at times, and Kim wasn't about to drop her guard completely. Not even for a talkative, friendly hermit named Harry.

But as she lay there in bed she couldn't help wondering who Harry really was. What had brought him here, to Tom's farm? What had happened in his past that he didn't want to talk about? Was it just the war? Was John in the photo his best mate who'd died? Had that changed Harry's life? Or was there more to this intriguing man's story?

Chapter 3

1968

'A BIT of a fixer-upper,' said John as he took in the old house, which spoke of years of neglect. Its roof flapped in the breeze, the noise ringing out like a hammer to an anvil, and its front door hung from its hinge like a lopsided mouth. Weeds grew through the cracks in the cement drive, bushes and shrubs pressed against the sides of the house, and spider webs festooned the verandah.

John glanced at his wife, Beth. She looked a little out of place in her city outfit, a soft knee-length blue dress with pockets at her waist. A frown was equally out of place on her delicate face, with her blonde hair held back with a thin headband and her curls sitting on her shoulders. He'd been fascinated watching her set her hair for the first time, but now he was used to it.

'It's charming,' she said.

He knew she thought differently, but the fact that she chose to look on the bright sight made him love her even more.

John strode up to the front door and pushed it open. It fell off completely and he had to stand it up against the wall. Dusting off his hands, he strolled back to his wife.

'Come on now, Mrs Parson. Let me take you inside.' John swept her light frame up in his arms as if she was a child. 'I want to carry you over the threshold.'

'Oh, John,' she said, giggling as she held him tightly.

She smelt like fresh roses. He still couldn't believe she'd married him.

'There we are.' Once inside, John almost decided against putting her down as the floor was so dusty. 'The kitchen is through here, and the bedrooms off to the side,' he explained as they walked through. 'We won't have to live with it like this for long. The bank said it shouldn't be a problem to get the loan to buy the farm and then we can fix this place up properly.'

Beth stopped, turned to face him and caressed his cheek. 'I know, John. We'll be fine here. I want to be wherever you are. I want a pet lamb and lots of dogs, maybe even some cats to keep the mice down.' She smiled and then walked to the back door and pushed it open.

The rear garden was even more overgrown than the front, and the path to the toilet looked like a jungle trek. It would be the first job on the list. John turned to Beth to explain exactly that when he was struck by her smile and the sparkling cornflower-blue of her eyes.

'Smell the air. It's so different. I'm going to love it here, John. You don't need to worry about me. You know I'm nothing like my sister.'

John had to agree. Beth's sister was a city girl through and through, while Beth's inclination to try new things would stand her in good stead out here.

'And that smell, what is it?'

'It's the wattle over there, see?' he said, pointing to the bright yellow pompom flowers that covered the tree beside the outhouse.

'Oh, wow. It's gorgeous.' Beth turned to him and her delicate pink lips turned up in a coy smile. 'So, Mr Parson. When do we start?' Her fingers slid between the buttons of his shirt as she pressed herself against him.

His body responded. Everything about his wife turned him on. Her smile, her touch, her scent. Reaching around her, he cupped her bottom, pulling her closer, before sinking his face into her neck to kiss her soft skin. 'How about right now?'

Beth's giggle set his heart racing. This was their new beginning.

John woke up early, after another restless night. He watched Beth sleeping peacefully, her hair fanned out across her pillow, and took some comfort in the sight before sneaking out of bed. He quickly got dressed and made a coffee before heading out to check on the sheep.

In the last month they'd worked hard, his Bethy beside him with her shirtsleeves rolled up, scrubbing like a woman possessed. She was one determined lass. The way she'd cleaned walls and floors, carted out dead rodents, made new curtains for the windows, helped shift in furniture and still had tea ready at night showed just how much she wanted their farm life to work. He'd told her she didn't have to prove anything, and that he didn't expect her to work so hard, but she wouldn't hear of it. Beth would give him that steely gaze and straighten her slender shoulders before walking off to her next task. Between the two of them, they'd turned the old house into something liveable.

John got into his pale-blue Holden EH ute. Well, in actual fact it was his dad's ute, but since he'd come back to the farm after finishing school it had become his. There was something relaxing about driving around the farm in the early morning: the way the sunlight caressed the land, bringing everything to life, and the fresh smells of the previous night. For these few moments he could enjoy, take pleasure in and almost believe this was his future. But all too soon reality set in. His future on the farm, his new wife, his life had been sorted until the post arrived last week, bringing with it a letter he'd never counted on.

Already his thoughts had ruined his mood and the magic of the morning had disappeared. John checked the sheep and then did some jobs at the shed before returning to have morning tea with Beth.

His parents' Morris Major was parked out the front when he arrived back at the house. It was older than his ute, a Series II in a soft green. John walked past it and up the path to the front door. His hand paused on the handle – he was reluctant to go inside. Yet the voice inside his head said he couldn't avoid what was about to happen. With a deep breath he entered the house.

In the kitchen, Beth had the kettle on and was getting out the cups. She was wearing a light lemon-coloured dress and her hair was out. She'd made an effort.

His mother, Norma, sat at the table with a carrot cake, her

signature dish, in front of her. More consolation. His dad, James, sat beside her, looking around the kitchen, no doubt reminiscing about his childhood in this house. When James had married Norma they'd built a new house near the main road, which was at the other end of the farm. Now, as John entered, they all turned to him.

'Cuppa's nearly ready, love,' said Beth. 'Norma, why don't you cut up that delicious-looking cake?'

Beth handed his mum a knife. John turned away to avoid his father's eyes; he couldn't take the look any longer. The pity, the sadness, the anger. It swirled like dark rain clouds and the worst thing was, John knew his own eyes held the same. He found himself shuffling through the papers by the phone. Automatically he found the one letter he knew he had to read again for probably the hundredth time.

Commonwealth of Australia
Department of Labour and National Service – National
Service Registration Office

Dear Sir,

As a result of the national service ballot in which you were included you have been selected for service. In due course you will be notified of the arrangements for a medical examination to determine your fitness for service.

Please read carefully the notes on the back of this card.
Yours Faithfully,
Registrar

'Maybe you won't pass the medical?' his mother whispered. The hopefulness in her voice was the same as Beth's had been when, late at night, she'd whispered through her tears. But they all knew he was as fit as a mallee bull and that he was destined for duty. They all knew where that duty would lead him: to Vietnam. To a war he hardly knew anything about.

John felt a hand on his back and looked around to find his beautiful wife, smiling and holding out his cup of coffee as if it held all the answers. He knew that he could be leaving her alone for not just a few years but perhaps forever.

'Your parents need to talk to you,' she said softly.

With a sigh he took his cup and sat down with Beth at the table.

His dad got straight to the point as his mum passed round the cake.

'Son, we've tried everything, but we just can't keep the farm while you're away. We can't afford to put on a worker, and your mum can't run it on her own.'

John's mum hadn't really been the sort to help out with farming – she was a housewife through and through. He'd never ask his mum to even contemplate doing farm work. But with his father's bad back, they were out of options.

'You know I'd love to keep this place for you but . . .' His words faded away as frustration flashed across his face.

John understood his father's disappointment. This had been his farm, his life, and he'd worked hard so it could be passed on to John. Now all that had fallen through, thanks to one letter. Since its arrival, John had been making the most of every minute he had on the farm, the place of his birth, the soil in his blood. Already he was mourning its loss. Farming was all he'd ever wanted to do.

His dad was doing his best to make this whole transition easy on them. With a smile, he continued. 'But if we sell up, then we can put some money towards a nice house in the city for you and Beth. We'll get a place close by and help Beth while you're away, plus she'll be closer to her family and we'll be closer to your sister's family.'

He didn't need to explain further. John wasn't going to be around for two years, so Beth would need her own family for support. Especially if she fell pregnant. There was a possibility she already was. He hoped not. John didn't want to miss the birth of his first child, nor did he want Beth left to raise their child on her own.

His father continued, 'Your mum is really looking forward to being closer to your sister, especially now that Susan has little Cheryl. We really are sorry, son. I know better than anyone what this place means to you, and to me, but we can't afford to keep it. I've had a few people interested. Everything points to selling up while we can.' James massaged his temples, his face grave. 'I'm so sorry.'

They stared into their cups. They were all probably thinking the same thing – if it hadn't been for that letter, they'd be sitting here now celebrating the farm handover to John, as the bank's formal loan approval had come through just the day before.

'I understand, Dad. There's not much else we can do.'

Norma put her cup down with false cheer. 'Well, I'm rather

keen on a home in South Perth. Your sister's only a stone's throw away and the river is so close by.'

Beth nodded. 'Sounds lovely. I think we'd be happy with something in a similar area. We'd love a big backyard, but I'm not sure we could find one that matches this.' She smiled ruefully.

When it was time for his parents to leave, John helped his dad up out of the chair.

'Thanks, son. The back's really tight and stiff today. Norma wants me to go see some doctors when we move to Perth. See if there's something we can do to ease some of the pain.'

'That would be a good idea.'

'The sooner we can sell this place, the sooner we can buy. Be good to get settled in before you take off,' said his dad quietly. 'At least so Beth feels comfortable. I'll start ringing around for a buyer straight away.'

His words were like a knife to John's chest, a sharp reminder of what he was about to lose.

'When do you have your medical, son?' asked his mum as she joined them.

'I'll head into Lake Grace tomorrow.' The words sounded like they'd come from someone else, as if John wasn't in control of his own body any more.

His mum kissed him before helping her husband into the car, then they drove off.

John sat down on the edge of the verandah and watched the gimlets around the house moving in the breeze. His two new dogs played among the small trees, chasing the pink and grey galahs that tried to eat the spilt grain from when he'd last fed the sheep.

What was he going to do in the city? When or if he came back alive from Vietnam, then what? Become a labourer? Would that make him happy?

A warm hand slid into his and the smell of roses snapped him from his thoughts.

'We can always come back out here after you've done your service, John. We can make it work,' Beth said, as if reading his mind.

She reached up and caressed his face, running her fingers across his stubble and gazing at him with such love that he almost cried. But he didn't want to cry in front of her when he knew just how hard she was trying to be strong for him.

'You are so wonderful,' he whispered, before kissing her deeply.

'I love you, John. No matter where we are, I'll always be with you.'

And he realised that he might not have the farm he'd always dreamt about, but he had the most amazing girl, and his life was with her. As long as he had Beth, he had a rich life ahead of him. Besides, as Beth said, they could always find a way back to the country to farm.

John smiled, really smiled, for the first time since the letter arrived. 'I love you too, Bethy.'

Chapter 4

KIM pulled her ute up in the middle of the street in Lake Grace, right where the road split into two and a wide median strip began. This was the spot marked for her special kangaroo sculpture, for which she'd been commissioned by the Shire. With harvest she'd been too busy to get the kangaroo finished, let alone installed, but with the recent rain she'd powered on in her shed, welding until the job was done.

She was ready to install it today. Luckily it was quiet in town and no one was bothered by her parking in the middle of the street. After making sure the metal sculpture was secured properly in the lift machine on the back of her ute, Kim got it off the tray. It was bloody heavy. But it had turned out all right, even if she did say so herself.

Kim was so engrossed in what she was doing that she didn't notice the man who'd walked over.

'Here, do you need some help with that?'

Kim looked up as a pair of hands guided her sculpture to the ground safely. She'd expected one of the locals, but this guy was a tall unfamiliar hunk. He wore jeans, boots and a white T-shirt and looked like he was in his thirties or forties – it was hard to tell. His face was handsome and he was fit – actually, he was *really* fit. But it was the greys in his short hair and the few sprinkled across his chin that showed he was older than he seemed. Kim loved the look – like Brad Pitt, who was even better looking these days than when he was younger. Grey hair on men could be very sexy.

Kim unhooked her sculpture and smiled at the man. 'Thank you.'

'This is amazing. Are you the artist?' he asked, as he bent down to check out her kangaroo.

'Oh, I wouldn't call myself an artist,' she scoffed. 'It's just a hobby.'

'A hobby? Pffft. This is amazing! Look at these parts – old cogs, washers, bolts. It's gorgeous.'

He touched her sculpture lovingly, almost caressing the kangaroo. Kim felt a little bit proud. 'Thanks.'

He stood up and held out his hand. 'Sorry. I'm Charlie.'

'Kim,' she replied and shook his hand. His fingers were long and clean; her hand seemed grotty and stained against his.

'Let me help you move it. Is it going on that block?' he asked.

She nodded, and together they took a side each and slowly shuffled the sculpture to its resting place.

Charlie stood back, staring at it. 'How many have you made?' he asked.

'Sculptures? Um, just a few.' Kim went back to her ute to get her drill and some DynaBolts to lock it in place. 'The Shire would like more to be installed, but it all depends on when I have time to make them. People are coming to me with orders, but the farm already keeps me flat out.'

Charlie watched her bolt the roo in place. When she stood up he had a silly grin on his face, and Kim wondered for a minute if she'd put grease on herself.

'You're more handy with tools than I am, by the looks of it, especially if you welded this beauty together all by yourself. Sorry – you must think I'm a bit of a dingbat, some stranger coming up and going on. But I'm just in awe of this kangaroo,' he said. His soft blue-grey eyes sparkled.

Kim smiled. No, she thought he was sweet. Most blokes around here could weld, so Kim didn't feel like she had done anything special. 'You just passing through town?' He certainly wasn't a farmer with those hands. They weren't office-soft but they weren't labour-callused either.

'No, actually. But I am new to town. Just got a job at Elders Insurance. I'm having a wander around, seeing the shops and getting a feel for the place before I start.'

'Oh, right. I actually need to ring you guys. We got some hail damage in the last storm. That's why I'm here doing this – we're waiting for the crop to dry out so we can finish harvesting.'

'Well, I start tomorrow. I'll be waiting for your call. And probably half the district's. I hear it was a ripper storm that came through.'

It had been. Kim thought of getting stranded and staying the night with Harry. Matt had been upset that she didn't bring home any horror stories. Kim hadn't told him about the bolting of her door. Nor did she mention the bit about Harry being a Vietnam Vet. She sensed it was something private that had left more than one scar in its wake. But she'd liked Harry, and made a mental note to return to say thanks again. Besides, she got the feeling he'd enjoyed her company, even though he chose to live a solitary life.

'Yes, there were a few that got the hail.'

Charlie didn't seem to have anywhere else to go. Not that Kim minded. He was a bit of all right. Probably married, although he didn't wear a ring, she'd noticed. Then again, most guys here didn't wear rings in case they got caught while working. Was she being overly optimistic? Finding a good man around here seemed harder than farming.

'Kimmy!' yelled a familiar little voice.

A boy-shaped blur ran towards her and hugged her waist tightly.

'Hey, Billy! Fancy seeing you in town. Have you just been to Arjo's?' she asked the nearly nine-year-old boy.

'Yep, I had a hot chocolate with a marshmallow and then some cake too,' Billy said brightly.

'Yes, I can see that,' she said, pointing to his mouth, which had a chocolate ring around it. Kim brushed his fringe back from his forehead so she could see his bright eyes. 'Does your dad know where you are?' she asked.

'Yep. He said I could come and say hi.' Billy let go of Kim and patted her metal sculpture. 'I love her. What's her name? Is it Skittles?' Billy then turned to Charlie and frowned.

'Billy lives next door to me,' Kim said. 'Billy, this is Mr . . .?'

'Macnamara,' said Charlie. He held out his hand for Billy. 'Nice to meet you, Billy. Why Skittles?' he asked.

Billy shook his hand. Happy to be asked such an important question, he beamed. 'Kim has a pet kangaroo called Skittles, so this must be her.' He rested his hand between the kangaroo's ears.

'I bet the likeness is uncanny. You're very talented, Kim,' said Charlie.

'This roo is pretty awesome,' said Billy. 'But it's still not as cool as our dragon.'

'A dragon?' said Charlie with a curious waggle of his brows.

'Yep. Kim made it for my dad for his birthday. It's massive and it breathes fire and its wings are huge.' Billy stretched his arms out. 'It guards our farm.'

'Well, I'd love to see this dragon one day.'

'When you come out to see our hail damage you'll pass it,' said Kim. 'You won't miss it, will he, Billy?'

'Uh-uh. No way, mister.' Billy stilled for a moment. 'I reckon it scares lots of people away,' he said softly.

Billy's face turned towards Kim and she suspected he was thinking about his birth mother, a lost soul who'd recently reappeared and caused shock waves in the family.

Kim knelt down and put her hand on his shoulder. 'Yeah, that big dragon is your protector, Billy.'

'It is?' he asked. His eyes widened. Kim knew he carried an ongoing fear that his mum might try to take him away, as she had once before. It was a source of constant nightmares for him, no matter how much Billy's dad Drew and his partner Nat tried to reassure him that she couldn't upset their lives again. Only time would really help him to feel safe again.

Kim felt emotion building in her chest. Seeing distress shoot across Billy's face made her heart ache. 'And did you know it will come to life to scare off anyone who's not welcome?' she said. She hoped he was still young enough to believe, even if just to give him some comfort at night. 'You'll always be safe with Dragon watching over you, Billy.'

Billy gave her a cheesy grin and Kim felt much better. She'd made that dragon for Drew – an expression of her unrequited love, in a way – but now that he was taken, she was glad the dragon had a new purpose.

'Billy, time to go, mate,' yelled Drew, who was standing outside the coffee shop.

When Kim saw him, it still happened: that tightness in her chest, that swell of love and admiration. Then the sense of loss as his future wife stepped from the door and held his hand firmly. They both waved to her, so blissfully happy that Kim felt more alone than ever.

'Hi, Kim! Billy, time to go, mate,' yelled Drew. Kim waved.

'Bye, Kimmy,' said Billy as he ran off towards his dad and soon-to-be step mum.

Kim was about to shout out to watch for cars but Natalie beat her to it. For many years Kim had dreamt of becoming a family with Drew and Billy, and for many years she had been the main female influence in Billy's life besides Drew's mum. Would it ever get easier to see Nat step into that role? Kim watched them walk off holding hands, Billy between the adults, Nat in a gorgeous summer dress and heels. It was hard not to be jealous. Nat was womanly, beautiful, wore make-up and smelt amazing. Not like Kim, who lived in jeans and boots, smelt like grease and fuel and had never had a manicure. Was she ever going to find a guy who could look past all that, who would want her for who she was?

'Cute kid,' said Charlie.

'Um, yeah.' Kim tore her eyes away from them and hoped her face wasn't an open book. 'He's a great kid.'

'Do you mind if I take a photo of your kangaroo to show my sister?'

'Not at all. Does she like kangaroos?'

'Yeah,' said Charlie, taking out his phone from his pocket. 'And she's an artist so I know she'll love this. My mum brought us up around art galleries.'

'If they ever come to visit, you must take them to the Art Space,' she said, pointing to the building next to the coffee shop. 'We have some fantastic local artists, and new artists are always coming to town for displays and workshops.'

Charlie looked at the building, a sad smile on his face and his eyes a clouded grey. 'Yes, I'll have to check it out.'

Kim wasn't sure what she'd said but she could see that Charlie's mood had saddened, much like her own.

'Anyway, I'd better go. Still have heaps to do back on the farm. It was nice meeting you, Charlie. I hope you enjoy it here in Lake Grace. Thanks for your help. Much appreciated.'

She was used to busting her guts shifting stuff. Matt left her to handle everything on her own because she could, but every now and then it was nice to be offered help. Kim was all for a guy opening a door for her. This Charlie Macnamara bloke certainly seemed like a door opener.

'You too, Kim. I'll talk to you soon.'

Kim headed back to her ute, but something about Charlie's warm smile stayed with her. She got in and glanced back in his direction. He was walking towards the Art Space building. He looked really good in jeans, she thought as she watched him carefully.

Then he glanced behind and caught her ogling. Kim quickly waved, then focused on driving her ute home while a hot flush rose under her skin.

Chapter 5

CHARLIE walked towards the coffee shop, where he'd originally been headed before he'd seen a pretty lady in need of a hand. He'd only been in Lake Grace for half a day and already he was impressed. It was a neat, tidy town, with a pub he'd seen on TV – the town had put up a 'Welcome to Nat Fyfe country' banner in honour of the Dockers footy star. People said hello as he passed them, or lifted their fingers in the country wave as they drove past. Then to stumble across Kim with her amazing art – well, that had been unexpected. It felt like a sign he was in the right place.

In fact, meeting Kim straight up, a gorgeous, talented woman, made him wonder if his luck was about to change. She was definitely his type, but he knew what small towns were like. Someone like her would never be single. Maybe he'd be able to find someone up for some fun while he was in town. A bit of company, or just someone to distract him. Maybe Kim could be that person?

He felt like he was starting from scratch. He'd left behind

family and friends, yet he didn't want to reach out to any of them. He couldn't. This was something he had to do on his own.

Instead of going in to get a coffee, Charlie kept walking to the Art Space building. He felt a pull towards it – was it something familiar? A sense of nostalgia? A way for him to cling to his mum a bit longer?

The front of the large building was all glass, along with the doors, which were shut. Charlie cupped his hands up to the glass and peered inside. It was an open space with white walls, a cement floor and a high ceiling. Charlie leant back and read some of the flyers stuck to the window.

One advertised a ferrous workshop in a few days by local artist Kerrie Argent. He could picture the scene. Charlie had many memories of dropping by to visit his mum only to find her city house transformed into a workshop, with her artist friends and his sister Sarah and all her friends working together. Sometimes they were experimenting in different mediums, other times they'd be learning something new from an artist passing through. His mum had always loved art, but her creativity had intensified after his dad passed away twenty-five years ago. It became her emotional release and her house was transformed with the many pieces she'd made, along with Sarah's. And Sarah – well, she had different-coloured hair each time he saw her and wore a lot of her creations, from knitted stuff to dyed silks. It possibly rubbed off on Charlie, who had his own creative urges. He had started doing woodwork in his dad's small shed at a young age. The things he made were artistic, but he also got to use power tools and it made him feel closer to his dad.

Through the window he could see a display of wire sculptures that looked as if they had been knitted. It was unlike anything he'd seen before. It had a rural feel to it – maybe that was because of the wire? Tania Spencer was the artist and one of her pieces was labelled *The Web of Secrets*. It made Charlie think about his own family secret. It did feel like a web, little strings of lies that must have been woven together over time. A secret that had been kept from him. One he wanted to unearth.

His phone rang. Funnily enough, it was his sister, ringing for the sixth time today. She didn't know how to give up, but in a way it was reassuring. Sarah was clearly worried about him. Feeling a little bad, he decided to text her.

I'm fine, sis. Don't worry.

He'd now probably be bombarded with texts, but so be it. Lately he hadn't wanted to talk. Too much was going on inside his head and he couldn't make sense of it, let alone talk about it.

Sarah's reply came back quickly.

I do worry. You're my brother, forever, no matter what. I'm here anytime you need to chat. I wish there was something more I could do. I miss Mum too.

Charlie scratched his head as he turned and glanced down the quiet street of this tiny rural town. He didn't know where he belonged any more. He didn't know who he really was either. His mum, Rachel, had been his whole life. They were so close, especially after his dad died. Now he'd lost her too. And the awful thing was he now wasn't sure if she'd ever been his to begin with. He felt like he'd lost her twice.

When Charlie got back to his rental house, he grabbed a beer from the fridge. The three-bedroom home seemed far too big just for him. He sat on the simple sofa and stared at the last few unpacked boxes. They contained mainly books, as he loved to read, but he wasn't sure where to put them yet. He did have his sister's painting up on the wall though. It was a bright yellow canvas of a wattle tree that grew in their mum's backyard. It had been a special tree for them, and the vibrant flowers had always fascinated Charlie. Sarah had painted two versions of the image, keeping one for herself and giving the other to him.

A reminder of their mum. It was the first thing he'd put up.

The kitchen bench was his work space for the moment, and his laptop and the paperwork from his new job sat there waiting. He didn't have a desk yet so for now the kitchen bench would do. He liked having his things there anyway, as it made the house feel more lived in. The thought of work excited him; he was eager to make his mark, and not just have this job be a means to an end. Just because he was in Lake Grace for another reason didn't mean he was about to slack off in his new position.

Yet the phone call from his sister had rattled him. It had sent his mind into the dark place he tried hard to keep it away from. He loved his sister dearly, but he needed her at arm's length right now. They'd had a great life, growing up in the city with parents who were loving and free-spirited, and Charlie wouldn't forget that, ever. It had helped shape him into the man he was. But the passing of their mum had brought more than just gut-wrenching sadness.

The only problem was that the secret he'd discovered didn't tell the full story. Charlie only had one piece of the puzzle, and it tortured him. There were just too many unanswered questions, and there was no way he could continue with his life until he had some answers. Lake Grace was the key. Until he could unearth more of his history, this would be home.

Chapter 6

1968

JOHN bounced across the paddock in his ute. Suddenly he stopped, the motor running, his hands gripping the steering wheel. He sat as if deep in thought, yet nothing seemed to take hold in his mind.

The paper was on the seat beside him. He'd been doing okay until he'd seen their farm advertised for sale. He knew it was happening, yet seeing it there in black and white was painful. Like the final nail in the coffin, this was real. All he'd ever wanted to be was a farmer.

As each day passed he'd hoped that the war would be over or that for some reason he wouldn't be fit for duty. Yet he'd passed his medical and was just waiting on his training details. In the meantime he farmed as usual, trying to savour every minute. He remembered how it had been growing up on the farm with his sister, climbing trees, making cubbies in the bush and building rafts when the floodwaters came. They'd learnt to drive, and ride motorbikes; they'd played with the dogs and got as dirty as possible at shearing time. He'd wanted that for his children, but now they would be raised as city kids – that's if he was even lucky enough to have any. He couldn't guarantee anything at this moment. How could you look forward to the future when you had no certainty you'd even have one?

Sammy, sitting beside him, barked and he jumped. The kelpie was still only a pup, but she watched him as if she knew something was wrong. *Why are we just sitting here?* her dark eyes seemed to say.

'Just thinking,' he replied and rubbed her ears. 'What are we going to do with you, hey? The city wouldn't be fun for a girl like you. Would be best if someone out here could take you on.' But then he didn't want Beth to be alone. Maybe Sammy would be nice company for Beth?

John dropped his face into his hands and rubbed it until his cheeks were stretched and squished. He felt mildly better, and more awake.

'Come on, Sammy, let's go collect Bethy some flowers.'

He drove around the farm to where the wattle trees were still in flower and picked some yellow blooms. They didn't brighten his mood but he hoped they'd bring a real smile to his wife's face. He didn't like the pretend smile she put on when he was around. He knew she was hurting just as much as he was. How she had the strength to even try to put on a brave face was amazing. He hoped that strength would get Beth through his absence.

Sammy barked with joy as they drove home, her head hanging out the window and her tongue flapping in the breeze. Maybe he should ask Beth and see what she thought they should do with

Sammy. If the pup was going to be too much to handle in the city, he could ask his best mate next door if he'd take her. They'd been friends since they were old enough to ride their pushbikes to the boundary fence to play together. And Sammy was a farm dog, already showing a keen eye for rounding up sheep.

'You were gone a while,' said Beth as John walked up to the front door, Sammy hot on his heels.

Beth was frowning in a way that only happened when she was truly worried. He wondered if she thought he might have done something silly, like run away or, worse, harmed himself.

'I was just getting you these,' he said, holding out the flowers.

The smile he got was worth it, but it didn't remove that frown.

'I was concerned. It's hard to know what you're thinking or how you're feeling with everything that's happening.'

John sighed. 'I'm not going to go off and shoot myself, if that's what you're worried about,' he said, holding her gaze.

Beth rubbed his shoulders and studied him closely as they stood by the front door. 'It's not unheard of, John. I need to know you'll never go down that path without at least trying to talk to me first.' Her eyes filled with tears.

'I promise you, love. I'm not about to take the easy way out. I love you too much to put you through that. Besides, how could I possibly leave this world when you're still in it?'

A tear escaped and rolled down her cheek. John smiled and wiped it away with his thumb. 'We'll be okay, Beth.' He pulled her in to him, holding her tightly and raining kisses on her forehead. 'Come on. Let's have a cuppa and then I'll help you start packing.'

'Already?' she said, glancing up at him.

He kept her close as they walked inside. 'Well, we've settled on our new place in Perth, so we may as well move in.'

He felt her body tremble against his.

'There's a cabaret this weekend at the hall,' she said. 'We should go, be a good way to say goodbye to everyone.' She went about making their cuppas.

'Yeah, I guess so. I'm going to miss the dances at the hall.'

'I'm sure they'll have some in the city,' she said.

He agreed, but he knew it wouldn't be the same. There was something special about parking outside the old hall with its wooden floors, a live band playing quickstep and barn dance music, people he'd known his whole life having fun, and everyone going up to the granite rock afterwards to watch the sunrise. He'd miss that small community togetherness, the safety and familiarity of it all. The city was busy and alienating compared to the country. John didn't mind the city, but visiting was a heck of a lot different than living there.

'Susan called this morning to see how you were going,' said Beth, handing him his cup. 'I could hear Cheryl gurgling in the background. I can't wait to see her.'

'Susan will love having you close by.'

Beth grinned. 'Me too. You know I love babies, but my sister won't be having kids any time soon, and I don't want us to start until you're back. I want us to be a family, to go through it together.'

'You just don't want to be doing all the nappy changes,' he teased. He reached for her hand and held it. 'I know what you mean. And if that's what you want, then so do I.'

'Darling, let's have lunch by the rock today. A picnic just like we had last year,' said Beth, her face lighting up.

When John had first brought her to the farm he'd packed up a picnic (well, his mum had helped with the food side of things) and taken Beth to a special place where the granite rock rose up from the ground in the bush by the old house. The orchids had been in flower and Beth had been transfixed by them. Lizards had scurried about, birds had sung in the trees and soft moss had been growing over the rocks near pools of tadpoles. It had been such an amazing afternoon that John had proposed to Beth. Watching her marvel at everything that he'd grown up loving, and seeing the afternoon sun radiate around her as though she was an angel, he had been overcome. He hadn't intended on proposing; it had taken him by surprise. What had surprised him even more was the fact that she'd said yes. He was only nineteen then, and Beth eighteen. Their parents had eventually come around.

They'd been married in Perth at the church her family had attended since she was born. She'd worn a dress with a lace bodice and sleeves, and her sister had been her bridesmaid in a baby-pink dress of a similar design with a matching headband. Beth's veil had been quite big, and in one of the photos the breeze had made it look more so. John had been handsome in a black suit, a white shirt and a narrow black tie. They'd danced at the reception to The Doors, The Beatles and Engelbert Humperdinck's 'The Last Waltz'. And John hoped it was those memories that Beth would hold dear to her heart, no matter what happened.

John smiled. 'Yes, that sounds like a perfect idea.'

'You're not needed for farm work?' she asked.

'No. The truck's coming tomorrow to take the sheep and I can get them penned up first thing with Sammy. I think we deserve the afternoon off.' Leaning over, he kissed her. 'Have I told you how much I love you?'

'A few times,' she said.

Her hand rested against his leg and slowly worked its way up. Beth's eyes twinkled with mischief and he felt his desire spike.

'Mrs Parson,' he said, pushing his chair back and reaching for her, pulling her across to straddle him. 'What would your husband think?'

Beth brushed her lips across his neck, trailing kisses up to his ear, then whispered, 'We just won't tell him, Mr Parson.'

All John's big ideas about packing went out the window.

Chapter 7

KIM lifted the 36-foot front on the header as she reached the end of the run, switching off the GPS at the same time. Her header box was full and it was time to empty it into the field bin. As she drove the yellow New Holland TR99 header across the paddock she pushed down the two buttons to disengage the reel and rotors. She had music playing through the stereo from her USB, a collection of songs she'd selected just for this harvest. When you sat on the header for ten to fifteen hours a day, you needed a huge selection of music that wouldn't bore you to tears. Kim had a heap of Aussie rock, some current pop songs and some of her favourites from the eighties and nineties. The radio was also an option, and in the afternoon it was pretty much guaranteed you would hear Bon Jovi.

It was nice to be back on the header, getting the last of the crop off. This rain had given them no end of headaches, with each load being tested at the bin for falling numbers. Not much they could do about it – that's just how the cookie crumbled with farming. So much was out of your control.

As she reached the field bin, she stepped on the auger pedal and watched as the auger folded out like a teapot spout. She lined it up with the opening in the field bin and then started to unload just as a vehicle pulled up. Her sister-in-law Lauren had brought the kids out for a visit.

Kim couldn't get out of the header while the job was underway, so she waited for the visitors to join her.

Mallory, who was now eight, got out of the car in her work boots, black leggings, a bright pink tutu and a green T-shirt. She had her hair up in a high ponytail with a bunch of parrot feathers stuffed in the hair band. She was the first one to climb up the header steps.

'Hello, Aunty Kim,' Mallory said brightly.

'Hiya, Mallory. Look at you today. Are you a princess? I'll call you Pocahontas.' Mallory looked at her strangely and Kim tried not to laugh. 'Have you come for a ride?'

'Yep. Seth wants to go with Dad but Mum and I are coming with you.'

Seth was the junior farmer in training. At nearly ten he was already driving utes, tractors and even the header. Seth took to it all like a duck to water. He even dressed like Matt, with matching farm shirts and work boots. Seth was standing in front of the header waving his arms so hard he nearly knocked off his akubra hat. Kim waved back just as Matt turned up to unload his header.

They'd both talked about getting a chaser bin, which would make life easier, but that would also mean putting on a worker, and that was a hassle they just didn't want to deal with. Especially when you never knew what kind of worker you'd get – at a highly stressful time like harvest the last thing either of them needed was a novice backpacker. So the consensus had been to plod along as they were and harvest around the clock. Kim always worked later than Matt, as he had a wife and family to go home to. She only had two pet sheep, a kangaroo and her dog. They didn't care how long she was gone unless it was past tucker time.

'How's it going?' said Lauren after Kim opened the header door. She carried a small Tupperware container and a thermos cup. 'Coffee and cake?'

'Oh, Loz, you're a bloody legend.'

Lauren handed over the goodies and then manoeuvred to fit into the header. Mallory had to push up against the front window so Loz could drop down the side seat. It was rather cosy with them all in there. Loz sighed with relief as she sat.

'Mally helped me make the chocolate cupcakes this morning.'

Kim opened the container to admire the brightly decorated cakes. 'Wow, look at all those stars and sparkles. I might need a chainsaw to bite through that lot,' she said with a grin. 'Or my dentist on standby.'

'Eat one now, Aunty Kim.'

Loz hauled Mallory up onto her lap as Kim pulled out a cupcake. 'Would you like to put my auger in for me, Mally?

Kim ate a cake while her niece pressed the foot pedal to retract the auger. Mallory watched in fascination as it moved back into position against the header.

'Right, let's go!' Kim put the container on the floor, took a sip

of her coffee, groaned in pleasure and then pushed the lever forward, moving the header away from the field bin and back up to
the location of her last recorded GPS line in the crop.

'So, have you got the bridesmaid's dress yet?' said Loz.

Damn, thought Kim. Her sister-in-law had to start where it
hurt the most.

'Matt's tried on his suit,' Loz continued. 'Stud muffin, he is.
You two will make great partners, brother and sister all scrubbed
up.'

Kim screwed her face up at the 'stud muffin' description. Matt
was a muffin all right, but more like a banana one. 'No dress
yet. Heard nothing since Nat came around to take my measure-
ments. But it can't be far away.'

'Wow, made to fit, hey? That doesn't come cheap,' said Loz as
she brushed back loose strands of her auburn hair.

'Waste of money. I'm never gonna wear it again, that's for
sure. Don't even want to wear it the first time.' Kim pouted.

'Now, now. You'll look gorgeous and might even snap up one
of her city friends. Think of some hot, well-groomed man who
can sweep you onto the dance floor.'

Kim raised her brows at Loz. 'Did you just come from watching *Pretty Woman*? Mally, you need to make sure Mum isn't
watching too many romantic movies.'

Mally had helped herself to a cupcake. 'No, she wasn't. Mum's
been reading though. Lots!' she said with dramatic flair.

Kim smiled. You could never keep anything quiet with kids
around.

Loz laughed and played with Mallory's hair. 'I've just finished a great rural romance. You should read them, be right up your alley.'

'I don't have time to read,' Kim scoffed. 'I still have two more bloody roos to make.'

'Well, you shouldn't be so bloody talented then,' Loz teased. 'Don't forget the P & C AGM is on next week. Are you still keen to come and help out?'

'Yep. I don't mind taking on work if it helps keep it going. Besides, one day I might have kids. I'd hate for there to be no school or P & C by then.'

'Great. We can go in together. When's your next RRR meeting?'

Kim had joined the Rural, Remote and Regional Women's Network last year – well, she'd applied and been appointed by the minister for regional development and had started a three-year term. 'Not until March. It's when they announce the winner of the Rural Women's Award too.'

'Oh yeah, do you think we can come to that? The fact that you made it as a finalist is awesome. You know your brother's very proud – we both are. He's just shit at showing it. But he tells me just how cool he thinks his little sis is.'

'Really?'

'Yep. Hey, how come you haven't told Drew about it? I mentioned it the other day and he had no clue what it even was, let alone that you were a finalist.'

Kim shrugged. 'He has other things on his mind. Besides, I've hardly seen him to tell him. It's no big deal.'

'No big deal!' Loz scoffed. 'Bloody hell, Kim, if you win you'll have $10000 to help with your award plan, plus the Australian

Institute of Company Directors course and then all the accolades and acknowledgement.'

'Shit, Loz, did you swallow the whole website?'

'No, but I may have googled the award. It's a big deal. I'm tempted to send in a piece for the *Lakes Link News* so everyone knows.'

'You wouldn't dare,' said Kim, shooting daggers in her direction. Lucky the header could steer itself. 'I don't need to broadcast it. I probably won't even win.'

'Um, really? I think your proposal is amazing. There are heaps of kids in country towns who don't even understand how farms work or how meat gets to our tables – let alone city kids.'

Kim stared at her for a few seconds, disbelieving.

'Where does your lack of confidence come from, Kim?' Loz shook her head.

'Ha! I think Matt took it all.'

'You'll give anything a go, but put you against anyone else and you think you're not good enough. You're more than just a farmer!'

Kim found it hard to think of herself as anything but 'just a farmer', yet Charlie's calling her an artist popped up in her mind. And at her last RRR meeting Maree had told them all never to use the word 'just' when referring to what they did. 'Just bloody awesome' was the term Maree had used instead.

'And you're not "just a farmer's wife" either,' said Kim. 'I don't see you getting any praise for all that you do. You run around after the kids, you're on every bloody committee under the sun and then you're cooking for Matt and me. It's women like you,

Lozzy, who are keeping our communities together. Without you, we'd have nothing to call a community.'

Loz was gazing at Kim, her blue eyes sparkling. 'That's the sweetest thing anyone's ever said to me. Thank you. I feel like I do a lot, but none of it seems to count because it's not a job, per se.'

'Oh, I'd say keeping Matt fed was a bloody big job and just for that alone you should win an award.' Kim chuckled. She loved teasing her brother about his ever-growing waistline any chance she got.

'Your poor brother. Besides, it's not just me feeding him. Doris keeps making those sweets he loves. I've been trying to make Matt healthier options and then she turns up with vanilla slice, chocolate crackles, fudge brownies and cream puffs. And what's worse is I bloody end up eating them because they're in the house. But I don't have the heart to tell Doris to stop – I know how much she loves baking everyone treats.' Loz looked down at her hips and slapped her thighs. 'I'm going to have to take up hockey again, just to burn some of it off.'

'I don't think a treat now and again hurts anyone. Not if you're taking in the good stuff too.'

'Mum, can we make some chocolate crackles?' asked Mallory.

'Maybe later, darling. I think you've had enough chocolate for the moment.' Loz pulled a tissue out of her bra and started to clean Mallory's face and hands. 'So, Matt showed me some of the hail damage yesterday. What a crap year.'

'Yeah, I know. If it's not one thing it's another. But at least we had it insured.'

Loz sat up straight and smiled her crafty smile. It always meant trouble. 'Speaking of insurance . . . I heard around town there's a new guy at Elders. Heard he's a bit dishy too.' She waggled her eyebrows.

'His name's Charlie and he seems really nice. He's coming out shortly to see the damage for our claim.'

'No way!' Lozzy smiled excitedly. 'Today? I might have to hang around until he gets here.'

'But Mum, I need a pee,' said Mallory. 'And I want to watch *Sponge Bob*.'

Lauren rolled her eyes. 'Can you wait until Aunty Kim unloads?'

'Yep, not busting yet. But I don't want to be here for ages,' said Mallory, rolling her eyes.

Kim handed her a black whiteboard marker and her niece slid off Loz's lap to do some drawing on the large window.

'So, spill,' Loz said in a low voice. 'Single, cute?'

Loz was never subtle. Kim had tried for years to ignore her constant questioning about her love life. But she was someone you couldn't say no to – she won you over with her charm and persistence.

'Well, he is rather handsome. I'm not sure how old he is but I'd say around the forties.' Kim frowned for a second.

'That's no biggie,' said Loz. 'There's twenty years between Nancy and Gus, and look at how long they've been married. Age is no problem, not if he's good-looking.'

Kim shook her head. 'Yeah, well, someone his age and with his looks will most definitely be taken. And if he's single, then I'd have to ask what's wrong with him.'

'Hey, that's not nice. People don't ask what's wrong with you,' said Loz.

'I bet they think it. Nah, most of them just aren't interested in a butch farmer.' Kim saw Loz open her mouth, about to argue. 'You know what I mean. I'm not typical wife material. Guys out here want someone like you, who'll be there to look after them and who dresses nicely.'

Loz looked down at her clothes and pointed to her holey black shorts. 'Like me, in my three-dollar Target shorts and my two-dollar, out-of-shape, stained Big W T-shirt?'

'Yeah, but you get dressed up to go to town. Maybe I should do that, if I could figure out what looks nice and how to apply make-up.' Kim pulled a face. 'I've never worked it out.' Make-up had always eluded her. There were times she'd tried it, mainly at school when her friends had made her up, but in day-to-day life there just seemed to be no need. And Kim didn't go to events or parties, or even really take holidays. The farm was her life. The farm would never leave her for someone better, and the farm would never break her heart. Sure, Mother Nature would try when she threw flash floods or droughts at them, but that was never the farm's fault. 'I've prepared myself for the possibility that I may end up a spinster.'

'You could artificially inseminate, if you wanted kids? You don't have to have a man. You know we'd support and help you,' said Loz.

'Mum, what's imsenimate?' asked Mallory as she worked the whiteboard marker across the window.

Loz smiled and played with her daughter's hair. 'An adult term, honey. I'll explain later.'

'I know there's that option. But I have you guys,' Kim said, smiling towards Mallory, who'd drawn a massive unicorn.

If she was honest with herself, it was the companionship she craved the most. Someone to come home to. Someone other than her brother to ask her about her day. And someone to hold her close at night and keep her warm through the winter months.

If only you could pull out your life remote and dial in the right bloke to turn up at the allotted time. Ah, if only life was that simple.

Chapter 8

CHARLIE had been looking forward to today's job. As he drove along the gravel road towards Lake View Farm he tried not to think about the phone call with his sister earlier.

'Charlie, we really need to talk about that card,' she'd said.

He did not.

'I'm worried you're bottling it all up. I wish you'd talk to me,' she'd begged.

But he just wasn't ready to open that lid. Not yet.

'I'm okay, honestly, sis. I just need some time to myself. I don't think talking about what the card said is going to help. What will help is finding answers. You'll be the first I call if I do.'

He'd managed to reassure Sarah, at least for now. But that didn't stop the thoughts in his own head from circling like piranhas hungry for a feed.

Heading out bush to Kim's farm was a wonderful distraction. There was something magical about being out in the country. So far, he especially enjoyed the on-farm visits, where he had a chance to chat with friendly farmers. The paddocks seemed to go for miles, and the trees could go from massive gum trees to small mallees and scrub bush. The quandong trees, when their fruit went bright red, were his favourites; they always reminded him of Christmas with their green and red bouquets. Then there was the sky. He felt like an ant under its massive expanse as it arched above in an umbrella of blues. But in the morning or evening it could be a patchwork of oranges, pinks and violets. It was good for the soul to feel the breeze on his face, watching the trees sway and hearing the birds squawk, or if he was lucky, catching an echidna or kangaroo passing by. Maybe it was his spiritual side coming out, but he felt a great inspiration when he stood in the bush and saw nothing that was manufactured or put there by humans. No freeways filled with vehicles, no high buildings surrounded by roads and concrete, no bustling streets filled with strangers. Every day here he felt more connected to the land. And with everything in his head right now, these quiet moments in the bush were the moments of meditation that he desperately needed.

His thoughts were interrupted as he saw a massive dragon appear out of nowhere. Hitting the brakes, he quickly pulled over. That young Billy was right, the iron sculpture was incredible. Charlie would never have pictured Kim's dragon like this.

He pulled into the driveway where it stood and got out of his work car to take a better look.

'My god.'

It was all he could say as he walked around it, touching each rusty metal part that had been welded together to create such a magnificent sculpture. Something like this would sell for thousands in the city, and yet Kim had just knocked it up for Billy's dad. Must be someone pretty special, he thought. After five minutes, maybe more, he decided he'd better keep going. He took a few photos, one from every angle, shook his head in disbelief, then jumped back in his car. His sister would want to see this for herself. Heck, people would pay money to see it.

A few more minutes and he came across the Lake View Farm sign, made from steel. The letters had been cut from one large square of metal and underneath there were intricate cut-outs of a fence, trees and a tractor. The border featured rusty tools. It wasn't hard to guess who'd made it.

Kim's directions led him up the driveway, past two homes and the sheds, to a back track that swept right. From there she'd said he'd be able to see them working in the nearby paddock. Charlie could see the dust from the two headers as he got closer. Farmers had so much gear, he thought, as he saw two field bins with tractors, the ute with the fuel trailer, the old truck with a water unit on the back in case of fires, a big truck with two bins parked under the field bins to cart away the grain, a white Prado and then the headers in the paddock. Some farmers also had chaser bins, and others had more headers. There were so many different ways to run a farm.

One header was returning to unload. Charlie hoped it was Kim.

He parked out of the way and put on his Elders cap before getting out of the car. Even though it was hot he still wore his jeans to look professional, along with his red-and-black work polo shirt. And besides, most of the time he was in an air-conditioned office, car or header.

The header's auger manoeuvred outwards and began unloading. He couldn't quite see who was in the header but he started to walk across the stubble towards it. At the same time a puff of pink tulle seemed to float down the side ladder to the ground, followed by a woman with auburn hair.

They met halfway, the pink-tutued little girl skipping over the stubble rows that came up to her knees.

'Hiya, you must be Charlie, the new Elders bloke,' said the woman, who looked him up and down.

'Yep, that would be me,' he replied, shooting her a smile. It was hard not to. The woman had one of those faces made for smiling, with matching bright eyes. Even her voice was bubbly and welcoming.

She held out her hand. 'Well, I'm Lauren, but call me Loz. I'm Matt's wife.'

'Nice to meet you, Loz. And is this your gorgeous princess?'

'Mallory is my little farm princess, yes. We've just been for a ride with Aunty Kim,' she said, righting the feathers in Mallory's hair band. 'Kim's waiting for you,' said Loz, pointing her thumb in the header's direction. 'I've gotta wait for Matt to get back and pick up our boy, Seth.'

'Righto. Nice to meet you both.' He didn't want to keep Kim waiting.

'You too, Charlie. I hope you stick around.'

As he headed towards the header he wondered what Loz meant. *I hope you stick around?* Had there been a few Elders

Insurance blokes before him? He'd thought he'd taken over from a guy who'd been here most of his life. Oh well, he was still trying to put a lot of things together. In a small town many people were connected – it just took time to figure out the details, and it never paid to talk ill of anyone as most were related or friends.

With a little flutter in his chest he strode to the header and climbed up the ladder. He saw Kim through the glass door, and almost wondered if he should knock. She was in denim shorts and a black singlet, her hair in a side plait. Even through the dirty glass he could see her beauty. He opened the door.

'Morning. Permission to come aboard?' He was rewarded with a smile.

'Sure, Charlie. Pull up a chair,' she said.

It was a cosy cabin, and the little side seat brought him close to Kim. He tried to sit as near to the door as he could to give her some space. She probably didn't want some old guy squished against her.

Kim retracted the auger. 'I'll harvest up towards the patch of bad stuff first,' she said. 'I'd offer you a cuppa, but the kettle's on the blink,' she joked. 'Loz did drop off some cupcakes, though, so help yourself.'

She pointed to a container. Charlie bent down to pick it up, his leg briefly touching hers. The rush it gave him reminded him how long it had been since he'd had a close encounter with a young, attractive woman. Or any woman, actually. His marriage had been devoid of contact for years. For a moment he felt like he was seventeen again. Some days he had to look in a mirror to realise he was getting older by the minute, each grey hair a reminder. Forty-five had seemed like inches from death when he was a kid; now he'd reached it he realised how wrong he'd been.

In the container were brightly decorated cupcakes slathered with thick icing and sugar decorations. 'Wow. I'd best not. The sugar low after one of those is gonna be a killer.'

Kim's light, feathery chuckle filled the cab. 'Yeah, it's true. Should come with a warning sign.'

The container was nearly half-empty. 'But you had one anyway, didn't you? I take it Mallory helped make them?'

She laughed again. 'Yes, she did. And yes, I may have crunched my way through one. Not bad once you get past the sprinkles. Mallory ate a few herself.'

'Ah yes, I did see some chocolate smudges on her face. I love kids, especially when you get to spoil them without dealing with the after-effects.'

'I know, right?' agreed Kim. 'I love my niece and nephew. Being on the farm means I've been there every day of their lives, more or less. I feel like more than just an aunty at times. Which is great.' Kim paused for a moment, sucked in her bottom lip and then said, 'So you don't have any kids?'

'Me? No, just wasn't meant to be, I guess. Not for lack of trying. Sometimes life just doesn't go the way you'd like.'

'Yeah, I understand.'

'So you don't have any kids either?' he asked. It was one way to find out if she had a fella.

Kim scoffed. 'Ha, you'd think so, right? Out here everyone seems to have had kids before they're thirty. I'm twenty-eight, so I could still tick that box, but I don't see a single guy happening any time soon. The one that was is getting married shortly.'

Charlie heard the undertone in her flippant words. 'The one that got away?' he asked gently.

Kim turned to him, watched him for a moment and then shrugged. 'Nah, not really. He was never mine. And not to worry, he's deliriously happy, which is all I wanted for him. He's a good mate and that's what counts. Besides, it's too hard to find a guy when I'm already married to the farm.'

'Surely not. Someone like you struggling for a date? I find that very hard to believe.'

'Well, that's very sweet of you, but it's hard out here. Plus the farm keeps me busy. Drew's wedding will be the first big event I've been to in ages.'

'Maybe you need a more optimistic attitude,' he teased.

'An optimistic farmer? They're a rare breed, don't you know?' Kim reached the end of the crop and pressed some buttons as she steered the harvester towards a patch of crop further away. 'This is the worst of the hail damage,' she said as they got closer.

'It's amazing how it's just come through in strips. I was at your neighbour's yesterday and it was his paddocks on this heading that were affected the worst too.'

'It's just topped off a shit year, really. Canola was patchy and crap to harvest, barley was all screenings, and the wheat has been just as crap – what wasn't hail-damaged. We have a hundred tonnes to put through the seed cleaner when we finish harvest,' said Kim.

'Is this all you have left?'

'Yeah, we'll be done today. Then Matt and Loz are taking the kids to the coast for a holiday and I'll be chief bottle washer.'

'When do you take holidays?' he asked.

She laughed. 'What would I do on a holiday?'

They talked about the hail-damaged crop and even got out to take a look before getting back on the header. Charlie told her to keep harvesting until she had a boxful, as he didn't want to slow them down – or give up this time chatting with Kim.

'So why insurance, and why Lake Grace?' asked Kim.

The first part of her question was easy. 'Well, living in the city my whole life, I knew bugger-all about the country but have always been fascinated by it. I don't admit this to many people, but *McLeod's Daughters* was one of my favourite shows. The amazing scenery was just one of the attractions . . . Claire was always my favourite.'

Kim smiled, nodding her head. 'Totally. She was my idol.'

'Anyway, I ended up in insurance and went through a few different companies and eventually landed with Elders. I think it was the call of the country. I did trips out with some of the guys and knew I was in the right place. From that moment on I made it my specialty, even though I knew nothing about farming. I was eager to learn, and farmers are easygoing guys to chat with. It made for a great job and a welcome change from the big corporate clients I was working with before. So I did a stint in Narrogin filling in for a guy on leave. The country had her hooks in by then, and when the Lake Grace job came up I applied and here I am. Happy as a pig in – poop.'

Kim pressed her lips together to stop herself laughing.

'What?' he asked.

'Sorry. I'm not used to guys toning down their language in front of me.'

'Oh, don't worry, I can be as rough as the best of them,' said Charlie, worried he'd disappointed her in some way.

'No, Charlie. I think it's wonderful. I swear a lot myself but it's nice to see someone making the effort to be polite. It's flattering to think I matter enough.'

'You can thank my mum for that,' said Charlie. 'She swore like a trooper, but always said I needed to respect the old values. No swearing in front of kids or women.'

'I like the sound of your mum. Was your dad the same? Old-school values?'

'Yeah, he was a gentle giant. Treated Mum like a princess. It's probably why she never found anyone else after he died.'

'Oh, I'm sorry.'

'It's okay. He died in a car crash when I was eighteen. Since then it's just been my mum and my sister Sarah.' He stopped for a moment, wondering if he dared share the rest. Talking with Kim was easy. Maybe it always was with pretty strangers. 'Um . . .' He cleared his throat and tried again. 'My mum actually passed away recently and it's been a bit hard.' He felt his throat constrict and clenched his fists to fight it.

'Oh no, Charlie. I don't know what to say. I haven't lost anyone; I can't imagine how you would feel.' Kim rested her hand on his leg briefly and gave him a sympathetic smile.

'If you talk to my sister, she thinks I've come to Lake Grace because of Mum. That I'm running away.' My god, he had no idea why he was telling her this, and yet he couldn't stop himself.

'But I was there for her funeral, and helped sort out the house.'

The funeral had been harrowing. It had been small with just immediate family and dear friends. They'd all come dressed in bright colours, which had brought a smile to Charlie's face. Only a week later Sarah had practically ordered him to help sort out Mum's house. 'If we don't do it now, Charlie, I don't think I'll ever be able to do it,' she had said.

And so they'd started with the personal things, before Sarah's husband had got a few friends in to help clear out the furniture. The house was to be sold, as neither Charlie nor Sarah wanted to live in it and they couldn't bear to rent it out. Charlie suspected they both wanted the house to stay in their memories as it had been – filled with happy times with their mum, the years with their dad – but they couldn't keep it as a memorial.

And then during the cleaning they'd found the card. It was addressed to Charlie, and it had tipped his whole world on its axis.

Kim got to the end of another run and stopped the header before turning to him. Her brow creased with concern. 'Are you running away?' she asked.

It was like she'd slapped him. 'I'm not running.' That part was true, but under the scrutiny of her coffee-coloured eyes he felt compelled to say more. 'I'm searching. Searching for me, my place, where I belong.' He swallowed hard under her watchful gaze. There were more questions churning in those dark eyes but she blinked and turned away.

'I hope you find what you're looking for, Charlie. I think you're entitled to some time out – just don't forget about your sister. She'll be hurting as well.'

'Yeah, I know.' He took a deep breath and ran his hand through his hair. 'Well, Doctor Kim, how much do you charge for your header counselling service?' he said jokingly.

She started the header moving again, her lips curling into a smile. 'I deal in the only currency that works around here, Charlie, and that's the liquid variety.' She shot him a wink.

The buzzer went off to indicate the bin was full, and Charlie automatically turned to look at the box behind him through the inspection window.

'Right. Well, I think I can manage that. You don't mind me stopping around with a few beers then? I'd love to see any other creations you have on the go. I saw the dragon,' he said, suddenly remembering how he'd felt in its presence. 'I gotta say it was something special. Billy didn't exaggerate one bit.'

'Billy never does. I do have a few things on the go. You've got my mobile number – just give us a bell when it suits. After today I'll be home cleaning up gear and sorting the seed cleaning, so I'd love an excuse to stop for a beer,' she said as they made it back to the field bin.

She moved on the seat, her arm briefly brushing against his. Little shock waves ran through his body. He tried hard not to look at her singlet, but it was fitted and her breasts were beautifully on display. They'd be perfect handfuls. Damn. He moved his eyes to the wheat, and tried to focus on the shape of the golden heads. If he didn't he'd be showing his excitement pretty clearly as he tried to leave. Yet again, he felt like a teenager. The emptying of the header box gave him time to clear his mind. 'Thanks for the ride, Kim. I'll sort out that claim and get back to you.'

'Thanks. And don't forget those beers,' she said with a warm smile. 'I'll hold you to that.'

As he climbed down from the header and made his way back to his car, he knew that nothing would make him forget the beers. Any excuse to spend some more time with Kim. Maybe he could personally deliver the claim details too?

Then he stopped himself. Did he really think he had a chance? Was he just an old fool? So out of the dating game that he was reading this all wrong? Maybe she was just a girl who liked beer and company.

Charlie got into his car, looked down at his left hand and rubbed the faint tan line on his ring finger. It still felt like it was there, that gold band. He wondered if Kim could pick it. It probably didn't matter – a few more weeks out in the summer sun and it would be well and truly gone.

Chapter 9

KIM walked back from the header to pick up the ute. It had an air compressor on it so she could clean her header – or at least make a start on it. Cleaning up was never a fun job, but it had to be done. There were a few other maintenance issues she had to take care of too. There was nothing worse than getting to the next harvest and realising you hadn't fixed that problem.

It was a beautiful afternoon. The day was still warm but bearable, and the clouds floating past provided some respite from the sun. The sky reminded her of Charlie, his eyes the same soft blue. She could easily get lost in them. It was undeniably pleasant to have a chat with a handsome bloke, especially one who was so easy to talk to. Was it because he was older, or was it just his manner?

She couldn't help but smile as she thought about his next visit with the promised beer. Had there been some chemistry flying around in that header cab? Kim was sure there was something, but she was no expert. Yet some part of her felt that he seemed interested, even if it was just as a friend. Kim would gladly take that right now. With Drew so busy, she was missing their friendship, and it hurt a little. Maybe Charlie could fill that void? He certainly ticked plenty of boxes. Yes, she'd been without male companionship for a while – so much so that just the scent of Charlie had her hormones going crazy, helped along by the intimacy of the header.

Her phone started ringing, interrupting her thoughts. She fished it out of her pocket.

'Hi, Dad,' she said.

'Hi, sweetheart. Have you finished?' David's voice was gravelly but soft-spoken.

'Just an hour ago. We're about to start cleaning down.'

Her parents, who lived in Albany, usually came back to town during seeding and harvest to help out. They stayed in their old house, which was now Kim's, and her mum would cook meals for her while Dad would help them out with the farm work. It was nice to see them again, even if her dad was a little annoying in the header, still trying to tell her how to harvest, as if she hadn't done it many times before. Matt couldn't handle the lectures, so Dad ended up with her most times.

'Mum and I are going to come down soon. We, um, have some things to discuss with you,' he said, his voice suddenly uncertain.

Kim stopped walking and frowned. 'What's up, Dad? Is everything all right? Are you sick?' she said, her mind going into a panic.

'We were thinking of coming down on Monday, if that's all right with you, Kimberly?'

'Okay,' she said. 'But what's this about, Dad?'

'Nothing to worry about, sweetie. We'll talk when we get there.'

Kim could tell she wasn't going to get anything more out of him now. 'Okay. Oh, Matt and Loz are leaving tomorrow. They're off on holiday for a few weeks with the kids.'

'Oh, I forgot about that. Silly me. Well, we'll come down when they get back.'

What could it be that they needed to talk about? Kim could only think it was something bad, something to do with their health. Dad had never sounded more serious, and the fact he wouldn't say anything now didn't bode well.

'Okay, Dad, as long as you're fine. Say hi to Mum for me.'

'Good girl. I will. I better go let her know she doesn't have to pack just yet. You know what your mother's like, she probably has our cases full already,' he said with a chuckle.

'Go stop her then. Give her my love.'

'Will do. Bye, Kim. Love you.'

'Love you too, Dad.'

After Kim had hung up she stared at her phone for a while, her brow creased in thought.

'You right there, sis?'

Kim had only dimly registered the ute approaching. Her brother leant out the window, his dark hair receding ever so slightly. She teased him about it on occasion, but not today. Her heart wasn't in it.

'Yeah.' She put her phone away and stepped up on the side of his vehicle, catching a lift. Matt drove her back to her ute.

'You're right to clean the headers by yourself?' he asked. 'Loz wants me to pack the campervan tomorrow.' He grinned cheesily.

'Please stop. That looks more like a dog's snarl than a smile. Far too many teeth on show.'

Matt rolled his eyes.

'Yeah, no worries,' said Kim. 'I knew I'd be doing them both, what with you gallivanting off on holiday.' She made a face. 'The cleaning can wait till tomorrow. I was thinking I might go visit Harry and say thanks.'

'What, Crazy Harry? Are you mad?'

Matt was only teasing but Kim could tell there was some genuine worry behind his words.

'He's nice. And he deserves a proper thanks.' After the sobering conversation with her dad, she couldn't help but think of Harry all alone, with no one to care for him, to worry about him and check on him, except for Tom. 'Think I might take over a few beers.' Plus she'd liked chatting to him. It was as simple as that. 'Besides, if he was going to kill me, he'd have done it that night,' she said, slapping her brother's arm.

'It's your funeral,' he teased as he got out.

'You can't get rid of me that easily, bro. I'll see ya tomorrow.'

She left him choking on her dust. When she checked the rearview mirror he was flipping her the bird. She loved that idiot to death. They could yell at each other and then be best mates again seconds later. If something blew up more seriously, Lozzy was always on hand to help them sort it out.

Stopping at her work shed, Kim walked past her welding gear and the collection of rusty metal bits to where all her finished creations sat. She wanted to take one to Harry as a thank-you gift.

'You'll do,' she said, patting a metal dog she'd made. After loading it into the ute she went to an old fridge in the corner where she kept her beer supply and pulled out a six-pack.

Next, Kim headed to her house and went around the back. Jo was lying on her dog bed. 'Hey, Jo, up for a trip?' Kim bent down and patted her kelpie, who was greying a lot around her face. Her baby girl was now sixteen, quite old for a dog. Jo lifted her head and Kim could swear she smiled, her tail flapping against her padded bed.

Kim almost fell over as something nudged against her back. She turned to see Maverick, her pet sheep. 'Hey, boy. You missing the love? Sorry, you can't come. I'd be a laughing stock if I had you and Goose plus Jo on the back of the ute.' Her two pet sheep had grown up with Jo, so they behaved as if they were dogs. If Jo left her bed for too long it was guaranteed either Goose or Maverick would be there. 'Let's go, Jo.'

Upon hearing the command Jo got up and followed Kim. Kim couldn't help but marvel at her dog; she still seemed happy and had no ailments. There had been no trips to the vet in the last ten years. She was sure Harry would appreciate meeting her.

Together they drove out to Harry's place, Jo in the passenger seat because she'd earned her place. Kim hoped Harry was home; which was likely, seeing as he didn't leave the farm. Plus it was that time of the day when the jobs were just about over and the beer was cracked open.

Sure enough, she saw his ute on one of the tracks on Tom Murphy's land and followed him back to his house.

'What are you doing here?' said Harry as they both got out of their utes. It wasn't said harshly though. It was clear he was pleasantly surprised, and the big smile on his face made her feel welcome. Harry stood while his dogs jumped off the back of his ute and ran around him, yapping at their visitor. Jo had been fast asleep on the front seat of Kim's ute until then.

Kim held up the six-pack. 'Thought I'd come and say thanks for looking after me the other day. Plus I brought you something.' Kim gestured for him to come closer and pointed to her creation on the back of her ute. 'This is for you, to add to your pet collection.' He had so many dogs, what was one more?

'Aw, you didn't have to, lass,' he said before he actually saw the metal dog. But then he was lost for words. The look on Harry's face was priceless. He reached out and touched its ear, which was made from the metal point of a header comb. 'This is amazing. No one's ever brought me anything,' he said softly.

Kim looked away as she heard his voice crack. 'I figured this one would be as loved as your others,' she said, patting Molly, or was it Bindi? She'd have to ask Harry later.

'I will treasure it. Did you make this, Kim?'

'Yep. One of many. Just a bit of tinkering I do on the side.'

Harry looked at her strangely. Kim kicked at the ground with her boot and watched the dogs as they all sniffed her legs, no doubt smelling Jo.

'I'm glad you came. I've never met a girl like you before. You'd be a farmer's dream wife, I bet, being able to weld and work a farm,' he said, picking up his gift from the ute tray.

'You'd think. But I don't have much luck in that department,' said Kim.

'Hey, who's this girl?' he asked as he spotted Jo.

'That's Jo.'

Jo lifted her head and blinked at them as if to say, *Yes that's me*, and then put her head back down.

They walked to the house and Harry found a spot for his gift.

'Right here by the back door, so I can see her every day,' he said with pride.

Kim loved that he was so chuffed with it. 'Did you want a beer, Harry?' she asked.

'Nah, love, I've been hanging out for a cuppa tea. You keep your beers for yourself. I'll just put the kettle on. Grab a spot on the verandah and we can watch the sun go down.'

'That sounds like a plan,' she said, making herself at home on the edge of the verandah and opening a beer. Harry kicked off his boots and went inside to make tea.

Kim wondered if Harry drank at all. Maybe he was a reformed alcoholic? There was so much about him that she didn't know. Well, with a bit of luck she'd change that.

'Look what I found. Not sure if they go with beer but they certainly go with a cuppa,' said Harry as he came back out with a big mug and a packet of Tim Tams.

'They probably don't, but when there's chocolate about, I find it goes with everything,' she said, reaching for one as he held the packet out to her.

He chuckled and settled down beside her. And then, as the sun set across the wide-open sky, they talked like old friends, dogs sniffing around the garden and Jo sleeping soundly in the ute again.

Chapter 10

1968

THE cement step was hard against his backside, especially after half an hour. But John couldn't move. Where was there to go? So he kept sitting and staring out across his poky lawn and the boundary fence. The grass was even and neat and an asbestos fence edged their bit of land. This was all the land he had now. Almost made him want to cry.

'Hey, Johnny,' said Beth. He felt her hand snake around his shoulders as she sat beside him. 'I know it's not the view you'd hoped for. Not much of a view at all, really. I wish we could have found a house on a bigger block.'

Beth sighed and he felt the weight she carried. She tried so hard to please him. He leant his head against her shoulder, breathing in her sweet natural perfume. She reminded him of home. Only it wasn't home any more. This tiny house in suburbia was.

'I know, me too. But this house is close to family. And it's got everything you were hoping for. I know you, Bethy – you'll make this place our home in no time,' said John. The truth was he didn't care in the end what house they lived in or how big the yard was, because he knew if he came back, he'd return to the country. Return to the land.

'Are you sure you didn't want a family dinner before you go? Your mum seemed a little upset you didn't want them here to say goodbye.' Beth spoke softly as she entwined her fingers with his.

John looked into the eyes of his wife, which were such a bright blue they always knocked him for six. He'd told her they put a spell on him the moment he saw her. They still did. 'I just wanted more time with you. I've said my goodbyes to the family. It's not like I'm off to Vietnam yet, anyway – this is only the first part of my training. I'm still in Australia, just at the other end of it. And I'll be home again before you know it.'

A horn sounded from the front of the house and panic flashed across Beth's face. 'The taxi,' she said, launching into his arms. 'Oh John, I wish you didn't have to go.'

'I know, Bethy. I love you so much.' He hugged her fiercely. 'Come on. I better not leave him waiting.'

Beth stepped back, trying to hide the tears running down her face. 'Let's get your bag.'

He followed her inside, collected his wallet and took a last look around the house. Not because he'd miss his new home, but because he wanted to be able to picture where Beth would be when he talked to her on the phone. He'd been trying to capture memories to take with him, to keep him company on lonely nights.

'Call me when you can. I'll write to you too,' she said.

'I will.' John threw his bag into the boot of the taxi. 'I love you. I'll be back before you know it.'

'Probably after I've done all the painting,' she teased.

Her brave face was killing him. After another hug he climbed into the taxi and wound down the window.

'I love you, John,' she said.

As the car drove away he watched his slim wife standing on the kerb, waving with one hand while the other held a hanky to her face. He watched until the taxi turned a corner and she vanished from his sight. But not from his mind. This was their first time apart since being married. He hoped they were both strong enough to endure the separation ahead.

The taxi dropped him off out the front of the airport. He paid the driver then headed inside to check in. It was cool, large and open. He stepped across the stripy linoleum floor towards a large map on the wall, looking at the clocks there for the different countries. None was near Vietnam. But for now he was just heading across Australia – flying to Seymour in Victoria to travel to Puckapunyal army base for national service training.

After offloading his bag he sat for a bit on the padded chairs by the large windows, watching the planes, then went for a stroll around the airport garden, which had a large pond with some black swans. Little kids gathered at the edge of the water with their parents, watching the birds excitedly as planes came and went.

John felt like those little kids. This was all new to him. He'd never been on a plane – heck, he'd never been to the airport before. John looked down at his shaking hands. Yep, he was nervous too. He needed a drink to calm his nerves.

He soon found a bar inside, called The Orbit Inn. There were quite a few people there already, mostly blokes. Were they all heading off to training too? John squeezed in and found a spare stool by the bar and ordered a beer. By the time he'd finished it he'd found a guy to chat to. Dennis was also heading to Seymour, and introduced him to another mate he'd just made. By the second beer John was no longer nervous. Instead, he was having a great laugh with a group of guys. Some were country blokes just like him – he knew the towns they lived in. But there were plenty of bar patrons who were just city locals who'd come to the airport for a drink.

At some point John realised that the crowd had thinned out. 'Where did everyone go?' he asked Dennis. He was riding a beer wave of happiness.

'Probably to catch their flights. Hell, mine leaves soon,' Dennis said, squinting to read his watch.

'Oh shit, is that the time?' John blinked as he tried to focus on his own watch. 'Bloody hell, I've missed my flight.' He'd missed it by a lot.

'Don't worry, come with me. See if you can jump on my flight.'

They headed for the information desk as quickly as their drunken legs could take them.

With Dennis's quick talking John was allowed to board with him.

'You are bloody lucky, mate,' said Dennis as they headed outside to the tarmac and the fresh night air.

'More like lucky I had you.' The cold air sobered John up somewhat and brought home the reality of what had happened. How much trouble would he have been in if he hadn't got to training? He had a feeling they didn't sack people for not turning up. If only.

He and Dennis slept off their beers on the plane and arrived at the small runway in Seymour in the early hours of the morning. John was still trying to open his eyes and adjust to his hangover as he descended the plane steps to the tarmac. Even in his disoriented state, he didn't find it strange to see a couple of buses nearby and men in army uniforms all about. Men from the plane were getting on the buses as uniformed officers directed them. Nor did John take much notice of the man in uniform who had a patch on his arm that read 'MP'. That was until he approached John.

'Are you John Parson?' he asked. He looked stern and official.

'Yes, sir,' John replied, feeling he needed to be careful with his words as a sudden nervousness grew. He was feeling rather seedy and wondered if it showed.

The man latched on to his arm tightly, and directed him towards the bus. 'Come with me, Mr Parson. You and I will be sitting at the front of the bus on our way to the base.'

'But I need to find my bag first.'

'It's already on board. You were supposed to arrive a few flights ago.'

That's when it dawned on John that *MP* stood for military police. Shit, what had he done? The man in the perfect uniform looked less than impressed. He glared at John as if he was a flight-risk toddler.

It was a quiet bus ride. The first stop when they reached the Puckapunyal base was the guard house, where John found himself marched off the bus and into jail. The bus continued on to the barracks without him.

It certainly wasn't the introduction to the army he was hoping for. Because he'd missed his flight they thought he'd done a runner. Even though he'd turned up, it seemed he was still considered a flight risk. Maybe this was a common occurrence? Men called up for duty must decide they just didn't want to do it, and go AWOL. He could see how it would happen. It had crossed his mind.

John sat in the small cell for a few hours, trying to catch some shut-eye and ride out his hangover. But before long someone was banging on his bars.

'Time to get up, soldier!'

John opened his eyes. A soldier stood there watching him. This one looked important, but wasn't military police.

'I'm your platoon commander, Lieutenant Griggs. Are you planning on disappearing?' the man said frankly.

'No, sir. It was all a misunderstanding.' John stood up and walked to the bars to face the lieutenant. 'I had a few drinks at the bar and lost track of time. I'm not going to shirk my duties,' he said, trying to stand up straight. 'Sir,' he added, as the lieutenant squinted at him. The man's nose twitched and John guessed he smelt strongly of alcohol. It would all work in his favour.

'Right then. You're with me.'

John was let out and the lieutenant took him to the base, where he was sent straight in to pick up his gear, get his teeth looked at, get checked for colour blindness and then finally have a haircut. The staff weren't impressed at having to look him over in his current smelly state.

And so began basic training.

The NCOs he'd encountered briefly on the bus (he learnt that meant non-commissioned officers) had changed face once they settled back in the barracks. They made the new recruits stand, in their new baggy green uniforms and big black boots, to be yelled at like disobedient children. It was more like verbal abuse at times. It was a rude awakening for John, who felt like he was in a completely different world to the bar at the airport just hours ago. Where had he landed? Was he still on earth?

John couldn't remember if he called them sir or who was sergeant or corporal, and they used words he'd never heard before. Everything the NCOs said seemed demanding and urgent. The national servicemen – like John, those conscripted to fight – did drills in their lines. The corporals shouted instructions like 'Form three ranks upon the road. Number off – start from the right. Stepping off on the same foot. Quick march!'

John felt like he was back at primary school practising marching for their sports carnivals. Only this time it wasn't fun, and there were no parents cheering from the sidelines.

He didn't know a soul in his platoon but quickly learnt to keep his mouth shut. One of the redheads was mouthy and gave the corporal lip. The twenty push-ups he was given, followed by another twenty, were a useful lesson in staying quiet. No one ever spoke out again or backchatted, unless pushed to breaking point – and then they suffered the consequences.

As the days passed, the routine became easier. Parades and

morning runs were done early, then after breakfast the corporal would check their kit was up to standard. This meant bed as neat as a pin, boots shined until you could see your face in them. And then there were endless drills until they were known off by heart. Repetition was the key. Fitness was paramount too, and they went to the gym every day until they grew stronger. John enjoyed the rifle practice, as it reminded him of shooting back on the farm. The hand grenades were new but also fun.

The ten weeks flew by, and John liked his new leaner body. At night, when he had some quiet time to himself, he thought of Beth. He called her now again, and he'd read her letters and hold them against his chest. They were scented with her special going-out perfume, which was nice, but he craved her natural scent. He longed to sink his hands into her hair and kiss her. Unquestionably the hardest part about training was being apart from Beth.

He counted down the days until parade out – not for the completion of basic training, but because his family would be there to watch them display their drills. His Beth. She'd already promised to make the trek over with his parents, and it was like waiting for all his Christmases to come at once.

One morning John looked in the mirror, after wiping the steam away from the showers behind him. One of the lads was singing a Slim Dusty song, which made him think of the country. Another was yelling at him to shut up. It was just a normal day at the barracks.

He stared at the person before him: clean-shaven, with short clipped hair and muscled arms that were bigger than he ever could have got just working on the farm. What would Beth think of this John? Would he be too different? Would she like the army look? He hoped so. He also hoped that living in the city alone hadn't changed her too much either.

The worst thing was, John wasn't done yet. He'd been assigned to the infantry, which meant more training in Canungra in Queensland. Then, and only then, would he be deemed ready for war.

John wasn't sure if he'd ever be ready.

Chapter 11

KIM threw her bra onto her bed and then pulled on the strapless pink dress, doing up the zip under her arm. A feeling of absolute dread filled her at the thought of seeing herself in the mirror. Even looking down at this dusky-pink number was enough to make her freak out. Nat had dropped it round a day or two before.

'Oh, why do you make me do this, Drew?' she said out loud. Kim would have been quite happy wearing a suit and standing beside Drew as his best man. But no, tradition had her in a dress as a bridesmaid, which seemed ridiculous seeing as she hardly knew Natalie and would know none of the other bridesmaids, Nat's city friends. She was going to be the uncoordinated, uncomfortable ugly duckling in among the glowing swans. How could anyone look forward to that? And then there was the fact that everyone would be gawking at them. Kim hated being on display; the thought filled her with dread. She might as well wear clown shoes and a red nose – she was bound to go arse-up on her massive heels and have everyone laughing, so why not cut to the chase?

Kim took a step closer to her full-length mirror with her eyes shut, counting to three before opening them. Maybe she was expecting a miracle, but the reflection was enough to send her into meltdown mode. It wasn't her at all. She looked awkward. How could she pull this off? She was breaking out in a nervous sweat already and it was weeks before the wedding.

Her sock tan stood out on her bare legs, as did her singlet tan. Her chipped nails and stained palms looked like blokes' hands and her calluses kept catching the soft material of the dress like she had velcro fingers. And her boobs! They were like two ripe melons on display at the front of the fruit shop. Kim felt like she might as well be standing in her bra and undies. Why was she so churned up?

'Argh!' she screamed, letting out her frustrations as she flopped face first onto her bed.

'Kim! Are you okay?'

She jerked her face up just as Charlie appeared in her bedroom doorway with a six-pack of beer under his arm. He was in jeans and a dark-blue polo shirt with two buttons undone at the front, his face showing salt-and-pepper stubble. And his expression was that of a man about to rescue a girl from a dangerous situation.

'What's wrong? Is it a spider? Snake?' he said quickly as he scanned her room. 'I knocked on your door but when I heard the scream I rushed straight in.'

Now she felt like even more of a twit. Flopped on her bed in the pink dress with her clothes on the floor and her bra across her bed. Great!

'Snakes and spiders I can handle,' she said. 'But pink girly dresses, I can't.' She stood up and waved her hands over her outfit.

His eyebrows shot up as he assessed her dress. 'Oh, I don't know about that,' he said.

Kim saw his eyes brush over the garments on her bed and a blush rise on his face.

'I think you do pink girly dresses really well. You look beautiful.' Charlie's eyes came to rest on her.

She felt exposed under his gaze. 'A shame I don't agree. I feel like a chameleon stripped of its camouflage.'

'Would a beer help?' he said, holding the six-pack up. His mouth curved up, making little dimples appear.

'Yeah, it would. Just let me get out of this thing,' she said, gesturing at the dress. 'Sorry about this – um, you having to witness my meltdown. I got distracted looking for my dog outside, and then I thought I'd get this fitting over with before you arrived. Had to see if the dress needed altering.'

'I think it fits perfectly.'

Now it was Kim's turn to blush.

'I'll let you change. I'll go put these in the fridge.'

'That would be great,' she said. 'Kitchen's at the end of the passageway.'

Charlie nodded and then reached for the doorknob, pulling her door shut behind him.

Kim shook her head. Gosh, the poor guy, he must think she

was a right dingbat. Quickly she pulled the dress off, throwing it onto her bed like a work rag and getting back into her denim shorts, white singlet and checked shirt. She instantly felt ten times better.

When she came out Charlie was standing by the table in her old-style kitchen. Her mum had renovated the room not long before they moved to Albany, so now Kim was the lucky one who got to enjoy the stunning jarrah cupboards and black granite benchtops. The floor had also been redone in a soft grey tile that matched the walls. It was the best room in the house. A large eight-seater jarrah table sat in the middle of the room. Kim didn't need all those seats but it came in handy if she had Matt, Loz and the kids over for tea.

Charlie held out a beer and Kim took it from him as they both sat down at the table. 'Thanks, Charlie. So how've you been? Settled into the new job? Thanks for sorting out our claim so swiftly.'

'My pleasure. Yeah, the job is great. Settled in nicely. Great bunch to work with at Elders. Heather has been amazing.'

'Yeah she's a lovely lady. Easygoing and helpful.'

'I agree. She's gone out of her way to introduce me to everyone, and gives me a rundown on all the clients and who's related to who. She's a great assistant to have.'

'And Heather really would know everything – she's been in that role since I was at primary school. I'm so glad to hear it's going well.'

He turned and pointed to a photo on her fridge. 'This girl here seems comfortable in a dress.'

Kim looked at the photo of herself with Matt and Drew at Billy's first birthday party. She wore a pretty blue summer dress with strappy heeled shoes. 'That was a long time ago.'

'So what happened?'

Kim shrugged. 'The farm, I guess,' she said.

Charlie glanced at her sideways. She could tell he was waiting for more, that he knew it wasn't the whole story. Well, he'd be right, but she wasn't going to share it, at least not now. It was bad enough he'd seen her dress meltdown as it was. Why alienate him further?

Instead of pushing the issue, Charlie pointed to a photo of Jo. 'Is this the missing dog?'

Kim frowned, puzzled.

'You said earlier you'd been looking for your dog,' he clarified.

'Oh yep, that's Jo. I got back from work today and she wasn't here. I did a quick check around the sheds and Matt's place. She'll turn up though – she can't go far, she's sixteen years old.'

'Oh, wow. That's not a bad age.'

'I know,' she said. 'Mum and Dad got Jo for me when I was eleven, because Matt was going away to boarding school and they knew I'd need a companion. She was my best friend – still is.'

'Shall we go for a stroll and see if we can find her?'

'You don't mind? That would be great. I am actually a bit worried. It's not like her to wander off too far. Her legs aren't what they used to be and she might have got stuck somewhere. Matt reversed over her a few years back and fractured her pelvis on both sides, so she struggles to get up at times. But she's one tough old biddy. She doesn't even need medication except for some emu oil for her joints.'

'I have to meet this girl. Sounds like a trouper,' said Charlie as Kim steered him towards the back door, beers in hand.

As Kim pushed open the flywire door she turned to Charlie. 'Now just watch out for Maverick. He likes to headbutt people he doesn't know.'

As they stepped onto the verandah she could see he was just about to ask who Maverick was, but the question died on his lips when her two pet sheep made a beeline straight for them. As expected, Maverick looked like he was getting a charge up.

'Maverick, no!' she yelled and jumped into his path. She grabbed his head and looked into his funny brown eyes. 'Be a good sheep. This is my friend.' She rubbed his woolly head, and soon Charlie was doing the same. 'He'll behave now he's let you pat him. And this is Goose,' she said, pointing to the other sheep, which had a black patch on its nose and was trying to bury its face in her crotch. 'They think they're dogs.' She pushed Goose away.

'How long have you had these two?'

'A while now. Jo's the only mother they've ever known. They're handy at mowing my grass for me. Their mum died giving birth to them, and an eagle had begun chewing on them when I found them. I rescued them, treated their wounds and raised them – with Jo's help of course,' she said with a wink. 'But you wouldn't guess their rough start in life now. Can't see their scars for wool.'

'Such funny guys. Love their names.' Charlie touched their eartags, which were engraved with their names. He looked up as something else caught his eye. 'Oh look, it's a kangaroo,' he said in a whisper.

Kim laughed and he looked worried that she might scare it away. Instead she made a clicking sound with her tongue and the kangaroo came closer. 'This is Skittles. She's been with me ever since I hit her mum with my ute years back. Her mum died, but I found her in the pouch and looked after her. You can pat her, she's friendly as. The kids have mauled her with love so she can take anything.'

Charlie reached out and gave Skittles a pat between the ears. He looked like a tourist having his first interaction with a real kangaroo.

'First time, hey?' she asked.

'Yeah. Pretty amazing, aren't they? I've seen heaps but never this close. She's gorgeous.' Charlie bent down so he could look at her face more closely. 'Interesting name.'

'Matt suggested it after what I did to her poor mum. It kinda stuck. She's a good girl – I don't keep her locked up. Skits is free to go as she pleases, but she stays. I've seen her mixing with the other kangaroos down in the bush at the end of the paddock, but she always comes home. It must be the milk,' said Kim, and Skittles put her paws on her and rested her head against Kim's belly.

'No, I'd say she comes back for you. Looks like a close bond.'

They shared a smile in the afternoon light. 'I do love my animals,' said Kim. 'Come on. If Jo's gone anywhere it'll be to the patch of bush at the back of this paddock. She used to go hunting rabbits down there.'

Kim pushed open the small wire gate and stepped into the holding paddock. In one corner was a bale of hay for the sheep and a water trough.

'I love the way the afternoon sun makes the wild oats and dry grasses glow,' she mused. 'Something magical about this part of the day, don't you think?' She took a sip of her beer and glanced at Charlie, who was watching her with a funny expression. 'What?'

He smiled and shook his head. 'It's nothing. Well, actually, it's just nice to find someone who feels the way I do about Mother Nature. Moments like these are what I live for – they're what brought me out bush to begin with. All this space, the animals, the setting sun. What's not to love, right?'

Both his dimples appeared with his smile and Kim was struck again by how handsome he was. He was turning her shit afternoon into a great one.

'I couldn't agree more.'

They chatted as they strolled towards the bush, with Kim occasionally whistling or calling out for Jo. 'She's quite deaf so I don't expect her to really hear me. I'd need a foghorn for that.'

'How far in do you think she'd go?' Charlie asked as they reached the edge of the paddock.

The bush here was mainly shrubs and mallee trees, with a few big gum trees here and there. Animal tracks wormed through the bush and they followed one of these deeper in.

'We used to play in here as kids, Matt and I. We'd build cubbies, climb trees, make bike tracks and do all the other normal farm-kid stuff. Makes for the best childhood, you know, having such a big backyard.'

'I'm jealous. Growing up in the city is pretty different. The only escape I had was the park over the road, which I couldn't go to alone, or otherwise when we went to the zoo. I'd have given anything for this type of freedom.' Charlie found an old rope swinging from a branch and tugged on it. The rope gave way, rotten in his hand.

'Yep, we used to swing from that,' she said with a chuckle.

'Oh look, is that Jo?' said Charlie, pointing to a dark shape under a shady tree.

'Yeah, there she is. Dug herself a nice cool spot. Poor dog, the heat knocks her about a bit.' Kim cupped her hands and yelled, 'Jo!'

Jo didn't move.

Charlie stopped her with his hand. 'Just wait here,' he said.

She watched Charlie with eagle eyes as he walked over and patted Jo. 'Old girl, you rest up now,' said Charlie softly. His large hand stilled on Jo and she could see he was checking for a breath. Then he turned to Kim and his face told her everything she needed to know.

She'd prepared herself for this day – Jo was no spring chicken, and she'd known it was coming, and yet the reality of it hit her hard. Hot tears sprung, blurring her vision. 'Oh Jo,' she managed to croak out before the first large teardrop rolled down her face. She rushed towards her beloved companion and stroked Jo's lifeless body as Charlie crouched next to her.

'I'm so sorry, Kim,' he said.

His tenderness was too much – it broke whatever reserve she was holding on to, and as Charlie's arms wrapped her up tightly she sobbed like a child. She knew a huge part of her had been torn away. Jo had been her companion for so long she didn't know how she could face the day without her. No more chats, no more evening strolls together or rides in the ute. Jo was her family.

Soon she realised she was turning Charlie's shirt into a sodden mess and tried to rein herself in, but it was undeniably nice to be held in his arms. His scent surrounded her and his warmth enveloped her.

'I'm sorry, Charlie. I thought I was prepared,' she said, leaning back on her heels so she could wipe her face with her shirt. He let his arms drop and she felt their absence.

'Don't be. I totally understand.'

'Gosh, I must look a right mess,' she said, using the other side of her checked shirt to dab her eyes. Her face would no doubt be all red and blotchy, her eyes puffy. Poor Charlie, he really was getting the worst of her. She'd be lucky if he ever came back.

'Kim,' he said, reaching a hand up to her face. 'You're gorgeous, no matter what.'

They sat looking at each other with Jo next to them. Cockies screeched overhead in the trees and the leaves rustled with the breeze. Time stood still for a moment.

Kim wasn't sure what to say, but the tenderness in his touch and words felt real.

'What will you do with her?' he asked, breaking the intensity.

'I want to bring her back to the house so she's closer to me.' She glanced at Jo's lifeless body and bit her lip hard as her eyes grew moist with fresh tears.

'Righto.' Charlie gave his beer to Kim and stood up so he

could gently lift Jo's body from the ground, cradling her in his arms. Her legs were stiff – she'd been gone for a while. 'Let's take her home then.'

'Oh, Charlie, you don't have to do that. I can take her,' said Kim.

He shook his head. 'No, let me do this for you. It's okay.'

Kim nodded and looked down at Jo in his arms. Her fur was soft, her ears flopped over and her eyes were closed. Kim touched the tan spots above her eyes. Jo was the smartest dog she'd ever known. She would miss the way those spots moved when Jo tilted her head and listened to Kim.

'I miss you already, Jo,' said Kim, and her bottom lip quivered. She swiped her hand across her eyes as they started their trek back towards the house.

Kim forced herself to keep looking ahead because if she glanced at Jo then more tears would come. She couldn't stop them. Her heart was so heavy and her body felt like lead.

Back at the house, Maverick, Goose and Skittles watched them curiously. 'Bring her into the old laundry. I've got a hessian sack we can wrap her in,' said Kim. She didn't want the other animals to see Jo like this.

They wrapped Jo up carefully and left her in the outside laundry on the verandah.

'She can stay there until I've dug the hole. It shouldn't be too hard after the rain we just had,' said Kim as she went back outside to get a shovel.

'Here,' said Charlie, following her. 'Let me help. Show me where you want it.'

Kim nodded and led him out to the pet cemetery, off to the side of the house next to the fruit tree enclosure. 'All our pets are here: lambs, dogs, birds, kangaroos, and even Matt's fish.'

Kim pointed to a metal cross with the name 'Jinx' welded onto it. 'Jo will go right next to Jinx, who was one of her pups. She died from a snakebite.' That day had gutted her. Jinx would have kept her company with Jo gone. If only.

'Parents shouldn't have to outlive their kids,' said Charlie. 'Jinx has a beautiful headstone. I'm sure you'll have something special made up for Jo in no time.'

Kim gave a sad smile. 'I will. I'll make sure of that.' She drew in a deep breath. 'Right, anywhere along here will be fine, thanks, Charlie.'

'Yep, onto it,' said Charlie as he launched the shovel at the dry dirt.

They took turns with the shovel, chipping away until there was a hole they could fill with water. After a few weeks of hot sun the ground wasn't as easygoing as she'd hoped. While that filled up, Charlie got them another beer and Kim pulled up the weeds that grew around Jinx's grave and the new one.

Charlie came and sat beside her, passing over a beer.

'I'm sorry, this probably isn't the afternoon you were expecting,' said Kim. 'You've copped the lot.' She gratefully took the beer.

'No, it hasn't, but in a way I'm glad I was here. I hate to think of you dealing with this alone.'

His blue eyes shifted to grey in the dying light. The sun had already set behind the bushes at the end of the paddock, and the two of them were now basking in its afterglow. She didn't want Charlie to go home just yet.

'Thanks, Charlie, I appreciate it. And I'm glad you're here, even if it means you witnessed my dress debacle.'

'Debacle, is that what you're calling it?' he asked with a chuckle.

'Yeah. Who does that over a dress?'

'Someone who's out of their comfort zone,' he replied.

Kim looked at him strangely and he laughed.

'You forget, I grew up in a house with a moody sister and a mum who was trying to cope with the loss of her husband. There were meltdowns most days and I was the one who tried to keep the peace. Debacles don't scare me.'

Kim grinned. 'Good to know.'

'As for your dress situation, may I suggest you ease into it?'

'What do you mean?' she asked curiously.

'Well, have you any events coming up? Birthday parties? Engagements?'

'I have an awards night in the city,' she said, wondering where he was going.

'Perfect. Use it as practice. If it's in the city, I'm guessing you're not going to know many people there?' Kim shook her head. 'Great, even better. They won't know you. Go to this event and wear a dress,' he said.

'But I don't have any, not any more.'

'Go shopping and find a dress that you feel a little comfortable in. And some nice shoes that aren't too high.'

'So, dressy but not too dressy,' she said.

'Yep. Get comfortable in a dress you've chosen first, wear it, own it, feel confident. I know you'll look amazing no matter what you wear. But it's up to you to realise it and accept it.'

'Wise words from the great Charlie,' she joked. But he had a point. 'I like the sound of that. I'll give it a go.'

'Do you need a partner for this event? Could I come?' he asked.

'Scared I won't go through with it?' she teased. 'I'm a finalist in the Rural Women's Award.' Kim went on to tell him about her idea to help teach kids farming and life skills through Camp Kulin.

'That sounds amazing! Who's going with you?' he asked.

'Just Loz. And you . . . if you want to.'

'I'd love to. When and where?'

Kim smiled. 'I'll email you the details.' Charlie clapped his hands together and got up, reaching for the shovel. Kim reached for his jean-clad leg, stopping him. 'Thanks, Charlie,' she said softly as she gazed up at him in the topaz haze of dying sunlight. 'Thanks heaps.'

Chapter 12

CHARLIE sank the shovel into the mud and dug out another heap. He could feel a blister or two forming on his hands, but he wasn't about to complain. He was having a great time – well, besides the fact he was digging a grave.

His heart had gone out to Kim, seeing her go to pieces – this strong independent woman who looked like she'd lost the world with the passing of her beloved dog. Just watching her now, standing tall but with tears in her eyes, he felt moved. She was an unusual combination of strength and softness, and it made him like her a hundred times more.

'Thanks, Charlie, I think that should do. I'll go get Jo.' Kim stood up and disappeared around the side of the house.

He glanced at his watch. He'd have to head home soon. But he didn't want to.

Kim came back and placed Jo gently in the grave. She said her goodbyes to her beloved mate, took off the dog's collar and then shovelled dirt over Jo as she lay in her final resting place.

'I can't believe she's really gone,' Kim said as she patted the last of the earth on the grave. 'It'll hit home tomorrow morning when I walk out to chat to her as I have my cuppa in the sun.' She was fighting back tears. 'It was our morning ritual.'

Charlie reached over and held her arm for a moment, an offer of understanding and support. To his embarrassment the contact stirred him in other ways. He was so damn attracted to her, it would be obvious if he wasn't careful. Quickly he withdrew his hand; now was not the time or place. But it was hard not to find her alluring. And part of the attraction was that Kim had no idea of her effect on him – or probably anyone, for that matter.

'Charlie?'

'Sorry?' Damn, he'd been away with the fairies.

'Did you want to stay for tea? My way of saying thanks.'

Inwardly he groaned. Why did he have to meet someone like her when he was least ready for it? 'I'd love to, Kim, but can I take a raincheck? I have to get home – there're a few things I have to attend to. But I appreciate the offer.'

'Yeah, sure. No worries.' Kim turned away from him and wiped her grubby hands on her shorts.

He felt awful, as though he'd hurt her. Charlie got the feeling she hadn't asked anyone over for tea in a long time, and his refusal might mean she wouldn't try again. 'I wish I could stay. Can I come another night? I hate cooking for one,' he said. She turned around and he was relieved to see her grin.

'I know what you mean. Sucks, hey? Sure thing, let me know when you're free and I'll have you over for my famous lamb shank pie.'

'Oh, gee, now you're talking. Sounds mouth-watering.' The mood had improved, which he was thankful for. 'Walk me to my car?' he asked.

'Yep, sure.'

They headed around to the front of the house, where his car was parked by the waist-high fence.

'Next time you come, just park in the shed next to my ute. The spot's only ever used when my folks come to stay,' she offered, pointing to the two-car shed next to the house.

'Cheers, I'll remember that,' said Charlie. He opened his car door then turned back to Kim. 'Thanks for your company. And I'm so sorry about Jo.' He leant across and gave her a hug. It just seemed like the right thing to do, and if he was truthful with himself, he just wanted to hold her one last time. She was the most huggable girl he'd ever known.

They held each other for a few beats longer than he'd expected. There was something wonderful about holding someone tightly: the connection, the closeness, the contact.

Reluctantly, Charlie pulled away when he felt himself stirring. 'See you soon. Take care.'

'Bye, Charlie, thanks for everything.'

He watched her waving in the rear-view mirror until she disappeared into his dust.

Not long after leaving Kim's, he arrived back at his new home. It was in a quiet street on the east side of town. Kids played in the streets and rode motorbikes in the large vacant block at the end of the road. His neighbours always waved and said hello. Most had come to meet him and introduce themselves. It gave him the feeling of being accepted and welcomed into this close-knit community.

He pulled into his carport, which was to the side of the cream-coloured house. The garden was slightly overgrown from the previous renter, but Charlie was slowly making headway with the weeds and dead plants. He enjoyed improving the look of it, and he realised his neighbours appreciated it too. Just yesterday Steph next door, the mother of twins, stuck her head over the fence to thank him for pulling out the scraggly bougainvillea that drooped over the fence and clawed at her kids as they ran past. She apologised for Jake and Max's noisiness, but Charlie actually liked hearing the kids play. It made him feel less alone.

As he got to the door he could hear the phone ringing. He managed to unlock the door and get to it in time. 'I'm here, I'm here,' he said as he put the receiver to his ear.

'This is the second time I've called. You were the one who said to call at seven,' said his sister, with an edge to her voice.

'I know. I'm sorry, Sarah,' he said, walking back to shut the door. 'I was out at a farm with a client and her dog died, so I helped bury it.'

'Oh, Charlie. How sad.' Sarah's voice had changed completely. She was an animal lover through and through. 'It was good of you to help.'

'There was no one else. It'd be horrible to bury your best mate on your own. Remember old fleabag Freddy? Took all three of us to bury him, remember.'

'Gosh yes, Freddy. How devastated we all were – just a mass of tears, setting each other off all the time. Losing Dad not long before didn't help us any. I loved that bag-of-bones dog.'

'Me too,' said Charlie, as he moved to the couch and sat down. He was feeling suddenly knackered, and a chat with his sister was going to wear him out even more. 'Are you at home, sis, or at work?'

'I'm home. It was a long day today. The kids wear me out but I love seeing their faces when they create art that really captures something of their lives. I think it helps a lot of them express feelings they have no other way of getting out.'

'You do good work, sis. I probably don't tell you enough, but I'm proud of you.' Sarah worked as an art teacher at a high school.

'Thanks, that's lovely of you to say. I hope you're not trying to deflect me from what I want to know though. I'm wondering how the detective work is going,' said Sarah.

'You always do cut to the chase, don't you?'

'One has to with you, Charlie boy. You beat around the bush and baffle me with bullshit sometimes.'

Charlie smirked at his sister's description. 'Well, the short answer is there's nothing to tell yet. I'm just taking my time, getting to know the town first, figuring out who I can approach. I've been checking out the Art Space in town, and I'm thinking of asking if they'd be keen for you to come down and do a workshop. Then you could visit and see for yourself what this place is like.'

Sarah sighed. 'From the photos you've sent me I doubt they'd need me. Looks like a town full of very clever artists. But I'd love to see some of their work firsthand. I met Kerrie Argent once, did I tell you? She came to Perth for Sculpture by the Sea. I heard later that her work went to Denmark. She got to shake hands with the prince himself. I'd love it if my art could get me that.'

'I may not be the prince of Denmark, but it gets my approval,' he teased. 'Anyway, Mum always said I was her prince.' The words came out without much thought and it wasn't until afterwards that he realised how confused they made him feel. But his sister didn't pick up on it.

'Ha ha,' she said sarcastically.

'I'll go and see the Art Space people and see if they'd be interested – that's assuming you'd be able to make time to come down?' he asked, feeling more tired than ever. He just wanted a hot shower and to change out of his muddy, doggy clothes.

'Yes, I'll make time – school holidays are easy. Anything for you, Charlie boy.' She paused for a moment. 'Do you think you'll find anything?'

He took a deep breath and blew it out. 'I don't know. It's a small town, so someone is bound to remember.'

'Okay, I'm not rushing you. Just curious. Take your time. You may decide you don't want to know.'

Charlie scratched his chin. Sarah was right: a part of him was still a bit unsure about whether he wanted to search at all. Was that why he hadn't jumped right in and started asking around? Or was he scared that once he did he wouldn't find anything, and his search would be over? He was so tired, he couldn't figure it out now. All he wanted to do was go back to Kim. Being with her made everything seem easy. He loved the quiet that she brought to his mind.

'All right, sis – I need to go and have a shower. I'll talk to you later, okay? Love you.' If he didn't get her off the phone now he'd be stuck for another hour listening to her talk about the next art project or a new protégé she'd been working with. She could talk the proverbial off a donkey when she got going.

There was a pause. 'Okay, Charlie. I'll call you again in a few days, same time.'

He could tell she'd been settling in for a big chat and was a bit thrown.

'Sorry, I reek of dog and I'm covered in mud. But we'll talk again soon. Bye.'

'Bye,' she said, before the line went dead.

He'd let her talk his ear off another night. Later this evening he planned to read the pamphlets he'd collected from the visitor centre, the ones that gave an outline of the history of the town. You never knew, they might give him a lead. Maybe the name Parson would pop up. Maybe it wouldn't be that easy. It was a long shot, but in a small town anything was possible.

Chapter 13

THE town was buzzing on Saturday morning as Charlie walked down the main street. It was a beautiful sunny day and the shops were a perfect two-block stroll from his house. Some thongs, shorts and a T-shirt made a nice change from his work gear. On the way he wandered around the old railway building, with its orange-tiled roof and spectacular garden full of orange roses in full bloom. They matched perfectly, and he figured it had been done intentionally. Next he passed the old Bankwest building – more orange, he realised – and the pharmacy, then Arjo's coffee shop, and then the Art Space.

Charlie stuck his head inside the door. 'Morning, ladies.' Despite Charlie being new in town, these ladies were well on the way to becoming friends. He loved popping in every Saturday for coffee and a chat. When he'd told them a few weeks ago about his sister, they'd welcomed him into the fold and had set in motion the workshop that would bring his sister to Lake Grace. He felt more at home with these ladies than he did in his own house.

'Charlie, good timing. Grab a seat, the kettle's just boiled. Black coffee, isn't it?' said Marjorie.

She was one of the caretakers of the Art Space, and in a way she reminded him of his mum. Not in looks – Marjorie had long grey hair swept up in a bun, and his mum had had short hair that was always changing colour. It was Marjorie's grace, the way she spoke, her passion for art and flair for creativity. And maybe it was the way she waved her hands around as she spoke and always greeted Charlie with a hug.

Marjorie came up to him now, hugging him and then gesturing to one of the plastic chairs set up around a white table. 'I'll be two seconds. Julie's just out the back sorting out our supplies for your sister's arrival. We're all so excited.' Marjorie ducked into the makeshift kitchen.

He took a seat and looked out the large glass window, watching the townsfolk come and go. The coffee shop next door was a popular spot.

'There ya go, my boy,' Marjorie said as she put down a cup in front of Charlie. 'Kim should be here any minute. She's popping in to say hello.' She put her own cup down and took a seat across from him.

Kim was coming here? His day was looking up. Charlie sat up in his chair and glanced at the street, trying to spot her tall, leggy figure. It had been a week and a half since he'd seen her, but that didn't mean she'd been far from his thoughts.

'G'day, Charlie,' said Julie, who'd appeared from the back of the building. 'If you're not in any rush, could I ask for your help with something?' She sat down next to him, the colourful scarf around her neck clashing with her equally colourful shirt. It was something his mum would have worn. It was nice to see Julie in something bright – he'd been starting to think she only owned black or navy clothes.

'Yeah, of course. What do you need done?' Charlie took a sip of his coffee as Marjorie opened a packet of chocolate biscuits. He reached for one. 'You know I work for chocolate biscuits,' he said, giving them a wink.

'I have a few boxes up high on a shelf I can't reach, and the ladder's at home. You'll reach them easily. Oh, hi, Kim,' said Julie with a grin. 'Just in time. Any longer and Charlie wouldn't have left us any biscuits.'

It took all of Charlie's effort not to snap his neck to see Kim the moment Julie mentioned her name. As he turned casually to say hello his words caught in his throat. Kim's long legs caught his eye, and he quickly took in her dressy shorts and black strappy sandals. These were teamed with a black singlet edged with lace, and her hair was loose over her shoulders. Wow.

'You look lovely, Kim,' said Marjorie. 'You off somewhere nice?'

'Just here,' said Kim as she sat down. 'Hi, Charlie. Fancy seeing you here.' Her coffee-coloured eyes looked mischievously over at him.

'He's become a bit of a regular,' said Julie. 'Art in his blood, this one. His sister is going to hold a workshop here, which will be great.'

'It's nothing,' said Charlie. 'My sister's been dying to come and visit me.' More like check up on me, he thought. 'Besides, she's fascinated by all the talent in this little town.' Charlie's eyes went to Kim.

'Don't look at me,' she said.

'Well, I am. You're one of the reasons she wants to come.' Charlie wondered if that sounded weird, like his sister was coming to check Kim out for other reasons. Like as a possible girlfriend for her lonely brother. 'She's in love with your kangaroo and I've told her about the dragon, so there's no stopping her now,' he continued quickly.

Julie and Marjorie went into the kitchen to sort out a cuppa for Kim and another plate of biscuits, giving Charlie a moment alone with Kim.

'Marjorie's right. You do look lovely today,' he said.

'Thanks. I thought about what you said, and I'm trying to get used to wearing different things. Small steps, right?'

Her eyes shone and his body tingled in response.

'Yep, that's right. How do you feel?'

'Awkward. It doesn't help that everyone I see asks where I'm off to. No one is used to seeing me out of my work gear. I feel really self-conscious.'

'Yeah, but soon they'll get used to it. They'd look at me differently too if I turned up in a lace top.'

Kim chuckled and he saw her relax.

'So how've you been?'

'It's been hard,' she said, glancing away.

Charlie was itching to reach across and touch her arm, initiate some sort of contact. He restrained himself, but sitting this close to her, smelling the sweet apple scent of her hair, was driving him crazy. He found himself tapping his foot against the floor. He tried to stop it but it started up again seconds later.

'Have you made Jo's headstone yet?' He had a feeling it would have been the first job on Kim's list.

'Yeah. Do you want to see a photo?'

'Would love to.'

Kim pulled out her phone from her shorts pocket. It looked new, and Charlie remembered Kim had said something about her old phone breaking. 'I sent Mum and Dad a photo of it the other day.'

She passed over her phone and Charlie looked at the photo. She'd cut Jo's name out of a piece of steel, and made a metal bone that hung underneath. It was charming and heartfelt.

'It's amazing. You really are a wonder with the welder.'

'Is that a new project?' said Marjorie, coming back with Kim's cuppa.

Kim passed her phone over to Marjorie, who put down the cup. 'No, my old dog Jo passed away the other day.'

'Oh love, poor old Jo,' said Julie.

The four of them chatted and polished off the rest of the biscuits, then Kim got up to leave. Charlie had a hard time hiding his disappointment.

'Thanks for the cuppa,' she said. 'I'd love to stay but I've still got to get to CCL Hardware and pick up some supplies – then do a grocery shop. I'll try to pop back in next week.'

Charlie stood up and walked her to the door. 'Thanks for that email about the awards night. As it happens I'll be in Perth then for a mate's engagement party, so the timing is good.'

'So you still want to come?'

'Don't sound so surprised. Of course I do! It's a big deal. And it's a great thing you're doing. I'm surprised more people don't know about it.'

Kim blushed, and he resisted the urge to caress her cheek with his fingers.

She shrugged. 'Oh, by the way, I'm having a bit of a barbeque next week before the awards. I'd love for you to come. Just Matt and Loz, the kids and Doris.'

'Ah, the famous Doris. I'll have to come to finally meet her.' Kim had told him a few stories about this fearless woman of the bush. A character, by the sounds of it.

'Great. I'll text you the details.' Kim flashed him a smile and his body reacted like it'd been hit with adrenaline. 'See ya.'

She left, and as much as he wanted to watch her walk down the street, he knew he shouldn't. Turning away, he went to find Julie to help her with the boxes.

'Hey, Julie,' he asked, after he'd got down the third dusty box of art supplies. 'Have you heard of anyone with the name of Parson living around Lake Grace?'

'Parson? It's not ringing any bells, but I'm actually from Wagin way originally. I only moved to Lake Grace once I got married. Why's that?'

'Oh, I'm just looking into something for someone. They thought there was a Parson family who lived out this way. I'll keep asking around,' he said, feeling a little deflated.

'Marjorie probably wouldn't know either – she's newer to town than I am, but go and ask my father-in-law, Mack. He's at the hospital in full-time care now, but his mind's still okay. He might know.' Julie opened up one of the boxes and coughed at the dust. 'Think I need to do some cleaning.'

'And I think that's my cue to leave,' said Charlie with a laugh.

Julie shook her head. 'That'd be right,' she teased. 'Thanks for your help, Charlie. Much appreciated.'

'No worries. See ya, Julie.'

He walked back through the Art Space past the works on display from a previous workshop. Although he didn't claim any great talent for art himself, there was something calming about being around it. He'd been raised in this sort of environment, and it was comfortingly familiar.

'Bye, Charlie,' called Marjorie as he reached the door.

He gave her a wave as he stepped out. He had time, so he might as well walk up to the hospital. It wasn't far, just up towards the dry salty lakes that edged the town.

He'd almost worked up a sweat by the time he arrived. The red-brick hospital was next to the medical centre and looked like it had just undergone renovations: a fresh paint smell lingered and there were signs of construction, with a final clean-up yet to be done.

Charlie looked through the big glass doors. No one was at reception. He pressed the buzzer and the doors opened. Inside it smelt vaguely like antiseptic and there was a big, wide corridor with a vinyl floor in mint green. It seemed as if no one was here, he thought, until he saw a nurse standing off to one side. Their eyes met.

'Hello.' She smiled, her eyes vibrant. 'Can I help you?'

'Um, yeah. I'm here to visit Mack.' He hoped she knew who he was talking about. 'Julie sent me,' he added as she sized him up.

'Sure thing,' she said with a smile. 'Come on, he's down this way. I'm Denny, by the way,' she said, holding out her hand.

He shook it. 'I'm Charlie. I'm new to town,' he said.

'Yeah, I guessed. Are you a relation to Mack?' she asked.

He glanced down to see that Denny only came up to his shoulder, and then wished he hadn't. She had very large breasts that stretched out her uniform, giving him far too much to see. Averting his eyes as they walked down the corridor he replied, 'No. I actually just moved here for a job at Elders. I'm here to see Mack as I heard he might know someone I'm looking for. I'm friends with Julie.'

'Yeah, Mack's lived around here his whole life. Poor Mack, he just got too much for Julie to look after, but at least here he's still close to his family and friends.'

They walked past the nurses' station, where a male nurse sat at a desk. Most of the rooms they passed had elderly people in them, from what he could see.

'Mack is in the common room; he hates to be stuck in his room. Some of the others are hard to move and they prefer to sit in their rooms watching TV by themselves. Old age can be a bitch,' she added, shaking her head.

'I hear ya,' said Charlie. 'My wife . . .' He paused for a second, realising his slip, and then continued so it wouldn't seem like a big deal. 'Um, her dad had dementia. It wasn't pretty. She felt like she lost him twice – once to dementia and then again when he passed away.'

Denny agreed as she directed him left at the very end of the corridor. They were in an area with two sections. One had a large table with a heap of chairs around it. The room extended beyond that, with windows that looked out onto a garden area with a birdcage. To the right of the dining table was another area, which had a TV cabinet and some cupboards with a collection of books and movies. There were couches and chairs against the wall and one of those mechanical chairs, in which an old man sat reading. A woman and a man sat nearby watching the TV.

'There's a few here. Are they all full-timers?' Charlie asked. He'd counted seven old folks all up.

'Yep. The only alternative is in Narrogin, and that's a long way from home for them, and a long way for family and friends to visit. Here they always get folks stopping by. It's nice to see, and it brightens their day.'

Denny clasped her hands together and smiled. Charlie could tell she was fond of the occupants in the room. She nodded to the man reading. 'This is Mack. Come on and I'll introduce you. Bear in mind he's well into his nineties.'

Charlie followed close behind.

'Hey, Mack. You have a visitor,' said Denny, speaking loudly.

Mack's face was lined with age, but behind thick glasses his eyes were bright. His hair was sparse and his hands sun-spotted.

'G'day Mack,' said Charlie as loudly as Denny. He held out his hand. 'Your daughter-in-law Julie sent me here.'

Mack put down his book. 'Is that right?' He held out his frail hand and seemed a little confused. 'How can I help you?' he said, eyeballing him.

Charlie gestured to a chair by the table. 'Do you mind?'

'Not at all. It's nice to see new faces,' said Mack as Charlie dragged over a chair and sat beside him. 'We get different nurses sometimes, which is a welcome change.'

Denny, who was just starting to walk away, turned back. 'Are you sick of me, Mack?'

'No, never. You know you're my favourite, Denny,' he said with a wink.

'Glad to hear it, Mack.' She headed back out to the corridor.

'Bloody good woman, that one. Why someone hasn't snapped her up I'll never know.' Mack paused for a second. 'Are you single?'

Charlie laughed. 'Julie tells me you've been in Lake Grace a long time?' he said, hoping to divert the old man.

'Yeah.' He nodded.

'I was wondering if you've ever heard of the Parson family.' Charlie held his breath. Just speaking the name out loud made his hands begin to shake and his heart race. Until now he thought he'd been doing a great job of staying calm. He was sure that this wasn't a big deal, yet his body contradicted him.

'Parson? They lived in Lake Grace?'

'Well, somewhere around here,' clarified Charlie. It was the best he had. Which wasn't much to go on. It was hard work to find a person when all you had was an envelope with a postmark listing the year and the name of the town.

Mack sat quietly for a moment, no doubt sifting through his memory. 'Sorry, the old noggin's not what it used to be, but I do recall a Norma Parson. I think she was a farmer out of town.

It's a bit hard to recall because she left the district back in the sixties.'

'Do you know why?' asked Charlie.

Mack's hand shook as he pressed it against his temple, his fingers like gnarled sticks. 'Sorry, mate, it's all a bit hazy. I do remember Norma, mainly because she was a looker and I danced with her a few times at some cabarets we had in town back in the day. Oh, she was married, of course, kids the same age as mine if I recall correctly. You always remember the pretty ones you dance with.' Mack's eyes glazed over as if he was reliving the moment. His head started moving to a beat only he could hear.

'Can you remember her husband's name, or her kids?'

Mack closed his eyes for a moment and Charlie wondered if he'd nodded off but then they opened as he shook his head.

'Sorry. I struggle to remember my great-grandkids' names, let alone anyone else's.' He looked apologetic.

'I totally understand. Thanks for your help, Mack. I appreciate it. I'll let you be.' Charlie rose and put his chair back against the wall.

Mack gave him a nod and kept on moving his head. Charlie watched him for a moment as he closed his eyes. He bet Mack felt much younger than he actually was. Old age was cruel at times. Some kept their mind but lost their body, and others lost their body but retained their mind. Charlie wasn't sure which way he'd prefer to go; neither sounded like much fun. A heart attack in his sleep at eighty sounded the better way to go.

'All done?' asked Denny, appearing from a room as he walked past.

'Yep. Thanks, Denny,' he said. She was a pretty woman, close to his own age, if he had to guess.

'I hope to run into you again. Nice to have new folks in town. Better than folks leaving. Town's getting bloody small enough as it is.'

'What? Nat Fyfe hasn't made a whole lot of Freo fans want to relocate?' said Charlie with a smirk.

Denny almost snorted. 'Ha, that's all we'd need. More people to paint the town purple. I'm an Eagles fan. Always have been, and won't change even for Nat. I've watched him play since he was knee-high to a grasshopper and still love to watch him play. Even if he did go to the dark side when he joined Freo.'

They stopped at the glass doors and Charlie laughed. 'A girl who quotes *Star Wars* and barracks for the right team. I think we'll get on well, you and I. Thanks for your help. I'll see you around.'

'Yeah, I hope so. Bye, Charlie.'

He walked out the entrance feeling a little less jittery than he'd been with Mack. Denny had taken his mind off his worries. She certainly had a way about her – maybe it was the bedside manner great nurses had. And now he knew for certain that there had once been a Parson family out here.

It felt like he'd slotted another piece into a massive puzzle. And he'd keep searching until he could slot in some more.

Chapter 14

KIM walked around with her head in the clouds after leaving Charlie. His presence, the way he looked at her and his lovely manner all had an effect. Actually, she felt more alive than she had in years.

That came to an abrupt end when she walked into the local hardware shop and came face to face with Travis Green. Actually more like body to body, as she bumped into him down one of the rows filled with bolts and nuts.

'Hey, Kim.'

Travis's hands held her arms where he'd grabbed her to stop her – or himself – from falling. He was in his usual farm clothes, shorts and a blue singlet. His dark hair was cropped and he had stubble across his chin. But it was his green eyes that spooked her the most. To think, a few years back she'd gazed into them after making love and dreamt of their future together. Now he felt like a stranger.

'Hi, Travis,' she said, moving away until his hands dropped

back by his sides. Kim nervously glanced around, hoping no one had seen them like that.

'Wow, you look amazing. It's been a while.'

Kim had difficulty concealing a shudder. She didn't want Travis to even look at her, let alone admire her. She wished he'd left town. But he was still here, and she was stuck having to run into him from time to time and pretend he hadn't messed her up.

'How's Sonia going? Bub three on the way, I hear?' said Kim, giving him a fake smile.

His eyelid twitched and she knew she'd given him a verbal kick in the balls. It might have been years since he'd been her lover, new to town, but it still cut deep, what he'd done to her. Oh yeah, he'd forgotten to mention his wife and child – and when Kim had found out, he actually had the nerve to ask if she'd still stay with him. Be his bit on the side? No chance. Kim wasn't one for confrontation but she'd let rip with Travis.

His head tilted to the side and he smiled. 'Yeah, they're okay.'

His eyes drank her in and she knew he was remembering intimate things. 'Good to hear. Bye, Travis,' she said and walked past him to the bolts in the size she wanted. But in her flustered state she couldn't remember which size that was. She could still feel his eyes on her, so she reached for some and pretended to be counting until she heard him shuffle away.

The bolts rattled in her hand as she put them back and then shook out her nerves. Just seeing Travis brought back so much. All her anger and sense of betrayal. She never wanted to be anyone's bit on the side. She wanted her own husband and partner, someone to spend the rest of her life with, not someone else's husband. She'd rather be married to the farm.

To this day Kim didn't know if Sonia had ever found out about the affair – which was exactly what it was, even though Kim wasn't aware of it until too late. Plenty of people around town probably knew about it, and that was something Kim had to live with. Knowing Travis, he'd probably had a few other girls after Kim. She'd heard rumours he'd seen a few barmaids on and off. Not much got past the locals: they saw when cars came and went and were quite good at putting two and two together.

With a sigh, Kim tried to gather her thoughts, but it was hard. Did she have 'gullible' stamped on her forehead? Her track record with men was atrocious. Her last two relationships had been built on lies, whether to her face or behind her back. Both men had used her.

Maybe that's why she had taken such a shine to Charlie. He always put her first, and seemed so considerate and sweet. She wanted to trust him. But bumping into Travis brought back all her insecurities.

'I will not let men control my life,' she whispered to herself. But not quietly enough, as the shop owner paused on his way past.

'You right, Kim?'

'Yeah, I'm okay. Just trying to remember what size I was after.' She gave him a smile. He nodded and continued on his way. Kim shook her head and mentally slapped herself. Next they'd all be calling her crazy.

Charlie opened the laptop on his kitchen counter and typed *Norma Parson Lake Grace* into his browser. The top hits were all the Norma Parsons on Facebook, then a company called Norma Parson Flowers in America, then a road named Norma on the Main Roads page, and then a lot of things relating to Lake Grace. But nothing to do with the Norma Parson he was chasing. He'd really hoped a first name would inch him further forward, yet he was no closer to unearthing this family secret than he had been yesterday.

Charlie looked at the plain notepad beside him. At the top he'd written *J Parson* in bold black texta. He picked up his pen and drew an arrow down and wrote *Norma Parson*. Next to Norma he wrote *Mother? Sister? Wife?*

So many secrets to unravel. Yet something deep down told Charlie this riddle was worth solving.

He glanced towards his bedroom door. In the top drawer of the plain bedside table was an envelope. It took all his willpower not to waltz in there and retrieve it. He didn't need to see it again; he knew it off by heart, and yet he still yearned to touch it, as though the secrets would reveal themselves upon closer examination. But he'd gone over it with a fine-toothed comb. Lake Grace and J Parson: the two clues that had led him here on this treasure hunt.

Charlie's phone beeped with a reminder he'd set. 'Damn.' It was time to get ready to head out for tea. Heather, his co-worker at Elders, had invited him over to her house for an afternoon barbeque. Her husband worked at the Farmers Centre further down the road. Charlie knew it would be a good way for him to better get to know the community.

He locked up the house out of habit, even though he often saw houses with windows open and no car in the driveway. Some folks on the main street still left their cars unlocked as they ducked in for coffee. He was sure that if someone ever did try to steal one they wouldn't get far, as everyone seemed to notice everything. New cars, new faces, people in places where they shouldn't be. Last week Marjorie had told him all about the latest hoon to leave black tyre marks all over town. He'd been spotted and reported to the police in no time. Charlie took comfort in this effective form of neighbourhood watch.

He drove the two minutes to Heather's place, which was over the railway line, not far from the local caravan park. The street backed onto a massive paddock that he could see had been harvested this year.

When he rang the doorbell, Heather's husband, Bruce, met him at the door.

'G'day Charlie.' His handshake was strong. 'Come in. Beer?'

'Thanks, I'd love one.'

They walked through the house out to the back patio. Heather was already out there drinking a glass of wine and watching the cricket up on a wall-mounted TV. It was a nice set-up they had.

'Hey, Charlie, pull up a seat. I hope you like cricket?'

Charlie shrugged as Bruce passed him a cold beer. 'I'll watch anything when I have a beer in my hand,' he said with a smile. He sat down and complimented Heather on the place.

'Thanks, Charlie. It's pretty easy to keep the place looking nice with the kids gone.'

It was moments like these, sitting with two people his own age who had grown-up children, when Charlie realised how much he felt left behind. People had raised a family by his age, and he hadn't even started. Marrying late hadn't helped, nor did having a wife who didn't want kids. It was probably his fault for thinking that she would change her mind eventually. He should have known better. Laura had always stuck to her guns.

'So Heather says you're searching for the Parson family?' said Bruce.

Charlie had mentioned the postmark to Heather in the office the other day. At first Charlie hadn't felt like telling anyone about the search, but he soon reasoned that the more people there were who knew he was looking, the more likely it was that he would meet someone who knew something. Besides, nobody had to know why he was looking. He usually said he was looking for some old relatives. No one had bothered to dig further than that, for which he'd been grateful. Now he sat up. Did Bruce know something?

Bruce must have seen the hope on Charlie's face and shook his head. 'Sorry, mate, I haven't heard of them. My folks brought me here when I was a kid. They moved on when I was seventeen, but I'd met Heather so I stayed. They might have come across the Parson family. I can ask them for you.'

'Thanks, Bruce, I'd appreciate that. All I know is that there was a J Parson who might have come from Lake Grace, or this area.'

'He or she could have come from a nearby town,' said Heather. 'Some people post mail here on their way through, or if they happen to be in town doing a shop. It's quicker than waiting that extra day for the mail run.'

Charlie nodded.

'Heather said it's a family connection,' said Bruce. 'I love those shows where they go looking for family history. I've been wanting to get on that ancestry website and do our own family tree, except I'm terrible with computers.'

'So am I,' added Heather. 'We keep meaning to get the kids to show us the ropes when they come home, but they never stay long enough. We should probably do a course, maybe see if the Community Resource Centre could set one up.' Heather raised a finger as a thought came to her. 'Hey, have you been to the CRC? They might be able to help you. Maybe they could find an old phone book and see if there are any Parson listings from back in the day.'

'Yeah, it's worth a shot.'

Relaxing back into his chair, Charlie took a sip of his beer and enjoyed the company of his new friends. Before long they were discussing cricket and laughing about work-related dramas, and Charlie enjoyed the moment of relaxation.

Chapter 15

1969

JOHN woke up, rolled over on his side and watched Beth sleeping peacefully, tucked under the yellow and orange floral sheets. Her hair fell across her face, and he carefully moved the strands back with a finger.

It was January, and it was hard to believe that in just three months he'd be off to war.

Although he was home it didn't quite feel like it. Home was the farm. But it was also Beth, and he'd tried hard to smile and be comfortable in the new house. The house was fine, but every time he stepped out the front or into the backyard he was jerked back to the realisation that the farm was no longer his life. He felt like a bird that'd had its wings clipped and been put in a cage. And the worst thing was, when Beth looked at him he could tell she knew how he felt. Her blue eyes would almost mirror his pain. Sometimes she'd take his hand and say, 'When you get back, we'll go looking for a farm.' And he knew she wasn't pretending. She wanted it too. Her eyes would sparkle when she let herself dream of getting back to rural life after his service.

How had he been so lucky to find her? She was his one true love, he was sure of it. That's why he knew he would survive Vietnam. God wouldn't give him Beth only to tear them apart.

'Are you watching me sleep again?' came Beth's muffled voice.

John smiled. 'Maybe. You shouldn't be so beautiful.'

She groaned and opened her eyes. 'I doubt that, especially in the morning,' she said.

To prove her wrong he planted kisses all over her face, eyelids and lips.

'Ah – I wish we could stay in bed all day,' she said as her fingers walked their way down his chest.

'Why can't we?' he said, propping himself up on his elbow.

Beth looked up at him with hopeful eyes.

'We've done all the family get-togethers,' said John. 'I leave tomorrow, so who says I can't spend the whole day lying next to my gorgeous wife?'

'Hmm, you might be right,' she said with a smile. Then her brow creased. 'But what if your folks come over? They'll probably want to see you one last time.'

'Then I'll answer the door in my dressing gown.'

Beth laughed and gently nudged him. John fell back against the bed and she shimmied closer and wrapped her body around his. It was the best feeling in the world. Her silk nightie had risen, her bare legs tucking in against his as her breasts pressed onto his chest, nipples hard. His body zinged with desire.

'Hmm.' He slipped his hand along her leg, up under her nightie, and traced his finger along the edge of her underwear.

Beth pressed herself against his hand and then sighed heavily. 'I hope nobody turns up,' she said as her cheeks filled with colour.

His wife moved quickly, sitting on top of him with practised ease. She grabbed the bottom of her nightie and pulled it up slowly over her head, exposing her breasts.

John reached up – how could he not? They were the most beautiful breasts, full and firm. The touch had him erect in seconds, which she helped along by moving against him in slow gyrations.

'Jesus,' he almost panted. She got him so painfully hard.

She pushed his hands away and held them in her own as she moved faster, her breasts bouncing in a way that had him mesmerised. He wanted those ripe nipples in his mouth.

When she finally let his hands go he reached up behind her back, and sat himself up a little so he could kiss her soft breasts.

Beth arched herself back as he licked and sucked, teased and kissed his way all over them. He needed to make sure he memorised them perfectly.

Then, when he could take it no more, he gently moved her over onto the bed and yanked off his pants as Beth wiggled out of her underwear. Then he sank into her warmth as his eyes connected with Beth's, so deeply it was as if their souls were intertwined. He moved slowly at first, focused on watching her. He stopped momentarily to put on a condom before finding his way back to her heat. She licked her lips, and he bent down to kiss them. Such a simple action, and yet it drove him to the brink. He couldn't hold on much longer, and he picked up speed.

Beth started making sweet, soft sounds, and he was gone.

'You're too good at that, babe,' he said afterwards as he lay beside her. 'I can't hold back for long. I'm sorry.'

Beth sent him a warm smile. 'I intend to remedy that. I believe we have all day.' Her eyes dropped to his manhood. Damn if he didn't feel himself getting ready again already. She was going to kill him today, he was sure.

His heart rate ratcheted up. 'You won't find any objection here. I think we should have breakfast in bed. But first . . .' John reached across and cupped her warmth, causing her to groan and press against his hand. 'I have some unfinished business,' he murmured as he found her lips.

John knew his parents couldn't stay away. Luckily, they arrived when he and Beth were out of bed and eating lunch, albeit in their robes with nothing underneath. Not to mention some serious bed hair and maybe a few lovebites.

'Oh, are we interrupting?' said his mum as they came into the house, glancing at John and Beth's attire.

'No, we've just about finished lunch,' said John as Beth grabbed their plates and headed off to the kitchen.

'It's nearly two-thirty,' said his dad.

James still wore his farm clothes despite having lived in the city for a good few months now. He'd found a job as a gardener for a few homes in the area. It was a part-time gig, but with more people interested he reckoned he could make a full-time job out of it soon enough. He found it wasn't too bad on his back, especially with his regular visits to the physio, and he could rest when he needed to.

'Well, I'm enjoying my last day at home.' John hoped he didn't sound put out, even though he was. He'd been having a great time alone with Beth.

'It seems like it,' said his mum as she looked his dressing gown up and down. Luckily he'd managed to get it tied up securely before he opened the door.

'Have a seat, I'll go and get dressed. You know where the kettle is, Mum,' he said. 'Help yourself to a cuppa.' He saw Beth dart to the bedroom to change.

His dad went straight to the rocking chair Beth had bought John while he'd been at training. John had a funny feeling his dad would be getting one before too long as well.

John headed to the bedroom, where Beth was already dressed in a pair of light-blue shorts and a white top. He was a little disappointed and reached for her. 'I was hoping to help you dress,' he said with a smirk.

She slapped him across the shoulder. 'Not with your folks here!' She smiled and pushed herself out of his embrace. Her eyes dropped to the tent he was making in his dressing gown. 'Best get him strapped down while you're at it,' she teased, before heading back to the kitchen.

He could hear his mother's and Beth's voices as they chatted. Quickly he pulled on some flared jeans and a brown shirt then joined his dad in the living room.

'I've been meaning to say thanks, Dad. For all the work you've done around the place since I've been gone. I appreciate you being here for Beth.'

'Oh, my pleasure,' said his dad with a beaming smile.

It wasn't all his dad's idea. Knowing the move to the city would be hard for James, Beth had taken it upon herself to ask for his help on projects like painting walls, fixing gutters, building new cupboards for the kitchen and anything else she could find. James was a hands-on man, and the work had kept his twitchy fingers busy and his mind off the move. John was happy with all the changes because they would only increase the house's value. It was in a good spot, and hopefully after his two years of national service it would be worth much more than they had paid for it.

'I've actually come to see how you want this back patio. Thought I'd get it measured up and order the materials for it.'

John felt a twinge of sadness. 'I wish I was going to be here to help you. Would be like old times, you and me working together.'

Father and son watched each other for a moment. Silent emotions passed between them. Neither knew how to express what he really wanted to say, but they knew damn well what they meant anyway. James blinked away tears when Norma entered the room with their cups.

The rest of the day went by in a flurry of plans and beers on the back verandah. His parents ended up staying for dinner and they had another tearful goodbye. Well, his mother did.

'Take care, John,' said Norma, holding him against her large bosom.

'I will, Mum. It's only more training. I get to come home before I'm shipped out to Vietnam.' His mum winced at the last word. She still wasn't ready for it. When he thought about it, was he? He didn't have a choice.

His parents left, Mum mopping at her face with a hanky while his dad tried to comfort her. As he shut the door behind them John sagged against it. 'I thought they'd never leave,' he said.

Beth frowned. 'John, don't be like that.'

'I know. I'll miss them. Just not as much as you,' he said, scooping her up in his arms. He held on to her tightly, drinking in the smell of her hair, the contours of her body and the feel of her breath against his neck. They stood like that for ages, just holding each other.

'Leaving you is the hardest,' he whispered, and felt his shirt grow damp from her tears.

Dear Beth,

It's strange being back at base with the boys. We're straight into core training with some specialised training on infantry and weapons. I got to lob some hand grenades! Such a surreal feeling. Not that long ago I was shifting sheep and driving the tractor, and now I'm playing with guns and blowing stuff up. It's been fun, although the training has intensified: five-kilometre runs, duck-walking up hills and crossing mud pits covered with barbed wire. We have to run everywhere, and if we're caught walking then it's twenty push-ups on the spot.

The other night one of our instructors, who has been to Vietnam, sat around telling us stories and initiated us all with an old smelly boot filled with whisky and other stuff. Let's just say it was a messy night and only afterwards did we realise he was probably having a lend of us. I have to go and polish my boots now and tidy up for inspection. We are off to Ingleburn, an Army base out of Sydney for more training and preparation.

I miss you.

Love, John xxx

Dear Beth,

I've made it to yet another state. Sunny Queensland – to Canungra for our jungle training. We've just got back from three weeks camping and tramping through the jungle, and it's hot, wet and muggy. I guess this is what Vietnam will be a bit like. Our instructors tell us stories and try to warn us about the hidden traps in the jungle ground, the tunnels and endless days of walking through mud and water. They say our socks will be forever wet! But it's hard to imagine before we are really there. We've been sitting skill- and knowledge-based exams plus having lots of check-ups and immunisations. I feel like the sheep at drenching time.

I think of the farm often. I dream that one day we will be back in the country, raising our children and growing old together. Is the distance making me a little nostalgic? Probably. I miss you like crazy, my love.

Love, John xxx

John counted down the days until he could see Beth again. He wrote to her often, describing camp and the lads in his platoon, how his shooting skills had progressed, the things they were being taught, plus the endless exercise. If she thought he'd looked good after his first lot of training, she'd be beyond impressed now. The idea of her hands on his muscled body drove him to distraction.

'Private Parson, are you paying attention?' shouted the lance corporal.

'Yes, sir,' he replied as he stood up straighter, his baggy green uniform neat and his black boots shining.

'Listen up, girls. You've reached the end of your training. The next step is to put your skills into action. Pre-embarkation leave starts tomorrow, and you have a week. Make the most of it, because then you'll be flying out from Sydney to Saigon. After that it's straight to the base at Nui Dat. That is when this shit is going to get real. Remember what we've taught you. It could well save your life.'

The lance corporal's words rang out over the ranks of motionless soldiers. Then they were dismissed, and all that was left was for John to say his goodbyes to his mates and head home to Western Australia. To Beth.

Chapter 16

KIM paused by the bathroom mirror and inspected the soft denim summer dress she'd pulled out from the bottom of her cupboard. She'd taken the bloody thing off and put it back on again five times before deciding to suck it up and wear it. Besides, it was only family and friends coming over to her place for a barbeque; she could handle that. And Charlie.

Is that why she was a little nervous? She'd even applied some make-up. Nothing full on – just a bit of eyeliner and eyeshadow in blue to match the dress. She was regretting it now. With a sigh she went back to the kitchen to finish making the salad.

'Yoo-hoo, I'm here.'

Kim smiled as she heard her friend's voice echoing down the passageway.

'And I've brought my famous potato salad too!' Denny appeared, carrying a bowl that she put on the table. She was wearing a fabulous vibrant-yellow dress, which enhanced her boobs and her hourglass figure, and she'd teamed it with wedge heels. Denny had no fear when it came to dressing up. She had a full face of make-up on and her hair was perfect.

'Oh my gosh, you look gorgeous, girl,' said Denny as she gave Kim a warm hug. 'About time you started tarting up!'

Kim inwardly grimaced. She didn't want to tart up for anyone, did she? Was she trying to attract Charlie? What was wrong with her work jeans? And for that matter, why wasn't her personality enough?

'I'm kidding,' said Denny, who was watching her carefully. 'But I love that you've made an effort. You're enhancing your already beautiful features.' She squeezed her arm.

'I feel a bit awkward, but I'm trying,' said Kim with a smile. 'You, on the other hand, look amazing – as always. I wish I had your confidence, Denny.'

'Confidence? Bah, this is me. Love me or leave me. I try to look nice when I'm out of uniform. I like to think of myself as a butterfly emerging from its cocoon.' She grinned.

'Well, I think you look quite sexy in your nurse's uniform,' said Kim, giving her a wink. They both burst out laughing.

'So what else needs doing? Thought I'd rock up early and give you a hand. Besides, it feels like forever since we caught up. I hate that life gets in the way.'

'I know. It's funny how months can pass and we barely see each other,' said Kim. The farm took up so much time, and Denny worked long hours at the hospital.

'When we do we sure as heck make up for it.'

And they did, chatting about what had gone on over the last few weeks. Kim told her about Jo.

'I'm so sorry. You should have called me,' said Denny, pulling a sad face.

'Hello?' Matt's voice rang out as he came through the front door, followed by Loz and the kids. The noise increased tenfold as hugs were exchanged all round. They'd got back from their holiday only a few days ago. Kim had missed them all heaps.

Kim took the large plate with a pavlova on it from Seth. 'Thanks, mate.'

'Can we go see Skittles?' asked Mallory.

'Sure can,' said Kim, and watched her niece and nephew head outside.

'Hi all,' came another voice. 'I called out but there was no reply.' Charlie entered the kitchen with a smile.

He wore jeans and a fitted black shirt, the sleeves pushed up to reveal tanned forearms. He looked fashionable and, Kim thought, swoonworthy. She had to stop herself from staring.

'No worries, come on in. You've met Matt and Loz, and this is —'

'Denny. Hello again,' said Charlie, giving a wave as he put down a box of chocolates on the table and his esky of beers by the wall.

'Oh, you two know each other?' said Kim turning to look at Denny. Her friend smiled back, nodding. They *definitely* had some more girl talk to catch up on. Was Denny interested in Charlie? She was thirty-eight, closer to Charlie's age than Kim was. And Denny always attracted men with her figure and pizzazz.

'We met the other day by chance at the hospital,' said Denny, who moved closer to Kim and added quietly, 'I didn't know you two knew each other.' She waggled her eyebrows.

Matt shook Charlie's hand and Loz followed suit, before turning to Kim and not-so-subtly mouthing 'wow'.

'This is going to be a long night,' said Kim under her breath. 'Hey, bro, can you fire up the barbie for me, please?'

Matt had a beer in his hand already. 'Righto, sis.' He headed to the back door with Charlie, while Loz grabbed the utensils, paper towel and oil and followed soon after, muttering something about men not thinking and forgetting the main bits.

Once the room was empty Denny eyeballed Kim. 'Okay, what have I missed? What's Charlie doing here?'

'Nothing. He did our insurance claim and helped me with Jo the other day. He's actually becoming a good friend,' said Kim, trying to keep a poker face.

'Really?'

Kim felt her eyelid twitch.

'Uh-huh. You do like him a little, don't you?' Denny whispered. 'Now the dress makes sense.'

Kim could have told Denny about the wedding, and trying dresses, but she knew that was just an excuse. Of course she'd been thinking about Charlie when she chose to wear this.

'How did you meet him?' Kim asked, neither agreeing with or denying Denny's assertion.

'He came by the hospital to see Mack.' Denny picked up two salad spoons to toss her potato salad.

'Mack? How does he know him?' asked Kim.

'He was chasing information on a family who lived in Lake

Grace years ago. Parson. Heard of them?' said Denny, putting some fetta cheese in her mouth.

'Parson? Nope. Wonder why he's looking for them.'

'I didn't ask,' said Denny. 'I probably shouldn't have been eavesdropping, but I was curious as to why a newcomer wanted to talk to my Mack.'

Kim smiled. Denny was so protective of her oldies. She had the biggest heart of anyone Kim knew, and loved those folks like they were her own grandparents.

'Hmm, interesting.' Kim added chopped capsicum to a bowl of lettuce. 'I thought you two might have hooked up. He's more your age than mine.'

'No, darling. I saw the way he drank you in the moment he set foot inside this kitchen. I knew I was outta the race then and there,' said Denny, her eyes lowered.

Kim had to try hard not to beam like an idiot. 'Really? You think he's interested?'

Denny's shoulders dropped and she raised her eyebrows. 'Oh my god, Kim, blind Freddy could tell. Don't sound so surprised. The reason you don't have guys falling at your feet is 'cos you're hidden away on this farm in the middle of nowhere. It's not because of *you*. You're a catch, Kim.'

Kim half laughed, half snorted. 'Then why did my last boyfriend dump me like a sack of spuds the moment someone nicer came along?'

'Honey, Chris was a tosser, and still is a tosser. And a busty barmaid who puts out is not "someone better".' Denny was waving her finger at her, doing a great Kardashian impersonation.

'Has Charlie made a move yet?'

'No,' said Kim. 'Should he have? Should I?' She pulled a face as it dawned on her. 'Hell, I wouldn't know what to do, it's been so long.'

'Chill. Don't do anything yet. Just be yourself and have fun.'

Kim looked at Denny with gratitude. Her friend's short blonde hair was shining like spun gold and her face was creased in a smile. Kim valued Denny's friendship so much – she was level-headed, funny and knew what it was like to be single in this place. Some days it felt like they were the only two in the area without partners and kids. 'You're the best, you know that?' Kim hugged her.

'Come on, let's join them outside,' said Denny as she poured herself a large glass of wine.

Kim grabbed a beer and they headed out with the meat on a tray. Matt had the barbie cleaned up and ready to go.

'What's up with Maverick and Goose?' said Loz, pointing to the sheep. Both were standing by Jo's padded bed, heads down.

'They've been like that since Jo died. They used to fight over getting onto her bed the moment she got off. Now they have it to themselves, but they won't get any closer than that.'

'Ohh,' said Denny, her bright-red lips curving down.

Kim could feel her emotions churning. 'They miss her,' she managed to get out before sipping her beer to hide the fact she was on the verge of tears.

'We miss her too, Aunty Kim,' said Seth as he wandered over to pat the sheep.

That made it even harder for her to keep herself together.

It was strange how one minute she was fine, and the next she wanted to sob her heart out. She was glad they were eating inside; she couldn't handle seeing her pets' sad faces.

'Let's get this meat on, shall we?' said Loz, nudging Matt in the ribs. 'Would be nice to eat before midnight.'

'Yeah, all right, all right. I'm on it.' Matt snapped the tongs at Loz before loading up the barbie with sausages and steak.

'Kim! Yoo-hoo, Kim?'

'We're out the back, Doris,' Kim shouted back through the door.

Doris stepped outside. She was wearing her good purple trackpants and a plain green T-shirt. On her feet were her old double-plug thongs, which displayed her incredibly long, curled-up toenails. Matt had once threatened to take to them with his grinding gear, which had caused Doris to fall off her chair in fits of laughter.

'I've popped some cream puffs on the table,' she said, brushing her fringe from her eyes.

'Oh, you're a bloody legend, Doris,' said Matt.

'Let me get you a beer,' said Kim.

'I brought my own,' said Doris as she went back inside. When she returned she had a big bottle in her hand.

'Doris, straight into the king browns. A woman after my own heart,' said Matt, giving her a wink. 'By the way, this is Charlie. He's the new Elders Insurance man.'

Doris wiped her hand on her trackpants and held it out, shaking Charlie's hand firmly. 'Nice to meet ya, Charlie.'

Charlie had a big grin on his face. 'Likewise, Doris. I've already heard about your cooking skills.'

'Bah,' said Doris, waving him off. 'Someone's gotta make sure this lot eat properly.'

'I'm testament to that,' said Matt as he rubbed his round belly.

As the others began to chat, Doris pulled Kim aside. 'Can I see where you've buried the old girl?' she asked.

'Of course.' Kim thought they'd be able to sneak away but Loz, Denny and the kids heard and wanted to come too. When they got to the grave it felt like another funeral. It was almost too much to bear, especially when Mallory took off the pink plastic tiara she was wearing and hung it from Jo's headstone.

'I miss you, Jo,' she said, placing both hands on the mound of dirt. Then she looked up at Kim. 'Do you think she's gone to heaven yet? I dug up our pet bird Eric after we buried him and he was still in his box.' Mallory pulled a face. 'He was a bit smelly and dirty.'

Loz looked at Kim, surprise and humour plain on her face. Then she just raised her hands and shrugged before turning back to her daughter. 'Honey, animals leave their bodies behind when they go to heaven. So please don't go digging up any more dead animals. Come and ask Mum instead, okay?'

Mallory looked up innocently. 'Okay.' Then she got up and skipped off towards Skittles, who was chewing on some grass by the fence.

'Oh god, she's a bloody corker. A princess and a tomboy rolled into one,' said Doris. Denny had her hand over her mouth and was trying hard to keep her splutters to a minimum, but before too long they were all laughing.

'What's so funny?' said Matt as he and Charlie joined them.

'Just your daughter,' said Loz. 'Have you finished cooking?'

'Yep. We wondered where everyone had gone. Poor old Jo. She was a top dog.' Matt's mouth twitched as if he too was fighting back a wave of sadness. The funny moment passed.

'Righto, let's eat then,' said Kim, and led the charge back to the house.

They squeezed in around the table, with Doris at the head and Matt at the other end with Loz and the kids. Charlie was between Denny and Doris with Kim opposite. The idea of playing footsies with him under the table had never entered Kim's mind. Until now.

As they ate Doris gave Charlie the third degree, while Kim listened intently.

'So how old are ya?'

'I'm forty-five,' he replied as he poked a bit of potato with his fork.

'I'm thirty-eight,' said Denny. 'Oldies compared to the rest of this lot,' she continued, gesturing to Kim and her family.

'Don't you include me in that "oldies" business,' said Doris. 'You're only as old as the person ya feel, or so I'm told.' She reached over and squeezed Charlie's thigh, which caused him to jump.

He looked at her and then burst out laughing – and then nearly choked on his food. Kim jumped up and got him a glass of water, which he gladly took. 'Oh Doris, you're a card,' he said.

She shot him a gappy smile and reached for her big bottle of beer. It was probably getting quite warm by now but Doris didn't seemed fazed as she took a swig.

As she put her bottle down she studied Charlie's hand as it rested on the table. Then she reached out and pulled his hand towards her. Kim had no idea what was about to happen – one never knew quite what Doris was capable of. Was she going to kiss his hand? Charlie looked slightly terrified.

But Doris just looked at it closely, tilting it in the light. 'You married, boy?' she said, letting his hand go. 'Ring been on that finger.' She didn't miss a bloody thing.

Kim's eyes went straight to Charlie's hand, as did Denny's.

'Oh yeah, you said you had a wife,' said Denny, nodding her head as she remembered.

Now that it was pointed out Kim could see the faint line on Charlie's finger. Holy shit, he was married? Her eyes went to Charlie, who squirmed in his seat.

'I am, yes,' he said. 'But we're separated, getting a divorce.' His eyes moved to Kim. 'Laura and I grew apart,' he added.

She knew he wanted her to know that, but it was still a shock. Why hadn't it come up in conversation? There'd been plenty of opportunities. Kim couldn't help feeling slightly deceived. He was married – to Laura. The name rolled around her head like an echo.

'Divorce is a thing these days. Back in my time you stayed married till death did you part, regardless if he was a wanker,' said Doris.

Kim turned back to her plate, piling up her fork with potato salad, but she could feel Charlie's eyes on her. Her face started to burn. 'Anyone for a refill?' she asked, pushing back her chair and grabbing her empty beer bottle.

'Me please, sis,' called Matt.

Kim got her brother a cold beer and put one on the table for herself, but went to the bathroom instead of sitting down. She needed some time to think.

She leant against the sink and looked in the mirror at her flushed face. Gosh, it wasn't like she and Charlie were dating. They were still only new friends, really. Besides, he was forty-five: he'd had plenty of time to live and love before now. She should have expected something like this.

Her face looked pale. Damn. She'd just have to go back out there and act like she was fine. It wasn't the end of the world. Straightening her back, she tilted her chin up and returned to the table. Denny and Charlie were in conversation but his eyes flicked to her as she sat down. Kim turned to Doris while opening her beer. 'Have you got a frock for Drew's wedding yet, Doris?' she asked.

'I haven't had a chance to get to the shops. I'm not really sure I should go to the wedding.'

'Drew would be devastated if you didn't. You kept those boys alive after Alice went. How about I see what I can find you in the local shops? I'm thinking you'd look good in a nice pair of pants and a top.'

Doris thought about it for a moment. 'I reckon I could do with a new pair of pants.'

Kim kept up conversation with Doris until it was time to serve dessert. Doris had brought her famous cream puffs and Kim had made a strawberry cheesecake. Oddly, she found she'd lost her appetite. She couldn't bring herself to look at Charlie. Luckily

Denny was keeping him busy talking about art and music.

Doris was the first to leave, reminding them all she had animals waiting for her. Then Loz and Matt left to get the kids into bed.

'Shall we sit out back?' said Denny. 'That way we don't have to look at all the leftover food.'

'Good plan,' said Kim, standing up. She'd half hoped Charlie would leave with the others, but then she wanted him to stay. She wasn't sure what she wanted, actually – perhaps only for the confused feelings to go away. They were messing with her head.

Charlie went to the bathroom, leaving Denny and Kim alone in the kitchen.

'How are you?' Denny asked, moving closer and touching her arm.

'Fine.'

'Come on, I'm not silly. You didn't know he was married, did you?'

'Did you?'

'Actually, he did mention a wife when he was at the hospital, but I'd forgotten about it. If I'd known you two were a thing I would have mentioned it to you. But he's separated,' she said eagerly.

'Doesn't mean much. Travis tried to spin that line a few times. Look how that turned out.'

'Yeah, but Charlie's wife's not here with him. Give him the benefit of the doubt. He seems genuine. And I'm usually a good judge.'

Kim laughed. 'Depends on how much wine you've had.'

Denny chuckled too. 'You got me there. Speaking of which,

not sure how I'm going to pull up tomorrow at work if I have any more. I better head home.'

'You sure?'

'I'm sure.' Denny winked cheekily. They hugged just as Charlie reappeared, and Denny hugged him next.

'Got work tomorrow, Charlie, so I'm gonna catch up on my beauty sleep. See ya round.' She headed to the front door.

Kim felt momentarily awkward alone with Charlie. 'I'm gonna give this to Skittles,' she said, picking out some of the left-over cheese from the salad.

Outside she leant against the verandah railing and threw the cheese out in Skittles' direction. 'A little treat just for you, Skits,' she said as the roo moved towards the food.

The air was crisp and fresh, which made a nice change from the stuffy kitchen. Charlie leant beside her on the verandah railing, and the scent she caught was alluring, spicy and male. Her heart flipped.

'Thanks for the invite. I had a great time,' said Charlie. 'Doris is everything you said she'd be. A diamond in the rough.'

He smiled, and Kim's insides went to mush. 'Yeah, she's a classic.'

The silence of the night engulfed them for a few moments. There was just the sound of Skittles moving around in the grass and the breeze blowing through the leaves of the nearby trees.

'Kim,' said Charlie, turning to face her. 'I was going to tell you about my marriage, but because it's over I hadn't thought to bring it up. I'm sorry if it came as a shock. I've been on my own for a while now.'

Kim shrugged. 'It's no biggie,' she said. Finally she felt her confusion draining away. 'I didn't realise you were that much older than me.'

'Are you calling me old?' he teased.

'Old enough to have been married.'

'So are you,' he said with a smile.

'So you never had kids?'

Charlie shook his head. 'No, it never happened for us. We were married late, when I was thirty-eight. Laura wasn't in any hurry for kids. Just as well in the end, I guess.' Charlie shrugged. 'Life never turns out how you plan it.'

Kim felt relieved. Was it because it presented a clean slate for her? And any future kids? Heck, her brain was moving too fast. Next she'd be picturing a big white dress. Shit. A warning siren was going off in her head. *You've been down this path before,* it said. *Remember Travis?*

She turned to face him, leaning her hip against the rail. 'I feel ya there. I always thought I'd be married with kids by now. Like my bro and my parents were.'

'I would have expected that. I was rather surprised to find you still single.'

'I've had boyfriends. Had one for a few years, Chris. I thought it was serious.' Kim took a steadying breath and then charged on. 'That was until I found out he'd hooked up with a barmaid in town. What's worse, I realised it had been going on for a while. And she was everything I wasn't, you know? She'd get around in heels, fashionable outfits, and she always wore make-up. A bit like Drew's Natalie. I think men just prefer a girl who looks like a girl, if you know what I mean.' Kim didn't like talking to people about her private life and yet here she was telling Charlie about Chris. She pressed her lips together so the next sob story about Travis didn't find its way out.

'Is that where the fear of dresses comes from?' asked Charlie, his forehead creased.

'I don't know. Maybe. Maybe I feel like a fraud in a dress. 'Cos I'm not that kind of girl.'

'That knobhead ex of yours really messed with your confidence, hey? And Drew falling for his city girl didn't help, did it?'

Kim could only look up at Charlie. How did he understand? She doubted any other bloke would have got it.

'Oh Kim.' Charlie reached out and cupped her face in his hands. 'You are the most exquisite girl I've ever met. That's exactly what I thought that first day I met you, when you were in your work clothes installing your kangaroo. And you had a bit of grease here,' he said, running his thumb across her cheek.

She closed her eyes. Was she hearing him properly?

'And then, when we sat on the header, it was hard for me to keep myself together. You don't have to wear make-up or get about in fancy clothes to be noticed, Kim. I noticed you the moment I saw you.'

Kim's heart was pounding as she tried to take in his words. He liked her as she was. She opened her eyes and gazed at Charlie in the dim light filtering from the back door.

'I must say, seeing you in that pink dress also made my day,' said Charlie with a grin. 'But it doesn't matter what you wear, Kim. I love spending time with you, being in your company.'

He bent his head down so their foreheads touched. 'Do you hear me?' he asked.

She felt his breath brush her face, more intimate and powerful than a kiss.

'I do,' she replied as her hands wrapped around his waist, almost of their own volition. He let go of her face and brought her into a tighter embrace. She rested her head against his chest, listening to the dull thud of his heart.

'Hmm,' she murmured. 'I do enjoy this.'

'What? The hugs?' he whispered against her ear.

'Yep.' There was something magical about being held so tightly. She could have stayed in his arms all night. 'I'm glad you're coming to the awards night next weekend.' Kim's lips brushed against his shirt as she spoke.

'So am I. You should be really proud to have made it to the finals.'

Kim smiled. 'It doesn't seem real. But I am proud of it. I think the project'll be great for the kids. We have a unique way of life out here.'

'Yeah, you do. I wish I'd been born in the country,' said Charlie.

He moved his hands lower across her back and she snuggled against him. She realised that they were moving gently, swaying, as if they were slow-dancing.

Half an hour passed like this, holding each other and talking softly.

Kim yawned, and Charlie pulled back to look at her.

'Am I keeping you up?'

'No, sorry. It's not you. I've been getting up at four each morning to work.'

'Oh.' Charlie cupped her face in his hand again. 'You poor thing, why didn't you say?'

Kim smiled sheepishly. 'Because I was enjoying myself.'

Charlie's eyes danced with joy and his lips curled up. 'Ditto,' he said, pulling her back against him.

He breathed deeply, and then she felt him kiss the top of her head. It was pure bliss. He wasn't trying to feel her up or get her to bed. That in itself spoke volumes.

'But I don't want to keep you up too late, as enjoyable as this is. Thank you again for a perfect night.' He let her go and headed back inside to get his esky.

Kim followed him to his car out the front of the house. The front floodlight was on, allowing them to see the pathway to the front gate and beyond.

'Drop me a text when you get home,' she said. 'Roos are bad along the stretch back to town.'

Charlie put the esky in his car and then turned back to Kim. 'Will do. Night, you.'

They hugged again, taking their time. He kissed her cheek as they pulled apart and Kim felt her skin zing from the contact. What would it be like to kiss him?

'Night, Charlie.'

She watched him drive away, hugging herself in the cool night air. When she could no longer hear his car she turned towards the house. 'Come on, Jo,' she said automatically as she glanced down at her side.

Oh damn. She could have sworn she felt Jo's presence beside her.

Kim went back inside, tidied up a bit and was crawling into bed when her phone buzzed. She picked it up and smiled. It was from Charlie.

No Skittles skittled. Home safe. Night you.

She texted back, *Good to hear. Sleep tight.*

She set her alarm for 4 a.m. Being tired tomorrow would be so worth it.

Chapter 17

KIM was feeling nervous. Her parents had arrived in town, and she couldn't help remembering the phone call with her dad a few weeks back. What was this 'talk' that he wanted to have? The timing wasn't great either, as Kim had to leave tomorrow morning for the awards night in Perth. All of it was making her a bit jittery.

'I feel like I've been summoned,' said Matt as he walked towards the front door of Kim's place. For most of the morning, he and Kim had been out shifting sheep and sorting fences. Their folks had called the moment they arrived, asking them to come in for a cuppa and a chat when they had a chance.

'I've known about this chat for a few weeks. Dad wanted to come down earlier but you guys were on holiday. It's had me worried,' Kim said, following him to the door. They both kicked off their boots.

Matt's eyebrows shot up as he opened the door. 'Do you reckon one of them is sick?' he whispered.

Kim shrugged. She had no clue.

'Here they are,' said their mother, Anna, as they walked into the kitchen. She was sitting at the table with Loz and their father David. The surface was covered with iced buns, chocolate muffins, vanilla slice and chunky chocolate biscuits.

'Doris has been, hasn't she?' said Kim.

Loz nodded. 'Yep, and the kids are staying with my folks for a few days, so you get to keep it. I can't have that in our house, or Matt will eat it all.'

Matt scoffed. 'Yeah, like I wouldn't have any help.' He squeezed Loz's shoulder on the way past.

'Great, so I get all the extra calories to myself?' said Kim, taking a seat and reaching for a bit of vanilla slice. Her mum poured her a cup of coffee. 'Thanks, Mum.' She took a quick sip as they all sneaked sidelong looks at each other around the table. 'So . . .?' Someone had to start the conversation.

'I suppose I better spit this out,' said David as he shifted in his chair. He reached for Anna's hand before he spoke again. 'Your mum and I are selling the house.'

Matt and Kim glanced at each other, wondering where this was going. Were they coming back to the farm? Were they moving into a home for the elderly?

'We've bought a caravan. We're going to become grey nomads and travel around Australia,' said Anna quickly. David frowned. 'Oh, you were taking too long!' she said. He rolled his eyes.

'You're going travelling?' said Matt. 'Well, that's great. For the year?'

'For as long as it takes us,' said David. 'It could be five years.'

'I think it's an awesome idea. You two need to enjoy your life, and if that's what you want, then go for it,' said Kim. She was relieved it wasn't something serious. And then she wondered if that meant she might never see her folks again. What if one of them died on the trip? What if they never came home?

By the look on Matt's face she guessed he was thinking the same thing. Only Loz seemed truly excited. Then again, she'd been deliriously happy when Anna and David moved to Albany. Anna had been reluctant to hand over the reins to Loz while she was there, causing some friction.

They sat around the table discussing their plans until their cups were empty.

'What are we going to do with all this food?' said Anna, who hadn't touched any of it.

'I know,' said Kim. 'I'll offload some of it to a friend.' She packed up a selection of sweets into a container.

Later in the afternoon, after she'd finished some repair work on the boom spray, she grabbed the container of goodies and drove off to visit Harry.

Kim wasn't sure what it was about Harry that she liked. Maybe it was his gentle manner, or his wealth of life experience – even if he kept most of his stories to himself.

When she arrived at his house she found him and Tom on the back verandah having a beer. Well, Tom was; Harry had his usual mug full of tea.

'Feel free to visit anytime,' said Harry with a wink as he helped himself to the treats she'd brought.

'I second that,' said Tom.

'I would have thought you'd get lots of goodies, Tom,' Kim

said as she cracked open the beer Harry had fetched her.

'Nah, the missus has me on a diet. She's worried about diabetes and my blood pressure. I know how those skinny models feel now: bloody hungry.' Tom helped himself to another biscuit.

When all the treats had been eaten, Tom headed off home, leaving Kim and Harry to chat. She told him about how old Jo had died, and he was heartfelt in his sympathy. There wasn't anyone more attached to his dogs than Harry.

'She was a beautiful girl,' said Harry, remembering Jo from her last visit.

'It's been pretty hard,' admitted Kim.

They sat in silence for a while. Kim enjoyed the silence but she knew others didn't. Denny detested silences and would always fill them.

Kim just didn't see the point of telling everyone everything unless they asked, and even then she didn't give much away. Loz once told her she was like most blokes in this respect. But silence sometimes expressed more than talking ever could.

For weeks Kim had had a burning question for Harry, but she was unsure how he'd react. Her curiosity got the better of her. 'Hey Harry, do you mind if I ask you a question about Vietnam?'

Harry's lips twitched and he cleared his throat. 'I'm not really sure. I haven't talked about it in a long, long time.' He turned towards Kim, his brow creasing. 'What is it you want to know?'

She could see he was afraid and curious at the same time.

'I'm guessing it was awful over there. I was just wondering if your move here was because of your experience. Does it still affect you?'

Harry was nodding as she finished, but didn't speak straight away. She would give him all the time in the world.

'Aye, it was horrible, love, and it changed my whole life. PTSD, they call it, only it took many years before it had a name and folks were diagnosed with it.' He scratched his chin and looked out over the land, at the setting sun. 'This is my sanctuary. It's probably what saved me from going crazy.' He turned to Kim. 'I made some great mates over there. Most of them are dead now.'

Kim saw the pain flash across his eyes before he blinked and turned away. It seemed so raw still, and she wondered if she'd just caused him to relive a bad moment. She suddenly felt awful. 'I'm sorry, Harry. I don't mean to open up old wounds.'

'It's all right, lass. It's nice to remember the good times. My best mate was killed there. Gosh, we had some laughs, but I can't forget his death. Especially as I was right there. He died in my arms.'

Harry looked down at his hands, and Kim could see they were shaking. She wondered what he was seeing in his mind. Had he tried to save his mate? Was his mate John, the one from the photo? Did he have any more photos? But she let her questions die away. She wouldn't ask Harry anything more. Seeing him so rattled was gut-wrenching enough. 'I'm sorry. I've lived a blessed life in comparison.'

They sat in silence for a while longer and she watched him slowly relax. His dogs came up to nudge him. Maybe they picked up on his emotions? If they did, they certainly helped him recover his spirits. Before long he asked her what she was doing over the weekend and so she told him about the awards night, to be followed by Drew's wedding the weekend afterwards. Next they discussed the seeding year ahead, and talked about chemicals and weeds. It was typical farmers' talk, which Kim loved.

An hour later she left with a fresh beer for the drive and an empty container. The sun was halfway past the horizon and would be completely gone before she even made it onto the gravel road towards home.

Packing was usually something Kim could do in under a minute, easy. But not this trip. Not when she had to pack a fancy outfit. Kim was planning to buy something in Perth for the awards, but Denny had brought over a heap of her dresses just in case Kim couldn't find any she liked. Now Kim was trying to decide which ones to take, and then there were matching shoes and jewellery to consider. Kim wasn't used to jewellery. She didn't wear rings, bracelets or necklaces in case they got caught during work. Wearing a ring was the easiest way to lose a finger. She did like earrings, though, and had some nice hoops and a gorgeous pair of pearl studs that she saved for special occasions. But now she was staring at the pile of dresses, overwhelmed. In the end her mum had come in and saved the day.

'Take a couple of black dresses – black is a safe colour – and team them with black shoes. Go with your pearls for the ears,' she said, before disappearing and coming back with a beautiful but simple pearl necklace. 'Borrow this. See, that's all you need. Elegance isn't hard.'

'Thanks, Mum. I appreciate your help.'

Her parents were going home tomorrow. Kim had asked them to the awards but it would mean an eight-hour trip on top of the drive back to Albany.

Loz arrived not long after Kim had finished packing, and together they loaded up Kim's blue Holden Commodore. Anna and David gave them both a hug as they saw them off. 'Good luck! And *enjoy* yourself,' said her mum.

'We will,' replied Loz, getting into the passenger seat.

Kim's Commodore was a bit of a relic but it was the first car she'd ever bought – brand-new, no less. She mostly used her ute, so the Commodore hardly got driven and was still in top condition.

Before they made it to Perth they swapped seats and Loz took the wheel. Kim hated driving in the city and Loz was used to it from years of shopping trips and taking kids to appointments so it seemed the best option. Besides, Kim's nerves were starting to kick in. Maybe it was the city itself having its usual effect on her, or maybe it was the idea of going in and out of dress shops all day. Or maybe it was knowing she'd see Charlie later. If she was going to go shopping, she could at least get some stuff she wanted. She'd kill for a new pair of jeans, and some of her flannel shirts were wearing thin.

When she suggested this to Loz she was whacked on the arm. 'Not on my bloody watch, you're not!' Loz said. 'Nat gave me a list of great stores to go to for dresses.'

'Really?' Kim groaned. 'And you think I'll be able to afford anything from those shops? I don't wanna pay a few hundred bucks for a dress I'll wear once. Just take me to Target and I'll find one in there. And can't we stop at Carousel? I'm hanging for a HJ burger.'

Loz screwed up her face as she thought. 'I hear ya. But Nat's got good fashion sense. She always looks so lovely.'

Kim laughed. 'She's been brought up with fashion, Loz. Plus she's happy to spend truckloads on her outfits. You know I hate paying even thirty bucks for a pair of jeans. I'm a country chick who wears boots most of the time. I wouldn't know fashion if it bit me on the arse. I just need a dress that's gonna look okay and that I'm comfortable in.'

'Yep. Righto.' Loz glanced at her sideways as they came to a red light.

Loz probably thought she was upset by the mention of Natalie. But it wasn't that. Well, not entirely. Kim disliked comparisons between the city and the country, especially when they played into the default idea that city people were better educated and more stylish than those from the country. It reminded Kim of another of her bugbears – country folks sending their kids away to Perth for a better education. Kim liked country schools and the small, safe communities in which they were rooted. In fact, she'd be thrilled if any kids of hers decided to stay in the country and have a family. But if they wanted to go off and be an air force pilot or a doctor, kudos to them too. She'd never hold them back.

God, she almost laughed at herself. She didn't even have a partner, let alone kids. *Hold your horses, girl,* she told herself.

When they arrived at Carousel shopping centre after the three-and-a-half-hour drive their first stop was for food. 'You know what?' said Kim with sudden determination, halfway through her burger.

'Oh dear. What?' said Loz as she sipped on her Coke.

'Stuff looking for a dress. One of Denny's will do. How about we go watch a movie instead? The new Star Wars one is out.'

Loz giggled. 'You reckon? I've been dying to watch that. Matt will spew if I see it before him.'

'I know, hey?' said Kim, thinking of all the taunting she could dole out to her brother.

'Let's do it. I'm ready for some Maltesers.'

By the time they got out of the cinema and checked into their hotel on Hay Street, they barely had time to shower and change before the awards ceremony. They ran around the hotel room in their underwear, trying to get dressed and do make-up at the same time, giggling as though they'd been on the wine all afternoon as their nerves started to take hold.

Kim's phone buzzed and she looked at it as she put her earrings in. 'Oh, it's Charlie. He's waiting downstairs to escort us there.'

'Hopefully he knows where we're going!' said Loz as she applied her lipstick quickly. 'Right, all ready? Got money, phone, key to get back in?'

'Yep, yep and yep. How do I look?' asked Kim.

'Gorgeous. I love your hair. You hardly ever wear it out,' said Loz as they left the room.

'Um, that's because I'd get grease in it otherwise,' Kim said with a laugh. Suddenly her ankle gave way, and she clutched Loz to stop herself from falling. She was wearing simple, black high-heel shoes that went with the fitted black-lace dress she wore.

'Shit, do you think I'll make it through the night in these?' said Kim after righting herself.

'Maybe. But your feet are gonna kill later on.' Loz pulled a face as they rode down in the lift.

'Blisters too, probably.'

Kim checked out her reflection in the lift's mirrored walls. The dress had capped sleeves and a V-neck that showed off her mum's pearls, and fell to just above the knee. She realised that by running late she hadn't had time to get worked up over her attire.

'There's Charlie,' said Loz as the doors opened. 'Oh, wow.'

Chapter 18

'OH my god,' mumbled Kim as the lift doors opened to reveal Charlie before them. His dark-blue suit fitted him perfectly and his black shirt was slightly unbuttoned, showing a hint of chest hair. His hair looked freshly cut and styled. He was like nothing you'd find at home.

They were so preoccupied that the doors had begun to close again before they got out. They must have looked like complete drongos. Trying to recover some decorum, Kim walked towards Charlie. She was concentrating on each step across the shiny floor, but it was hard when Charlie was so handsome. He wore the suit ridiculously well.

'Hello,' she said, smiling awkwardly as her hands ran down the sides of her dress. Her mouth had gone dry, making it hard for her to say anything else.

'You look amazing, both of you,' he said, holding out an arm for each of them.

Kim wanted to tell him how divine he smelt, but she kept her cool. Mainly because walking was taking such an effort.

'Are you excited? Feeling comfortable enough?' he asked as he walked them from the hotel out onto Hay Street.

'Um, I'm doing okay.' Charlie was a great distraction from her clothing anxieties. Besides, the way he'd watched her as she left the lift was something she'd never forget. The dimples in his cheeks and sparkle in his eyes were totally worth the dress and the poxy heels, she thought, wincing as the shoes pinched. 'Just don't go too far, will you? You're a handy crutch.' Kim almost lost her footing again and gripped his arm. With a groan she added, 'I should have practised wearing these around the house.'

'Don't worry, I won't leave your side.' He sent her a heated gaze and pulled his arm in so he had hold of her securely.

Loz leant forward so she could smile at Kim. She was wiggling her eyebrows with all the subtlety of a schoolgirl. 'Nor mine,' she said. 'It's not often I have a sexy man on my arm. Getting Matt into a suit will have to wait till he's dead. He didn't even wear one for our wedding.'

Loz kept up the small talk on their short walk down the street to the Chamber of Commerce and Industry building, where the event was being held. A security guard was by the lifts, and he told them which floor to head to.

As they got in the lift with another couple dressed up in cocktail wear, Kim ran her hands down her dress again nervously. Then she played with her hair, scratched her arm, and fanned herself as she felt another wave of heat come over her. Charlie moved his hand and began to brush the skin on her arm with his thumb. His eyes watched her intently. She felt her body relax as the tension drained away.

'Well, this looks fancy,' said Loz as the lift doors opened and they made their way into the mingling crowd of well-dressed people. There were men in suits, women in cocktail dresses, and waiters serving drinks and food.

A waiter approached and held out a tray with tiny bread circles topped with something.

'I think it's smoked salmon,' whispered Loz as she grabbed one. Kim shook her head and the waiter walked away.

'Too nervous?' asked Charlie.

'No, she's afraid she'd spill it on her dress,' said Loz, and Kim laughed.

'Got it in one,' she said. 'I'm a bit of a klutz and not great at staying clean. But yes, I'm also too jittery to eat,' she admitted. Some women waving in her direction caught her eye. 'They're the RRR girls. Looks like I'm needed for a photo. Do you mind?'

'Go for it,' said Loz. 'I'll be chasing waiters – for the food,' she clarified. 'I'll keep Charlie company.' She winked.

'We'll be here,' said Charlie reassuringly.

Kim took a breath as she left his side and walked across the room, following the women to the outside balcony. Here, the rest of the board of the Rural, Remote and Regional Women's Reference Group was gathering.

'Kim, it's a photo for the paper. You need to stand at the front, seeing as you're a finalist,' said Maree, the chairperson.

While the photographer was getting ready, Kim took the chance to catch up with the girls from RRR. Some had flown down from Kununurra or Geraldton, or across from Esperance.

The network covered the whole state, and Kim loved seeing her far-flung friends. They might come from different areas and have different backgrounds, but they all shared a passion for helping regional women. The connections they'd made and the resources they had made Kim proud. They all wanted to make a difference, and she felt honoured to be linked with them.

Once the photos were done, it was hard to get back to Charlie and Loz as there were so many people to talk to. Past winners, other finalists, politicians and sponsors of the event and award. Introductions, handshakes, new faces, a quick chat – it was kind of like what Kim imagined speed dating would be like.

And then, suddenly, it was time for the award's announcement, and everyone was ushered into a side room filled with chairs. Kim found herself seated up the front with the other finalists, but Charlie and Loz managed to snag chairs behind her.

The brilliant MC was past RIRDC winner Jacki Jarvis, who was highly entertaining. After a quick introduction, she began to announce the names of the finalists. A projector screen displayed their photos, nestled in among all the banners from the sponsors. Kim squirmed in her seat when her photo came up. And then the runner-up was announced, and everyone clapped as the name was read out, a worthy winner from down south.

Kim felt a hand on her shoulder. It was Loz wishing her luck. Then, without warning, Kim's was read out, and Loz was clapping like a madwoman behind her and urging her to go up on stage. The girls beside her were clapping and congratulating her too, yet Kim was still trying to process what had happened.

She glanced up at the screen. There was her picture with

'Winner' underneath. She'd won?

'Kim?' said the MC, giving her the nod to join them.

'Oh shit,' she said under her breath as she stood up. How was she going to step up onto the stage in heels?

Somehow she managed it. Standing on stage in front of a crowd of people all watching her was totally surreal. Bloody hell, she hadn't even prepared a speech! Faces were buzzing before her like a swarm of bees, making her disoriented – until she saw Charlie. He smiled and nodded as if to say, *You've got this.*

With a deep breath, she said the first thing that came to mind. 'Wow, I did not expect this at all.' She cringed, getting used to her voice through the microphone. 'I'm so grateful and honoured to be here among some amazing rural ladies, and blown away to have won. Thank you so much. Camp Kulin, for those who don't know, does a fantastic job of teaching children essential life skills, and does an especially important job helping kids affected by trauma. It's an amazing program to have in our wheatbelt area. With this award, I'll be able to develop a book and an educational program through Camp Kulin to tell the stories of children and young people living on farms. This, along with trips and tours to local farms, will help provide much needed leadership development and a better understanding of our rural industry. I don't want to see our communities, the rural communities that I love, disappear. This is a step towards our rural future, supporting our way of life and strengthening our regional industry. I am overwhelmed and truly honoured.' Somehow she remembered to thank the sponsors, the event organisers and the other finalists.

The applause that followed was deafening, and she was sure

she could hear Loz whooping loudly for her.

Next was a barrage of photos with important people – politicians, sponsors and the other finalists for all the papers – and then so much more talking. She had a long chat with the Honourable Mia Davies, whose electorate was the central wheatbelt, and then Mary Nenke, who was also a RIRDC winner, manager at Cambinata Yabbies and the president of Farming Champions. To be in a room full of passionate rural people who gave up hours and hours of their time to help advance, support and nurture the rural way of life was inspiring.

By the time it was quietening down, Kim was starting to feel shattered. She hadn't talked so much in years. Or perhaps ever.

'You okay?' said Charlie as she felt his hand caress her back. 'Congratulations, by the way.'

He pulled her in for a hug and Kim let it linger longer than was normal. No doubt Loz would be asking questions later, but for now Kim needed Charlie's touch like oxygen. She sagged in his arms. 'I'm exhausted. Talking is tiring when you don't do a lot of it. I've been trying to be my best around all the VIPs.'

Charlie pulled back to look her in the eye. 'You've been amazing. We are so proud.'

'Oh my god, you're a superstar,' said Loz as she approached and wrapped her arms around Kim. 'Congratulations, clever lady. I knew you'd win.'

'Thanks, Loz. Thank you both for being here.'

'Wouldn't have missed it for the world,' said Loz. 'I'll go find us some more wine to celebrate. Especially while it's free,' she said, setting off on her mission.

'I need some air,' said Kim. 'Come out to the balcony?'

Charlie took her arm and accompanied her without a word. Once outside she felt like she could breathe a little better, but the air was a mixture of car fumes and food smells from nearby restaurants. She missed the crisp night air from home.

They leant against the balcony and gazed out over the nearby gardens and the state cricket ground. The lights of the city were in full glow.

'The lights are pretty,' she said.

'Yeah, it's not bad. You were great up there. Good speech,' said Charlie, who slid closer to her and nudged her shoulder.

'Thanks. I was freaking out a bit. Then I saw you guys and it helped to have friendly faces in the crowd.' She paused. It was now or never. 'On that note, there's something I've been meaning to ask you,' she said. His eyebrows shot up curiously as he waited for her to continue. 'Drew's wedding is next weekend, and I can bring a partner. Would you like to come with me?' Kim's heart was pumping so loudly she felt sure he could hear it.

Originally she'd planned to go on her own, but it would be great to have someone in her corner. Someone to keep her distracted from Drew's delirious happiness. Of course she was happy for Drew, but still it hurt being the one left out. Drew was so busy that she barely saw him these days.

Any wedding hurt when you were single and unlucky in love, but it hurt even more when the one you had pined for was marrying someone else. Kim couldn't stop thinking of that movie, *My Best Friend's Wedding*, where the best friend lucked out. That was Kim. Only she had to keep reminding herself she never had Drew to start with. He'd only loved her as a friend, a sister. And she'd rather have Drew in her life as a friend than not at all.

'Tell me what's going through your mind first,' said Charlie as he reached for her hand, rubbing circles on her palm with his thumb.

Kim closed her eyes for a moment, enjoying the touch. Drew had never touched her like that. It was such a simple gesture, yet so powerful. She glanced at Charlie. 'Lots, I guess.'

'The wedding? Don't want to do it alone?'

'Not really. But I'd like you there as my date, not as a prop,' she said. 'I understand if you don't want to, though. I'll be stuck doing bridesmaid duties for most of it. If it'll swing it, I'll make sure you're at Loz and Matt's table for dinner.'

He smiled and let out a little chuckle. 'Yeah, that sounds all right to me. I don't mind weddings – plenty of opportunities to dance with pretty ladies.' He nudged her gently.

Kim pressed her lips together so she didn't smile like a buffoon. 'Thanks. You really are my saviour. How can I repay the favour?'

'Easy,' he said. 'I could use another one of those hugs of yours.'

'Oh, I'll pay that gladly,' she said, moving into his arms with ease. The city lights paled as she closed her eyes and used her senses to savour the moment. The press of his body against hers, his secure arms around her, his tantalising scent of spice and something earthy – then there was the sound of his heart beating and the feel of his breath against her neck. She calmed and relaxed into him.

'Hmm, now *that's* more like it,' he said.

Kim opened her eyes, wanting to see him. She was overcome with new feelings, and was having difficulty identifying them. What she felt for Drew was nothing like this. Her body never tingled, not like it did with just one glance from Charlie's twinkly grey-blues. And she'd had hugs from Drew, but they didn't have the same effect as Charlie's, which seemed to calm her soul and give her an adrenaline rush at the same time. Was this thirst for Charlie lust, or was she experiencing something much more?

She gazed at his lips, so close. If his hugs were so brilliant, what would it be like to kiss him? Was there a reason he hadn't tried to kiss her yet? Should she kiss him? Maybe he was as unsure as she was?

He began to move towards her and her breath caught in her throat as she anticipated his kiss. It was as if the night had sucked them into a different universe, just the two of them. But his lips found her forehead instead, pressing gently against her skin for a long moment, and then he pulled away and cleared his throat.

Someone nearby laughed loudly and Kim was reminded they weren't alone.

Loz stepped out onto the balcony. 'Here ya go. I brought a plate of snacks, too,' she said.

Kim couldn't meet her eyes as she reached for the glass Loz handed her. Had she seen them? Did it matter?

'This is the last of the food. Shall we sneak off for some Italian tucker at that place down the road? Are you going to join us, Charlie?' asked Loz.

'It sounds great, but I'll leave you two to celebrate. I'll walk you there, though.'

Kim ground her teeth as questions churned through her mind. Why didn't he want to stay?

'Oh, that's a shame,' said Loz. 'Are you booked up?'

Good old Loz, thought Kim. She wasn't afraid to ask personal questions or be a little nosy.

'Yes. It's an old mate's engagement party at a restaurant in the city,' he said. 'I told him I was going to be late but he'd kill me if I didn't turn up.'

Of course! Kim mentally slapped herself. He'd told her about the engagement party when she'd first asked him to come.

'Oh well, it's only eight-thirty. That's not too late. Shall we make tracks?' Loz asked, touching Kim on the elbow.

'Good idea. Now that this is all over I'm finding myself rather hungry.'

The three of them headed back through the dregs of the awards crowd to the lift and got out on the ground floor, setting off for a nearby Italian restaurant. Kim was quiet for most of the walk. What with her feet screaming in pain and her brain flashing questions faster than she could make sense of them, she couldn't hold a conversation.

'How about we get it to take away and go back to our room, kick our shoes off and watch a movie?' said Loz. 'Do you know how long it's been since I've had a hotel room without kids?' Her hair shone in the streetlight and her eyes were alive with excitement, and perhaps a little too much wine.

'Sounds perfect. Especially the part about kicking off shoes,' said Kim.

'Righto, I'll go order us a selection. Night, Charlie,' said Loz, giving him a quick hug as she headed into the restaurant.

'It smells great,' said Charlie as he watched Loz disappear. 'I better get going.'

Kim didn't want him to leave. She couldn't help but reach out and adjust his jacket as an excuse to touch him.

Charlie covered her hand before she drew it away, holding it against his chest. 'I'll see you back home. Maybe we can go out for lunch?' he asked.

'I'd like that.' Kim smiled as she gazed into his eyes. It was a surreal feeling: here she was in the city, all dressed up, standing so close to someone so handsome, someone who made her heart race.

Charlie pulled her into his arms one last time. 'I really have to go,' he said, but he didn't move. His arms remained around her, and if anything they grew tighter. He sighed heavily and moved so he could kiss her forehead again.

'Goodnight, my awesome rural winner,' he said as he finally stepped back. 'See you soon.'

Then he headed off up the street at a brisk pace. Kim watched him go. Damn it! She should have kissed him! It irked her that she was so scared of being rebuffed that she hadn't tried.

Fifteen minutes later it was still messing with her head as she and Loz got back to their hotel with their dinner.

'So, are you going to tell me what's happening with you and Charlie?' said Loz as she put their food down on the table.

'Shit, Loz, you could have waited until I got these bloody heels off!' Kim removed the evil shoes and sighed loudly. 'Oh my god, that feels so much better.' She lifted the lid off one of the takeaway containers and groaned. 'Smells amazing.'

Loz opened the other container. 'Stop changing the subject, but you're right. Yum,' she said as she put a piece of pasta in her mouth. 'Let's eat, then you can tell me all.'

Kim couldn't chance spilling food on the dress. She quickly took it off and put on a baggy shirt, then picked up a fork. Once she was halfway through and starting to feel the sleepy effects of the pasta she finally replied. 'There's nothing to tell. Charlie is a great friend.'

'Who you hug a lot. I'm not silly, I can see the spark between you two. Any hotter and you'd need a room.' Loz smirked.

Kim smiled sheepishly but didn't say anything. She wasn't used to this kind of girly chat.

Loz tried prodding a few more times and then gave up, mainly thanks to the Nicholas Sparks movie she'd found on TV. But Kim's mind was still buzzing with questions. Why hadn't Charlie kissed her? Actually he'd had a few chances. Was he really interested, or was she so out of the game she couldn't tell?

Her phone rang and she jumped. She still wasn't used to her new phone and the funky ringtone Seth had picked. 'Oh, it's Drew,' she said to Loz, and headed outside to the balcony so she wouldn't interrupt Loz's Scott Eastwood love fest.

'Hey, Drew. What's up?' Kim assumed it was something to do with the wedding.

'Kimmy, I'm just calling to see how you went tonight. You killed it, didn't you?'

'Did Loz text you about it?' she asked.

'No.' He sounded hurt. 'When my friend is up for an amazing award, I'm interested.'

'Oh.' It was all she could say. They might be friends, but what with the farm and his wedding, it had been months since they'd really talked.

Drew sighed. 'Look, I know I've been really busy and we haven't caught up much. I know that things have changed a lot, but you'll always be my friend, Kim. I think about you often, and I miss our times together. I want you to know I'm still here for you, and that will never change. You're family to me, Kimmy,' he said.

Kim sniffed as the tears poured down her face. She was taken completely by surprise. His words had touched a part of her that had been feeling left out, alone and friendless.

'Are you crying?'

'No,' she squeaked as she sniffed again.

'I'm sorry.' His voice was soft and he sounded upset.

'Don't be,' she said. 'I really needed to hear that. I miss you too.'

'I can't believe you're crying. You never cry,' he said with concern.

'I know, I'm just being silly. It's been a big night. I won, actually,' she said, trying to change the subject and pull herself together.

'You won! You bloody ripper, I knew you would. You're amazing. I'm so proud of you, Kim. I want to hear all about it when you get home, okay? Come by the farm – you're always welcome. Billy misses you too.'

That made Kim start crying again. Gosh, she was a right mess tonight. 'I miss Billy too. I might swing by and see if he wants to come for a bike ride. Oh, and I'm bringing someone to the wedding, if that's okay.'

'Oh, yeah, sure. I'll let Nat know.' If he wanted to know who, he didn't ask. 'I'm glad you're coming. It wouldn't be the same without you. It will be hard enough without Mum.'

He didn't say any more although Kim could imagine what he was thinking.

'Anyway, I better let you get back to partying,' said Drew.

Kim laughed. 'Yep, pasta and a movie is as good as it gets for us. I'm buggered from trying to sound intellectual in front of all the politicians and bigwigs. Can't wait to get back home.'

'You come and tell me all about it, okay? Promise?'

'I will. Night, Drew.'

'Night, Kimberly,' he said and hung up before she could bust him for using her full name.

Kim wiped her face and smiled as she opened the sliding door to head back inside. Loz was propped up on her pillows, passed out while the movie blared away. Her sister-in-law had made good use of the free wine.

Kim sat on her bed and stared at her phone. Did she dare ask Charlie the one question that was causing her grief? She'd never be able to ask him face-to-face. She wasn't normally this brazen, she thought as she typed out a text.

Don't you want to kiss me?

Quickly she hit send and then regretted it. What if he doesn't? If only you could delete a text from another person's phone.

Her phone rang and she yelped. It was Charlie. She jumped off the bed and went back to the balcony, Loz still sound asleep.

Her finger shook as she answered the call. Was he angry?

'Hello?' she said softly.

'Of course I want to kiss you,' said Charlie. His voice was rushed. 'You drive me crazy, Kim.'

'Really?'

'Yes, really. The only reason I didn't kiss you tonight is that I didn't trust myself to stop, and I couldn't afford to miss my mate's party.'

'Oh.' Her mind raced as she imagined a hot kiss leading to a hotel room with naked bodies. She smiled as heat ran through her body, pooling between her hips.

'I have to go. I rushed outside the restaurant to call you, and my friends are watching me. I just wanted to tell you that yes, I do want to kiss you, very much. I'm hoping to have a chance one day soon, if that's all right with you,' he said. His voice sounded unsure for a moment.

'Oh, it's all right by me,' she said, grinning into the phone.

'Good. Glad we got that settled. Night, Kim.'

'Night, Charlie.'

Kim stared at her phone before holding it against her chest. Taking a few deep breaths, she tried to calm the adrenaline buzz darting under her skin but it was no use. She had to admit she liked this feeling.

'Soon,' she said aloud into the night full of lights and stars. Charlie had said he'd kiss her soon. She was so excited she felt like skipping.

As she headed inside she got a text from Charlie. She turned off the lights and crawled into bed before she read it.

Very soon.

Chapter 19

1969

JOHN had had just about enough of goodbyes. This time had been the worst, because it was for real. He was taking his first flight overseas to fight in another country from which he might never return.

'Please stop crying, Mum,' he begged as his family gathered around him at the airport.

She only cried harder and reached for another hanky.

His dad held out his hand and John shook it, before he was pulled into a tight embrace.

'Take care out there. Come home in one piece. I love you, son,' said James, his voice cracking with emotion.

'I will, Dad.'

James backed away, turning his head from them all as he wiped at his eyes.

Then it was Beth's turn. She stood with her arms hugging her own body, grip tight. Strong she was, his little angel. Tears rolled down her face.

'I know,' he said as he gently took her arms and pulled her into his embrace. 'I love you.' There wasn't much else left to say.

'I love you too. Always,' she whispered, while trying to keep her sobs at bay.

Letting go, he walked to the immigration doors and went through. He didn't look back. He couldn't. He needed all his effort to march towards the plane while his chest seized up like he was in the throes of a heart attack. As he fought off tears he counted his steps. He couldn't think about what he was leaving behind. He couldn't think about the possibility of this being the last time he saw his family. He couldn't see his wife's heartbroken face for fear of unravelling himself.

Dear Beth,

Hello my love. Well, here I am in sunny Vietnam. I made it through the flight to Sydney by sleeping a little and thinking of you. At Sydney we boarded a Qantas commercial flight, called the Skippy Squadron, and stopped over in Darwin. I'm getting to see more of Australia than I ever thought I would. We also had a stopover at Singapore before arriving at Tan Son Nhut Airport. Guess I'll get used to all these funny names and spellings. From there we got on a massive American Hercules plane for a very noisy ride and a rough landing on a short runway at the base at Nui Dat. After the flight I was feeling a little nervous, but I could tell I wasn't the only one. There were plenty of pale and scared-looking faces.

Nui Dat is right in the middle of a jungle, and even though it's protected by fences and bunkers, I still felt exposed. Some

*men were gripping their guns just a little too tightly. I'm sure
they were feeling just as scared. We felt like sitting ducks for
the Viet Cong. Luckily Lieutenant Colonel Nash, in command
of regiment 5RAR, came moments later. He told us a bit
about the Nui Dat base which is in the Phuoc Tuy Province.*

*Darling, this place is nothing like home. The base is
made up of sandbags and scraps of wood and tin. Soldiers
in their baggy green uniforms are everywhere, and the
Huey helicopters are always overhead. I was taken to my
new home, called 'the lines' – a row of tents, one each side
of a track. It's a strange place, so different from home and
everything I know. A small tent, which I share with three
other soldiers, is my new dwelling. Home is still where
you are, Bethy. I miss you.*

Love, John xxx

'Your bed is in this tent.'

John thanked the lieutenant and carted his bags and equip-
ment inside. There was a plywood floor below, propped up on
pallets, as well as four stretchers and a single light bulb.

'Hey, we have a reo,' said a bloke as John walked inside.

He'd quickly learnt that 'reo' was short for reinforcement.
Apparently it would take him around a hundred days before
he'd lose the title.

'Lance Corporal Harrison Johnston – they call me Harry,'
a bloke said, holding out his hand. 'Where you from, mate?' He
was a tall bloke, a few years older than John, by the looks of it,
with sandy-coloured hair.

John dropped his gear by the bed Harry indicated. 'I'm from WA. Name's John Parson.'

'Get outta town. I'm WA too.' Harry turned off the music coming from his tape player. 'This bloke here's Daniel McLaren,' said Harry.

A young guy much like John lay on his stretcher shirtless, in just his dog tags and pants. He held out his hand, not wanting to move from his position. He had a tiny black moustache, which was a little on the thin side. 'Call me Macca.'

'And the other bloke's Peter Garland – we call him Judy. He's out at the PX at the moment.'

'PX?' said John.

'It's the Post Exchange. Don't worry, you'll pick up the names quick,' said Harry.

'So are you going to the Hoa Long dance tonight?' Macca asked with a smirk.

'No, should I?' John asked.

Harry slapped his back. 'No, mate. It's a trick tried on all the reos. They get you dressed up in your polyester uniform and make you wait at the main gate for the bus to the dance, but it never comes,' he said with a laugh.

'Worked on you, didn't it, Macca?' came a voice and John turned to see a bloke come in through the tent flaps.

'Fuck off, Judy,' said Macca.

'You looked so pretty in your dress uniform, waiting.' Judy dodged the water bottle thrown at his head. 'Harry, you had to go and ruin it – I would have loved to try it on this reo as well.'

Harry turned to John. 'Watch Judy, he's ever the prankster.'

He turned back to Judy. 'And his name is John Parson, not reo.'

Judy was a tall, scrawny bloke with wing-nut ears made all the more obvious by his short back and sides. He pulled off his green shirt, threw his floppy hat onto his bed and sat on the floor beside Harry. 'So what's it to be? Johnny or Parso?'

John shrugged. 'John is fine,' he said.

'Righto,' said Judy. 'Johnny it is.' Then he pulled out a pack of cigarettes and lit one up.

John settled in and got to know a bit about the guys he was going to be living with. He'd taken a shine to Harry, and not just because he was from country WA like himself. Harry had a gentle way about him, and was clearly helping John settle in. And he loved to laugh as well. Time passed quickly and before John knew it, it was lights out at ten-thirty. His first day in Nui Dat was over.

'Wake up, sunshine,' said Harry as he shook John's arm.

'What?' said John as he tried to open his eyes and figure out where the heck he was. It all came back to him pretty quickly when he saw the tent ceiling and the men beside him getting up.

'It's six o'clock. Time for the pill parade,' said Macca.

John got up and followed them to the compulsory parade where anti-malarial pills were handed out and taken while the roll was called. Then the men went down to the mess for breakfast and ate out of dixies, square aluminium trays. It wasn't bad tucker – cereals, baked beans, sausages, tomatoes, and even grapefruit.

'Grab them while you can,' said Harry pointing to the grape-fruit. 'They're not always available.'

They dropped their dirty dixies into a half 44-gallon drum full of water and detergent as they left the mess. John stopped by the Q store to collect four sets of jungle greens and a steel trunk.

Dear Beth,

Not much is going on here. I spend a lot of time cleaning my gun. They're not allowed to be loaded inside the wire, which means inside the Nui Dat boundary. I've filled a few sandbags, pruned the grass in front of the gunpits and sprayed malathion around for the mozzies. I thought we had mozzies bad back home after the rain, but it's much worse here. I won't complain again! I came face-to-face with my first mongoose too – they live wild in the rubber plantation next to base. They're like small weasels with a long tail. Every night we attend a compulsory parade, much like the morning one, where we have to take Paludrine and Dapsone for malaria. Sometimes it feels like the biggest enemy we have is the mozzies.

I'll have to thank Mum for the biscuits and remind her that they do feed us here. It's not too bad. Tucker is often ham, lamb, roast beef or pork, and the desserts are nearly always jellies, fruit or ice-cream. Lots of dehydrated or canned foods too. We have ration packs for when we go on operations. But there are days I would kill for your vanilla slice.

The heat and humidity don't make it much fun, especially if we are doing physical work. Judy generally walks around without his shirt, wearing a sweatband around his head.

Everyone at camp keeps a record of the time left until they can go home. The day you go home is 'a wakey'. So I've started my own calendar. I'm now down to 350 and a wakey! Harry tells me I have to get to around 260 and a wakey before I can lose my reo label. It all seems so far off, but as I cross off the days I know each one brings me closer to home and you.

I hope my parents aren't smothering you too much. Just tell them you need some space if they do. I understand they can get a bit much. Tell Dad – he'll make sure to steer Mum away if you need.

It's lights out in five minutes so I best get organised. I love you.

Love, John xxx

One morning a few days later the lieutenant colonel informed them that their battalion was going on a patrol to get used to the jungle. 'It will be valuable revision in fire and movement and the basic skills of the infantryman,' he said, addressing them all. 'It will also serve as an effective introduction to the type of terrain over which the battalion will operate in the ensuing months.'

There were plenty of reos in the battalion. As they stood around at the headquarters prior to heading out, Harry pointed them out to John.

'How do you know?' John asked him.

'Look at the way they hold their guns, ready to shoot at a moment's notice. And check out their knuckles.'

John looked down to check his own knuckles. Yep, they were white with tension as he clenched his weapon. He took a breath and tried to relax. Harry had assured him that they shouldn't come across anything untoward today.

It was mildly reassuring.

The jungle was creepy, especially since John was used to wide open paddocks. In some places the foliage was so thick he couldn't see more than four or five metres in front of him. As it was the dry season, the terrain was hard, which he was thankful for; the thought of trudging through wet mud wasn't so appealing. Each footstep he tried to make as silent as possible.

'Gotta watch out for pansy pits and hidden tunnels,' said Harry quietly.

John had heard about the tunnel rats, Australian soldiers who did search-and-destroy missions underground in the Viet Cong tunnels. 'A pansy pit?'

'Yeah, a deep hole filled with sharpened sticks that can skewer you if you fall into it,' said Judy. 'Only thing is that some don't die from that, so the Viet Cong put their shit on the sticks so the infection will hopefully kill you later.' He shook his head. 'Bloody sick is what that is.'

It sounded horrific.

One minute they were walking along, John watching his every step, and the next minute there was a high-pitched scream, which brought them all to attention. Luckily no one fired off a round as it was one of the other reos.

John looked up as the reo dropped his gun and ran around yelling, 'Shit, get it off, get it off!' He'd walked into a massive spider web and a huge spider was on his face. It was something out of a nightmare, and John was glad it wasn't his face. Some blokes nearby laughed, and everyone relaxed after realising the threat.

Operation Bordertown lasted three days. They returned to camp on foot on the third day with no casualties, even though they'd had two contacts with small parties of Viet Cong at night. John hadn't been anywhere near that action. Back at base, they had to clean their weapons carefully, breech open, magazine out, and check that the breech was clear as they didn't want any accidents on base.

'It pays to double-check,' said Harry. 'Don't want any ADs.'

John's brow creased as he tried to figure out what AD stood for.

'Accidental discharge,' Harry explained, and then went on to tell him a few stories about bullets missed and guns accidentally going off at the base. One time one had actually hit a fellow soldier in the lines.

John didn't want to be one of those stories. He made extra sure to check his gun.

That night, after the pill parade, they got word from HQ that they'd be going out on another operation: Operation Ulladulla. It was a big one, with four rifle companies going out for up to five weeks in the north of Phuoc Tuy Province.

'It's pretty much a search-and-destroy,' said Harry as they sat in their tent later that night. 'You'll be right, mate. I'll keep an eye on ya.'

John was holding the letters he'd received while they'd been out in the jungle. There were three from Beth, one from his mum and another from his sister with photos of her baby. The boys ribbed him for getting so many. But he was glad he'd got them; they helped take his mind off the new operation. He was nervous, but also keen to put some of his skills to the test. 'Thanks, Harry. I'll watch your back too,' he said with a weak smile. Then he settled down to write a letter to Beth.

Just in case.

Chapter 20

IT had been a crazy few days. Not only was the farm busy, but Kim had been inundated with calls and interview requests after the award. Charlie's sister was in town for her workshop at the Art Space, so Kim and Charlie hadn't got around to catching up since the awards night. But that hadn't stopped him calling her each night to see how her day had been. It was nice to chat with someone who wanted to listen.

'I'm off to Drew's,' she yelled out to her brother as she climbed into her ute.

Matt raised his hand in acknowledgement before turning back to finish fixing the fire lighter he'd made for the back of his ute.

As she drove to Drew's farm she felt relieved that she was finally going to see him. She'd been staying out of the way, leaving Matt to help Drew with the wedding preparation. But after Drew's phone call she realised that a true friend didn't leave a mate in need. Sure, she'd made some metal bits and pieces for the wedding, but it was fair to say she'd been failing in the friend department. Time she grew up.

Kim pulled up outside his house and saw Turbo run out through the gate to bark at her. The moment she opened her door and called out to him he stopped, ran over and jumped up on her, wagging his tail. 'You're all bloody bark, aren't ya, boy.'

With the dog following her she walked down the path to the house, smiling at various welding creations of hers in Drew's garden.

'Hello, stranger,' said Drew.

Kim looked up to see Drew, Nat and Billy sitting on the verandah together, Billy by Nat's side. Well, until he saw her.

'Kimmy!' Billy ran to her, his arms outstretched.

She hugged him as he clung to her like a little monkey. Kim had trouble with the lump welling in her throat. She'd missed this kid something fierce. 'Hey, buddy,' she croaked.

Billy leant back to see her face. 'Where have you been all my life?' he said.

Kim laughed as she blinked away her unshed tears. 'Farming. What about you?'

His shoulders sagged. 'School,' he said glumly.

'Come on, I'm sure it's not that bad. Seth and Mallory love having more friends and different teachers.' With the small Lake Biddy school closing down last year the local kids had to catch the bus into Lake Grace.

'It's okay. The bus ride sucks though.'

Kim's eyebrows shot up at a word she'd never heard from his mouth before.

'But I have a new friend called Eric, and he likes motorbikes too.'

Kim let him go. 'Well, that's cool.'

Billy grabbed her hand as they walked to where Drew and Nat sat.

'So you finally graced us with your presence,' teased Drew.

Kim ignored him. 'Hi Nat. How're you going?'

'I'm good,' said Nat as she tucked her neat blonde plait back over her shoulder. She looked amazing in trackpants and a checked shirt, one Kim had seen Drew wearing before. Kim found it easier to talk to Nat when she was dressed like this. 'A little stressed with wedding prep, but we'll get there. It's good to see you. Drew's been sulking about his lack of welding ability.'

'Hey, don't tell her about my failings,' said Drew.

'I already know you can't weld. I've known since the moment you picked up a welder,' Kim said with a smirk.

Drew screwed up his face. 'Come on then, there's a few free beers up at the shed with your name on them. But,' he stressed, 'I need some welding advice.'

'Was it really that hard to ask for help?' she teased.

'Yes, it was. Besides, you've already done so much for us.' He stood up. 'Come on, let's get a beer. We'll be back later, love,' he said to Nat.

'No worries. Did you want to stay for tea, Kim?' Nat asked sweetly.

'Say yes, say yes!' said Billy. 'We're having fried rice. Mum makes the best one, with real prawns.'

It was weird to hear Billy call Nat Mum, but seeing her eyes light up when he said it made it perfect. It was meant to be.

'I'd love to, but Doris has invited me for tea. I have her wedding clothes,' said Kim.

'Oh,' said Billy, pouting slightly.

'But I'm sure I can fit in a quick motorbike ride around the track if you're keen?'

'Awesome.' Billy turned to Nat. 'Can I?'

'One quick one, but wear your helmet,' Nat warned.

Billy and Kim followed Drew down the path to the shed, with Billy trying to match their strides. She smiled. It was nice to be missed. Just because Billy had Nat didn't mean she was forgotten. She still had a place in his heart.

Drew was happy to wait while Kim and Billy did three laps of the bike track. Billy won all three, even though Kim was actually trying, and once they pulled back into the shed Drew had a cold beer waiting for her.

'Thanks.'

She drank half of it in the first go. Drew raised his eyebrow.

'What? It's bloody hot outside and Billy is hard to catch,' she said.

Billy beamed. 'You did okay, Kimmy. Maybe next time you'll win,' he said.

'Why thank you, Billy,' she said, giving him a wink.

'How about you head back to the house now, mate?' Drew said. 'Kim and I have some welding to do.'

Kim shot him a look.

'Okay, Kim has some welding to do,' Drew corrected.

'I messed it up. I don't think I should be around the welder at the moment.'

Billy gave Kim a big hug and started walking back to the house. Drew crooked his finger at her and she followed him further into the shed, where his workshop was.

'Ta-*da*,' he said, presenting a metal arch that didn't sit straight and had big blobs of metal on all the joins.

'Hmm, you tried hard,' she said, and he laughed.

'Too hard maybe.'

Drew went to pick up a drawing from his bench. The piece of white paper was smudged with grease. Kim did her best not to notice his nice butt in his work shorts and his bronzed, muscly arms. Or at least she did her best to appreciate it all as a friend would.

'This was the plan,' he said. On the page was a hand-drawn arch. 'Nat tried to make it simple for me. This is the size she wants, big enough to fit us both underneath.' Drew scratched his chin. 'I think I've left it too late,' he said with a grimace. 'Can you fix it?'

Kim did some quick calculations in her head. 'I'll go one better and make a whole new one, okay?'

'You can do that in under two days? Oh, Kim, you're a bloody legend.'

'It can be my wedding present. Then you can stick it in the garden afterwards.'

'Yeah, Nat would love that.' Drew was smiling like a goose. 'Do you want a hand?'

Kim put up her hand. 'No. I've got this.' She chuckled.

They sat down on some old plastic milk crates to finish their beers. She was taken aback by the first thing out of Drew's mouth.

'So who's this plus-one you're bringing? Do I know him?'

Kim rested her head in her hand. Really? He wanted to have that conversation?

'Come on, Kim, Nat needs to know to put his name on the table.'

With a sigh she lifted her head. 'It's Charlie, from Elders.'

'The insurance guy? Isn't he . . . old?' said Drew.

'A little. But he's actually a great guy. I'm starting to think age is where I've been going wrong. The young guys I was seeing just weren't right, whereas Charlie – the guy has class, manners, he's thoughtful and so patient. Besides, he likes me. That is a huge plus right there,' she said with a smile.

Drew's eyes watched her seriously, his mouth twitching as if he had something to say.

'What is it?'

'It's nothing,' he said. 'No, well, yes, actually. I heard that Charlie was married.' Drew sat back as if he expected Kim to explode.

'Yes, he is.'

Drew's brow shot up.

'But it's not Travis all over again. Charlie's been separated for ages. He came to town alone.' Kim felt a little uneasy as she said it.

'If you're sure? I care about you, Kim. You were a mess after Travis, and I would hate for you to go through something like that again. You deserve better. Much better.' Drew reached out and patted her hand.

'I know. But he doesn't have Travis's cockiness and he really seems genuine. I want to trust him.' I *need* him to be telling the truth, thought Kim. To be taken advantage of a third time might just put an end to her dream of a life partner. It would be strictly pets if this went pear-shaped. She could be the female version of Harry with all his dogs. It didn't seem like that bad a life.

'There'll be more fish in the sea if this one doesn't work out, Kimmy.'

'Thanks, Drew,' she said. 'But I'm not so sure.' In her mind Kim was already planning her spinsterhood.

'So you really don't want my help with the welding?' he asked.

And that was the end of the Charlie talk, much to Kim's relief. They spent the next hour chatting like they used to about farming, machinery and their seeding plans.

When it came time to leave, they hugged each other and Kim walked away feeling, for the first time since Nat's arrival, that things were actually back to normal. She loved Drew and loved being around him, but she knew he was like a friend, or a brother. It didn't feel like she'd lost him any more. He would always be there, and he needed her friendship – and welding skills, she thought with a chuckle. Kim was happy to see him so happy. He deserved some happiness after everything he'd been through – losing both parents and devoting his life to Billy. This was Drew's time.

Kim was going to build him the most kick-arse archway ever.

With a smile, she headed straight over to Doris's place.

Doris's house was a ramshackle place, a bit rundown and very old-school. She still did her washing in a twin tub in the ancient laundry off the back verandah. She still used her outside shower and toilet, both covered with spider webs. The shower curtain was way past its use-by date, the walls were mouldy in places, paint was peeling off and the cement floor was cracking. The garden was just as haphazard, with Doris's vegetables grown in among plants and flowers, wherever she found some spare dirt. Nails were coming out of the tin roof, which was rusty and threatening to fall. And inside the floorboards were worn and her carpets beyond repair. There were big holes burnt in it close to the fireplace.

With her own eyes, Kim had seen Doris bring in a massive tree branch and put it into the open fire, pushing it further in with her foot as it burnt down. Certainly an unusual way of adding wood. As a result, ash coated most of the ornaments and shelves in her house. The place hadn't been dusted since the early sixties, by the looks. The kitchen was a time capsule, with a massive chopping block by the old wood stove. Doris's dogs were allowed inside and at times the chooks wandered through too.

Yet Kim loved it. It had been like that since she was a kid, and it suited Doris to a tee. She was a happy lady with a big heart.

'Glad you could make it, Kim. The roast is just about ready,' said Doris, greeting her with a big hug.

She wore holey black shorts with her favourite double-plugger thongs and a blue T-shirt. Her grey hair was short and standing up on one side.

'It smells yum,' Kim said as she pulled back from the hug.

'I've got some wedding clothes for you. The girls at Sand and Salt let me borrow them for you to see what you liked.'

'Righto. Let's check them out then.'

Kim waited in the lounge while Doris tried on the clothes she'd picked. It was much easier to bring the clothes to Doris than vice versa. Doris's ute was unregistered and she didn't like going into town much.

'Whaddaya think?' said Doris as she came out in black slacks with a dark-blue blouse.

'Wow, you look fabulous. Blue is your colour, Doris.'

'I'm comfortable in this. The other top looked like something one of my dogs spewed up.'

With her hair brushed and a bit of lippy, Doris would be unrecognisable. For a moment Kim wondered if Harry and Doris would get on. They were both homebodies.

'What do I owe ya?' Doris said.

'Nothing. They're on me. You've cooked us enough food to buy ten outfits.'

'You sure, lovey?'

'Dead sure.'

Doris nodded. She seemed happy enough with that. 'Righto. I'll get outta this fancy stuff before I ruin it.'

Doris brought out the other garments for Kim to return to the shop, then she headed into the kitchen to start serving up the roast. They sat down to the full spread: meat, roasted vegetables – in more oil than Kim usually liked but full of flavour – gravy and a side of peas.

It was after Kim had chewed on the last bit of pork crackle

that a question popped into her mind. 'Hey, Doris, do you remember any . . .' Kim had to think as she tried to remember the name Denny had mentioned. 'Um, Parson. I think that's the name. Used to live around Lake Grace.'

Doris was licking her fingers and paused to think. 'Parson. Yeah, there was a family way back. Norma and her husband. They were farmers. Had two kids.' Doris used some freshly made bread to mop up the gravy and chewed as she thought. 'A girl,' she mumbled through her food. 'And a boy.'

Kim leant forward, eager to hear more. She wondered again why Charlie was interested in them.

'If I recall,' said Doris, finishing her mouthful, 'the girl went to the city and the folks sold up the farm after the boy went to Vietnam.'

'For the war?'

'Yep. John, I think his name was. So many went to that bloody war. No good came of it. The poor soldiers who returned weren't ever the same.'

Kim nodded, but she didn't really know much about it. There were a few blokes around Lake Grace who were Vets, but she'd never spoken with them about it. It wasn't something you just went up and asked people about.

'Time for dessert. I made your favourite,' said Doris, getting up and putting their plates in a very full sink.

'Sticky date pudding?' Doris nodded and Kim just about trembled with delight. Doris made the best pudding and caramel sauce. 'I love you, Doris.'

Doris laughed, her typical dry cackle. 'It's nice to know I'm still good for somethin',' she said.

By the time Kim was ready to drive home she was feeling the size of a whale. Damn Doris! She had a bridesmaid's dress to fit into in a day and a half. She'd have to watch what she ate tomorrow. And of course Doris had sent her home with a Tupperware container full of leftover pudding. She'd give it to Matt in return for the day off to make Drew's archway. Not that she had to bribe her brother – she was entitled to take days off when she liked, but they did work as a team. But Matt's belly could certainly carry more pudding than hers.

Sitting in the ute, Kim undid the top button on her jeans and groaned. As she drove she tried to plan a design for the archway – probably something with swirls and love hearts. Now all she had to do was bring it to life.

Chapter 21

CHARLIE went to his office early on Friday morning. He had to get some of yesterday's work finished, send some emails and make a few phone calls to head office, chasing information about a car damage claim. Heather popped her head into his office just as he collected the paperwork for his visit to Simon Caldwell.

'I was just going to see if you wanted a coffee?'

'Sorry, Heather, I'm off to see Simon now. I've sorted that car claim with head office. It's all good to finalise. Any chance you could call Rodger and let him know, please? He'll want to book it into smash repairs.'

'Yeah, no worries. Say hi to Patsy if you see her. Simon's mum,' she explained, seeing the quizzical look on his face.

'Righto. See ya.'

Charlie drove out to Simon's farm, ten minutes from town, to have a chat about changing some policies. It was all pretty straight-forward, and Charlie gave Simon some estimated figures and promised to have the updated policies to him within a few days.

He'd been hoping that some of his farm visits would lead to more information on the Parson family, but most of the farmers he met hadn't heard the name before, probably because they were too young. Sometimes the moment wasn't right for Charlie to throw the question out there. He didn't want to start the town talking. But today, Simon invited him to stay for a cuppa at the house that he shared with his parents. Simon was unmarried, only just younger than Charlie, and ran the farm with a bit of help from his dad, while his mum kept him well looked after.

'Come in and grab a seat,' said Simon as he removed his dirty cap and hung it up on a hat rack by the front door.

Charlie followed him into the kitchen, where Simon introduced him to his parents, Bert and Patsy.

'Would you like tea or coffee, Charlie?'

'Coffee, white with one, would be lovely, Patsy. Thank you.'

Patsy moved across the old kitchen. He guessed she was in her sixties or a touch older.

'I've just finished baking,' she said, presenting a freshly made sponge cake filled with jam and cream.

Charlie's stomach grumbled loudly and Patsy chuckled. 'Sorry,' he said, 'breakfast was a coffee on the run this morning.' He watched Patsy cut a huge slice of cake for him.

'We can't have you starving. Eat up.' Patsy passed him the cake and turned back to finish the cuppas.

'I'm going to have to limit my farm visits,' said Charlie with a smile. 'It always seems to be smoko time, and you country folks sure know how to cook up a mean spread.' He actually loved this part of the job – it was nice to learn more about his clients, and they were always curious to learn more about him.

After talking about insurance for a bit, Patsy said, 'That's enough for now. I get tired of too much farm talk. Charlie, tell us a bit about you. Where are you from?'

He gave them the basic rundown as best he could, without mentioning both his parents were dead. It was always a conversation killer. 'My sister Sarah is here at the moment, which has been really great. She's been doing workshops at the Art Space while she's here. She mothers me a bit too much, but I can't complain that the house is clean and food is cooked for me. Makes a nice change.'

'I bet it does,' said Patsy, glaring at her son and husband. 'Be wonderful if some people would offer to give me a break every now and then.'

'Don't look at me, woman. You know I'd burn your kitchen down,' said Bert.

'That's 'cos your mum never taught you a bloody thing, and I made it worse by looking after you too well.'

'Ah, my love, that you did.' Bert gave her a wink and Patsy smiled, then raised an eyebrow at her son.

'I fend for myself when you and Dad disappear on holidays,' said Simon.

'Yes, dear. But it's the fact I come back to a grease-covered kitchen and a full laundry that irks me so.'

Charlie was trying hard not to smile. Time to change the subject. 'Sarah's workshop is today, actually, and I'm heading into town after this to run her back to Perth.'

For a moment they talked about the art centre and how great

it was for their little town. The timing seemed right, and Charlie decided to risk it.

'Bert, Patsy, have you ever heard of a Parson family who used to live out here?'

'Yes,' said Patsy. Bert looked a bit confused. 'Remember James and Norma?' she said. 'They were farmers. Norma came to our quilting club a few times but then they sold up and left.'

'Ah yes, James. He was stuffed, couldn't farm any more on his own. I remember.'

'Did they have kids?' asked Charlie.

Bert shrugged, but Patsy nodded. 'Yes, two kids. Daughter went off to the city. I can't remember her name but Norma talked a lot about her son John. He was the real farmer, but he got conscripted to Vietnam and that's why they had to sell up. I'll never forget her bursting into tears the last time she came to quilting club. I can't imagine how hard it was for them.'

Charlie swallowed the brick sitting in his throat. His heart was racing.

'Did he make it back from the war?' he asked.

'I'm afraid I didn't hear anything more about them after they left. They didn't have any family in the district, and I'm not sure who she was close friends with. My sister actually lived near them in Perth, and went to the same church as them before she passed away. I think she did mention once that something awful had happened. Maybe that was the son?'

What could have happened? Finding the answer would be like searching for a Skittle in a trailer load of M&Ms.

'Can you remember the year he went to war?' Maybe Charlie

could track this John fella down through war records. Find out if he was still alive.

Patsy frowned and he could tell she was getting curious about all his questions. 'Well, it was around the late sixties that we had the quilting club going. I'd guess anywhere between 1967 and 1970. Do you know the family?' she asked.

He'd been expecting it. 'I think there's a family connection, and seeing as I'm in Lake Grace I thought I'd see if I could find out some information. Thanks, Patsy. This is the most I've heard about them.'

'There are probably folks about who know a lot more. It's a country town – someone will have been their friend. I think they lived out south of Lake Grace. Ask around that way,' she offered. 'They had a farm, so the person who bought it would probably know something, or the neighbours.'

'Thanks, Patsy, much appreciated. And that is the best sponge cake I've ever eaten.'

Patsy blushed and then made him take half the cake home for later on.

Charlie said a quick goodbye and headed back into town. His mind was all over the place. He went back to his office, a small room with a window onto the main road through town, and tried to sort out Simon's policies. But he found himself staring at his computer, or the keyboard, or the pen in his hand. He reorganised his insurance pamphlets and re-sorted his pens and sticky notes on his desk. After a quick coffee he managed to make some headway but it was futile. He was knocking off early to take his sister back home but with his head how it was he may as well leave now.

'Heather, are you right here? I'm going to head off now,' he said, sticking his head into her office.

'No worries, Charlie,' Heather said. 'Say goodbye to Sarah for me and have a safe trip back to Perth.'

'If there's anything urgent feel free to ring me.'

'Don't worry. I've got it covered. Go and enjoy.' Heather waved him off and he was grateful.

Although he was technically senior to Heather, he treated her as an equal in the office. Her years of experience and knowledge were worth more than the wage she got paid. Plus, she encouraged him to be flexible with his hours, which he loved.

When he got home he charged through his house straight to his bedroom, to the simple white bedside table. Opening the top drawer, he paused before reaching for an envelope and sitting down on his bed.

The envelope quivered in his shaking hands. He ran his finger over the stamp with its Lake Grace post mark. His name was written in pen on the front, care of his mum. He flipped it over, his chest tight, and read the line on the back.

Sender: J Parson

Could it be John Parson? It had to be, surely. The only Parsons who seemed to have lived anywhere near Lake Grace were a family with a John Parson. Of course this J Parson could have just posted the letter in Lake Grace as he or she was passing through, but Charlie didn't believe that. His gut was telling him that he had the right J Parson.

As carefully as he could, he lifted the flap and pulled out the card to read it for the millionth time.

The front of the card had a tractor and a big green seven. Inside it said HAPPY BIRTHDAY in block letters. But it was the handwritten words in pen that held Charlie captivated.

> *Dear Charlie,*
>   *Happy seventh birthday, son. I think of you always.*
> *I hope you're happy and doing well at school. I'm sorry I've missed so many birthdays and haven't been the father you needed. You are with the right people.*
>   *Love always, Dad.*

Tears welled in his eyes again. It happened every time. He was a grown man brought undone by a child's birthday card.

Charlie wiped at his eyes. Carefully, he put the card back in its envelope and tucked it away in its special place. He couldn't get caught up in emotions right now. For forty-five years Charlie had had two parents, Robert and Rachel Macnamara. Then suddenly he'd found this card from another dad. What was he supposed to think? He tugged at his hair, wishing he knew. He wished his mum was still alive. She'd be able to explain it. Why was it kept from him?

His phone beeped with a message.

Ready when you are. At the Art Space. Ta x

Charlie sighed. He was thankful for the distraction. Some days it was like he was stuck in a whirlpool, spinning around and around, going over the same ground.

He drove to the Art Space to pack up all the stuff Sarah had brought down for the workshop.

'Hey, you,' Sarah said as he entered.

'Hey, sis. How did it go today?'

'Fabulous turnout,' said Marjorie as she walked past with one of Sarah's works. 'Best yet. We had over thirty-five attending the workshops, kids included.'

'Oh, that's great to hear.' He knew he sounded flat, and instead of engaging in conversation he went to wrap some of Sarah's frames for the car. He concentrated hard on the task at hand to keep his mind from wandering. After finishing a few frames, he looked up and watched his sister. For a 43-year-old woman she still looked great, and was fit from the long walks she loved taking. Bangles moved along her arms, and her long necklace of coloured beads swayed every time she bent over. Her hair was cut in a bob and streaked with vibrant reds, and her outfit was typically trendy: leggings and a loose tunic teamed with topaz ballet flats.

Sarah glanced up, caught his eye and smiled.

'You okay?'

'Yeah, fine.' He smiled. 'Bit sad to see you go already.'

Whether she was his sister by blood or not, they'd forged a deep bond over their lives together, and he never wanted anything to come between them.

Sarah smiled at him again. 'I know. Me too. I've had a fantastic time with you. You'll always be my big brother. You know that, don't you?' She lowered her voice. 'Whatever you find out, nothing will ever change that.' Tears glistened in her eyes.

Charlie pulled her in for a hug. 'I love you too, Sare. Forever.' He knew she also wanted reassurance. What if Charlie discovered a whole new family? New sisters or brothers? Last night she'd told him she was just as scared as he was by what he might find out. Whatever happened, he would always have his sister.

'Do you want to get takeaway from Arjo's before we leave?' he asked.

'Sure. What would you like? My shout.'

'A sweet-chilli wrap would be lovely, thanks,' he said.

'Yep, no worries. And a cappuccino,' she said with a wink.

He laughed. 'Yes, please. You know me well.'

Sarah left to go next door, and as she walked out Kim walked in. A ripple of shock passed through him, and he realised how much he'd missed her.

'Hello, stranger,' she said with a soft, uncertain smile.

'Hey.' By god, she drove him crazy. Her easygoing character, her natural beauty, her laconic humour, her lovely long legs . . . she was the full package.

'I'm sorry I missed your sister's workshop. Is she here? I came to say hello.'

'No, she's just ducked off to grab us lunch. She'll probably be twenty minutes. Can you wait?'

She pressed her lips together so sensually that it drove all his troubled thoughts away. He was dying to kiss those perfect lips.

'Yeah, I can, I guess. I've just come to town to grab some more steel. I'm making an archway for Drew and Nat's wedding.' She pulled a face. 'Drew tried but failed, so I'm doing a rush job before the wedding tomorrow.'

'That's cutting it fine. How's it going?'

She brushed her hair back from her face and he felt his body start to burn.

'Should get it done by tonight. It's actually coming together all right.' Kim smiled again.

How could he last any longer? The fact that she was a few feet away was becoming torture. He wanted to kiss her now.

'Oh, hi, Kim,' said Julie as she walked out from the back room. 'Marj and I are going to duck next door and have a sit-down lunch. You guys right here?'

Marjorie came out of the little kitchen with her purse. 'I'm ready, Julie. Oh hello, Kim, great to see you.'

Kim greeted them both as the ladies headed for the door.

'Have a nice lunch,' said Charlie, waiting until they were about to enter Arjo's before firmly shutting the door of the Art Space.

Kim's forehead creased as she watched him. 'What are you doing?'

Charlie smiled. 'Something I've wanted to do for a very long time.' Taking her hand, he led her to the back room. 'Soon is *now*,' he said, shutting the door behind them and pushing Kim back against it gently. He stood there for a moment, just inches away from her body, testing himself, making the moment last longer, enjoying the surge of passion running through him, the feelings he hadn't experienced in a long time. Those coffee-coloured eyes swirled with desire and he felt his legs start to shake. Her lips parted, waiting. Her tongue darted across them. Now she was just teasing him, but hell, it was working. He couldn't hold back any longer.

He lifted his hand, brushed back her hair and then caressed her cheek. With his thumb he touched her lips and she closed her eyes. Jesus, Mary and Joseph, he wanted her so badly.

He moved his lips against hers softly, as a prelude. But then her hands snaked around his waist and moved to his backside, dragging him closer, and he lost control. He deepened the kiss. Their mouths pressed against each other. He was rock hard, but didn't dare press against her. He needed to hold on just enough to remember where they were.

After a few seconds they stopped and watched each other. Kim smiled.

'It was worth waiting for,' she whispered.

He kissed her again, murmuring against her lips, 'I agree.' He held her face in his hands as their kissing became more playful. He loved what he saw in her eyes. In his whole married life he'd never seen that look of desire and devotion. The funny thing was, it didn't scare him one bit. It felt so right.

He closed his eyes and focused on the soft tenderness of her lips, the electric buzz of her tongue and her sweet, sweet taste.

They heard the front door creak open and quickly pulled apart, both flushed.

'You have to go out there and distract whoever it is for a sec,' Charlie said urgently. 'I'm here packing up, okay?'

Kim went to say something but he gestured to the obvious erection bulging in his jeans.

'Ah. Roger,' she said, smiling.

Her heated gaze did nothing to help his swelling. Not one bit. He gritted his teeth and tried to breathe calmly.

'Okay,' Kim said. 'I'll see you tomorrow at the wedding. Drive safely this afternoon.'

He nodded. 'I'll text you when I get back from Perth.' Risking tearing apart his jeans, he grabbed her for one last kiss, and then she was out the door.

Charlie leant against it, his breathing erratic as he tried to adjust himself. Shit, he felt like a bloody teenager. Doris was right when she said you were only as young as the person you feel. He smiled. Somehow he knew it was much more than Kim's younger body that was affecting him so much.

He could hear Kim chatting to someone in the main room. It wasn't Sarah, but she'd be back soon with their lunch. He shook his head in an attempt to clear it. Just as well he would be in Perth tonight. He'd be hard-pressed not to drive to Kim's place and ravish her. He had a feeling she wouldn't object.

Chapter 22

KIM walked out of the Art Space with a silly grin on her face. Were her feet even touching the pavement? She paused for a moment to gather herself before going into Arjo's to say hi to Charlie's sister, Sarah. An unbelievable feeling was coursing through her.

As she walked into the coffee shop, it wasn't hard to spot the newcomer. Besides, Kim knew everyone else in there. She went to the counter to order a coffee and a toastie to take away and then went to introduce herself to Sarah. Except she was on the phone. Kim stood nearby as they both waited for their orders.

'Yeah, Laura, he seems fine. I know . . . I told him to call you. I don't know what he's found out yet, but I'm sure he'll call when he's ready. You know Charlie,' said Sarah.

It was hard for Kim not to eavesdrop. She picked up one of the papers and pretended to read it but her ears were tuned in to Sarah's voice.

'You know he loves you to bits, he just needs some time to himself. It's been a shock, and it was the worst way to find out.

I just wish he'd open up to me a bit more, you know? Maybe if you came down here and visited him he'd open up to you. He wants to do it alone, but I think he could use our support. Yep, I agree. No, Laura, call me anytime, it's not a problem. You're family, and always will be. You're the only sister I've got,' said Sarah. 'I'd better go, our order should be ready soon. Yep, stay in touch. Love you, bye.'

Sarah tucked her phone away just as the girl behind the counter brought out her order.

Kim wasn't sure what to make of what she'd heard. She knew Laura was Charlie's wife, he'd said so himself. But he'd also said they were separated. Yet that phone call didn't sit well with her. It sounded like Laura was still in his life, and in his sister's life. Kim's belly rolled with uncertainty. Fear of betrayal reared its ugly head, and Kim didn't say a word as Sarah walked past. How could she? Instead she got her own lunch, which she didn't feel like eating any more, and went home. And what was this shock that Sarah had mentioned happening to Charlie? What was going on in his life? It made Kim wonder if she knew him at all.

When she got home she called Denny.

'Hey you, what's up?'

'Why does something have to be up for me to call you?' said Kim. Denny made a funny throaty noise and Kim realised she was right. 'Okay, okay. I need your help.'

'Fire away. I'm home for the day.'

'Can you get on Facebook for me and check if Charlie is on there, please?'

'Oh, a bit of Facebook stalking. Didn't know you'd sink that low, Kimmy,' she teased. 'I've got my computer ready.'

Kim had never been on Facebook, even though Denny kept telling her to try. Kim didn't have the time or the desire. All of her friends lived within driving distance, so she didn't really see the point. Plus Denny told her whatever goss she'd happened upon there anyway. She could hear Denny tapping away on her keyboard now.

'Okay, so what information are you chasing? I've found him.'

Typical of Denny to do it so quickly. She'd probably been on Facebook when Kim rang.

'I don't know. Anything, really.'

'Sweetie,' said Denny. 'It's not going to tell me if he's a serial killer.' She laughed but then stopped. 'Oh, it says his status is married. I'm sure he hasn't changed it recently though. Doesn't look like he uses Facebook much. It's all mainly other people wishing him happy birthday or someone called Laura posting links on his page.'

'That's his wife,' said Kim dryly.

'Oh. Do you think he's still with her? That he lied?'

Denny's voice was so heartfelt and filled with concern that Kim suddenly felt her throat constrict and tears burn her eyes.

'I don't know,' she said truthfully. 'I'm so confused. I don't want to get hurt again.' She went on to tell her about the phone conversation she'd overheard. 'Do you think I'm overreacting?'

'You know what they say: believe a third of what you hear and half of what you see. Or something like that. It could all be explained. Just go and talk to Charlie. Tell him what you're worried about.'

'Yeah, but I did that with Travis, and look where that got me.'

'Just talk to him. Ask him for proof. And if you're still not comfortable, call his wife up or ask him to call her. If he won't, then you know something's up.'

'Got the bloody wedding tomorrow. I wish I hadn't invited him now. Thanks, Denny. I gotta go – I need to finish this archway for tomorrow.'

'No worries. Sorry I couldn't help much.'

Kim hung up and knew Denny was right. She just had to talk to Charlie, but she was scared. Scared of what it might reveal. Because if she was truthful, she was in way too deep with Charlie already.

Chapter 23

1969

Dear Beth,

343 and a wakey! We're off on our first big operation, Ulladulla. This letter will probably come in parts as I write it out in the field. It's a big operation with A Company (along with a platoon of B Company) and a section of mortars. We're under the operational control of C Squadron 1st Armoured Regiment. I know probably not much of this makes sense to you but I'll try to explain when I can. And yes, I have been smoking. Not much else to do, and all the boys smoke. We can't out in the field though, unless you're clever like Judy, who uses his hat to help hide the smoke. He's actually doing that as I write.

We have just finished digging our sleeping pits in the ground for the night. We string up our hoochies over the top with some sticks as makeshift poles. All those years building cubbies in the bush as a kid have come in handy.

Now we've got to take control of a 35-kilometre stretch

of Route 15 from the west of Ba Ria north-west to the village of Tam Phuoc. When I get home I'll show you where Ba Ria is and where Nui Dat lies. I could draw you a map. Actually I might do that for you, then you'll have an idea where I am.

Harry is beside me, taping shell dressing padding to the butt of his gun. And Macca is picking the mud from his GPs with a stick. GPs are what we call our steel-capped boots. When they get wet and layered with mud they end up feeling like cement bricks. And it's started to rain, AGAIN! Judy is cursing while Harry is smirking. You could set your watch by the showers here – would have loved this regular rain on the farm. Imagine the crops I could have grown. But I don't think I could handle this tropical humidity all the time. If I'm not wet from the rain I'm wet from the sweat. My feet don't have toes any more – just big pale prunes, all shrivelled and wrinkly.

Harry's just told Macca off as he's scratching at his face again. His whole lower jaw is covered with red scaly patches. Doc said it's ring tinea and has given him cream to treat it. Macca is worried about his looks, but Judy reckons it's only improved his face. Never a dull moment here with these boys, love.

It's the next day now, and we're about to pack up for more tramping through the wet mud. We have all our webbing on, which is quite heavy, and have to carry our ammo, shell dressing, entrenching tool, machete, grenade, water bottles and rations for five days, small stove and hexamine fuel tablet. Then there's the shaving gear, mug, shelter, blanket, spare socks and our weapon. I'll get a photo

of me all loaded up so you can see what I'm describing. Lucky
we did all that training. We also have to share a load of round
belts for the M60 machine guns, plus carry flares, smoke
grenades, claymore mines and much more. I keep thinking
I shouldn't bore you with all the details, but you say you
want to know everything. Harry is the machine gunner in
our platoon, and has to carry extra rounds over his shoulders.
And the medics carry a big medical kit and the signallers carry
the radio with spares. So if you could see us now, you'd be
amazed at the stuff we can carry. In the thick jungle. In the
heavy-going mud and rain. Sometimes I think we are all
just crazy. Why do we even need to be here?

Up ahead it was starting to clear as they came to a river. John
heard Harry mumble something under his breath about 'more
bloody water'.

Suddenly the sound of guns echoed through the jungle and a
soldier five metres from John cried out as a bullet hit him. John
automatically crashed to the ground, with everyone else following suit or taking cover behind trees. Their platoon leader stuck
his head up for a quick look out front and another gun fired.
John saw the wide-eyed look on his lieutenant's face as the bullet
sank into the tree trunk beside his head.

John understood his fear, because right now his own heart
was racing so fast he felt faint. Soldiers called out for the medic,
while the shot soldier held his arm. Meanwhile, they were given
the go-ahead to return fire, and for the first time John got to fire
his gun.

Up ahead the river rolled past, its gurgling sounds now masked by gunfire.

The contact probably only lasted ten minutes, but it felt like hours. Leaves from the trees and shrubs fell shredded, while trunks were marked and chipped. Eventually the shots stopped and they waited. It was a nervous interval, and John's finger grew twitchy as sweat ran into his eyes. He tried to keep still but maintain his gun in position. Mud lined the front of his jungle greens as the rain kept falling gently from the sky. Soon he'd be lying in a puddle, not just mud.

A few shots were fired by his company to test the area ahead. None were returned.

John wondered if the enemy had moved on. How did they check? After another few minutes of anxious waiting, the lieutenant made them rise. Now they would be visible to the VC, if they were still there. Yet there were still no more shots. Had they retreated, or were they lying in wait for them?

'Right, Private Parson, can you cross the river and check it's clear?' said the lieutenant.

John almost squeaked in terror but managed to remain quiet.

Harry sent him a sympathetic look. 'Sorry, mate, you're the greenie.'

'Yep,' said Judy as he appeared beside John, his greens now coated in brown mud. 'You're more expendable. Don't take it personally.'

John glanced back to his lieutenant, who gestured him on. With tentative steps John walked towards the river. Only now, as he saw his life flashing before his eyes, did he realise it was his birthday. He was twenty-one today. Shouldn't he be exempt from this? You couldn't possibly die on your twenty-first. He'd known his birthday was coming up, but out on the operation the days had slipped away, losing their meaning. But it was sure as shit coming back to him now. Everything was: his birthday, Beth, his parents, the farm, his dreams.

His pulse was racing but he tried to keep his wits about him as he made it to the edge of the river. He checked the foliage on the other side. Nothing moved; there were no sounds, no rustling leaves. He stepped into the water, the current gentle. A few more steps, and water rose above his high boots and filled them. It didn't matter, everything was already wet, and with his long pants and his shirtsleeves rolled down he'd have some protection from leeches.

John couldn't believe all the things running through his mind. Shouldn't his mind be blank, focusing on the task at hand? He made it halfway across the river and there was still no movement. Water was up to his knees now but soon began to drop. He stepped onto the bank on the other side, his eyes peeled for any traps or mines.

He stepped further into the jungle, his eyes searching for hidden VC.

A body made him pause as his heart lurched. It was a Viet Cong soldier, only this one wasn't going anywhere. He was face-down in the mud, blood pooled around his body like a gallon of spilt wine. Bending down, John reached out, his hand shaking while he tried to feel for a pulse, bracing in case the guy had some life left in him. John wasn't taking any risks – who was to say he wouldn't roll over and with his last dying breath stab him or fire off a shot.

The wet skin of the man's neck was slimy under his fingers, but try as he might he couldn't find a pulse. For a second he allowed himself to breathe.

He saw heavy footprints in the mud, all heading further into the bush. The VC really had left this area. Leaving one dead behind.

John turned and signalled the company across. The coast was clear.

'Good job,' said Harry when he finally caught up with him.

'Got more balls than I thought,' said Judy, slapping his back on his way past.

'It's my birthday today,' said John. For some reason he thought someone ought to know now, just in case he did die. It was important to celebrate to some degree, wasn't it?

'Hey, why didn't you say so sooner?' said Harry. 'When we get back we'll hit the boozer.'

John smiled. He liked the thought of making it back to camp. He liked it a lot.

We're back from our trek, where we came under fire. One person was hit but he'll be fine. The only downside was I had to cross a river to check the VC had gone after the contact. Gee, Beth, I've never been so scared in my life. But as you can tell, I made it out okay. I saw my first dead VC though. It's probably the first of many, and is to be expected in war. Don't worry about me, though: I have the guys here looking out for me. The trek was so intense I even forgot it was my birthday. It was nice to get back from the jungle and find cards and letters from everyone. Especially yours. I will treasure that photo, my love. Thank you for making my day. Now I best go and post this letter before the boys take me out for a few. I'm looking forward to letting off some steam.

Love you always, John xxx

Dear Beth,

302 and a wakey!

Thank you for the photos of the patio, it looks amazing. I can't believe the size of the vegie garden you've created. You've got a real green thumb. It's great that you don't mind the folks coming over to help. Mum would be chuffed to give you gardening tips, I'm sure. I'm so glad you are keeping busy.

So you want to know more about camp life? Well, just yesterday Judy got up to mischief, as usual. Our dunnies are built like a long-drop, with five seats, and they're burnt off with diesel to keep them clean. (Not good if you need to go just after a burn-off as the seats get pretty hot!) Anyway, Judy, wanting a laugh, threw a smoke grenade down the chimney when the house was full. Harry and I had front-row seats as five blokes, one of them Macca, ran out quickly in a cloud of yellow smoke, trying to pull up their strides and wipe their watering eyes at the same time. It was so funny, but I'm glad it wasn't me. Poor Macca was furious – lucky Judy hightailed it out of there. No one is game to tell Macca who did it.

*We had no beers last night. The CO closed down the
boozer because he found a beer can in one of the drains and
claimed it was evidence the men were drinking in the lines.
Bit harsh, we thought. Tomorrow a band from Sydney are
playing at the Luscombe Bowl, the main stage here. The
boys and I are thinking of going.*

*As I write this letter the ground is shaking from bomb
explosions. There's an American B-52 strike on the Long Hai
hills about seven miles away from us. We can't hear the planes
as they fly really high but the bombs sure do rattle the ground.*

*There's a new station on my radio now – an Australian
army radio station has started in Vung Tau, which plays a
mixture of music and some Radio 2 programs like news and
sport. It makes a nice change from the American radio.*

*I got all my forms filled in to register to vote in the
election, seeing as I am now twenty-one. I'm not even sure
who I should vote for. You'll have to let me know in your
next letter, if it's not too late.*

*Um, what else can I tell you? Harry is great, as usual.
Showed me photos of his little girl. He's so chuffed, and it
makes me excited to start my own family. When I get home
we must take a drive out to his farm and catch up. Harry said
he'd try and help find me some farm work. We can spend ages
talking farming, much to Macca and Judy's disgust. They're
city boys and wouldn't know a tractor from a header.*

*Speaking of Macca, he said he saw two Phantom jets and
a Canberra bomber buzz the airstrip yesterday. Judy doesn't
believe him, but Macca keeps telling us how awesome*

221

and loud the Phantoms were in comparison to the bomber.
I think Macca's been trying to outdo me since I saw a massive
Chinook helicopter taking supplies to Long Binh. It literally
lifted a tank off the ground – a sight to behold.

As I rack up the days here, I'm getting close to losing my
reo title. But all I care about is that it's closer to this tour
being over. Miss you like crazy. Wish I was sleeping beside
you and not three noisy, smelly, wind-filled blokes. Can't wait
to stroke your hair and run my hands over your soft skin.

Miss you, my love,

Your husband, John xxx

Chapter 24

KIM was up early on Drew and Nat's wedding day, even though it had been a late night. She'd stayed up to paint the archway. As the sun came up, she poured a coffee into her thermos cup and went outside to soak up the morning rays. 'Best part of the day, hey, Jo?' she said. She spoke to Jo each morning because she felt sure her beloved dog was still here somehow. Jo would be looking up at her with excitement in her eyes, eager to see what the day would bring. Kim could see her as clear as day.

After the sun had risen she put on her boots, collected her fancy dress, underwear and shoes, and put them in her ute ready to take to Drew and Nat's place, where she'd be getting ready. The ceremony would be held in the backyard. Then she drove to the shed to put the archway in the back of the ute, being careful not to scratch her paintwork.

It was a quiet morning, with just the pink and grey galahs screeching up in the gum trees by the sheds. The sky was a pale blue with a few white clouds smeared across it. Kim kept the window down as she drove past Matt's house, the clean morning air filling her lungs and invigorating her senses. She wondered what the boys had got up to last night. Drew had stayed over at Matt and Loz's, along with Nat's brother Jason.

It was a perfect day for a wedding. If only Kim was feeling more excited.

She pulled up outside Drew's house. His mum Alice had been a great gardener, but after she passed away the garden had been neglected. Nat had been restoring it ever since and it was back to its best, if not better than it had been. Even now, as Kim walked along the path under the large shady lilac trees, she couldn't help but be impressed. She came out onto the large back lawn, so vibrantly green and clipped it looked like a bowling green.

Kim knew where the archway was going to go as Drew had given her the details. The lawn stretched out in a massive half circle, with two more lilac trees offering some height along the fence and the garden beds edging the lawn and rockeries. Rows of agapanthus with their nodding heads of blue and white came together at the top of the lawn. Drew had placed four large pavers just in front of them for the archway; later, a seat would sit there too.

Nat wouldn't need any decorations for the wedding, with the rockroses in full flower, hibiscuses in yellows and pinks, and lots of lavender, which complemented the gardenias on the verandah behind her.

Kim got the archway into its spot. It was heavy on her own, but she wanted to surprise them with it all set up. Then she put out the chairs on the lawn and rolled the red carpet down the aisle.

She was standing there, trying to decide if the archway needed some flowers, when she heard a gasp behind her

'Kim, did you do all this?' said Nat, walking down the red carpet. 'I was just coming to set it up . . . Oh my god.'

Nat walked straight past Kim to the archway, her white silk dressing gown fluttering. Her long straight blonde hair fell perfectly around her angelic face. After a long minute she spun around, her perfectly manicured hands at her mouth and tears in her green eyes.

'Oh, hey,' said Kim, suddenly embarrassed.

'It's okay,' said Nat, flicking away a tear. 'No make-up on yet.' She turned back to the archway and shook her head. 'It's perfect, Kim. It's more than I ever hoped for. Thank you.' Nat threw herself into Kim's arms and hugged her.

'I'm glad. I think the garden makes it, though. It's so beautiful.'

Nat pulled away and nodded. Her smile showed just how much joy Kim's gift had brought her.

'Alice would be so proud of what you've done here, and she'd be tickled pink about today,' Kim said.

Nat sucked in her bottom lip and took a deep breath. 'I wish I could have met her.' She blinked rapidly. 'Crap. I'm so emotional already. I'm going to bawl like a baby up there and ruin my make-up.'

'Somehow I don't think Drew is going to care one bit,' said Kim with a laugh.

'Come on, let's go inside and have some breakfast. Alisha has already opened the champagne,' said Nat with a grimace. 'She's my best friend from Perth and can be trouble.'

'I'll make sure you don't drink too much,' said Kim.

'Thank you. My nerves have kicked in and I'm worried I might not realise how much I'm having. Alisha is dying to meet you – I've told her all about you.'

Knowing Natalie, her friend Alisha had probably never known a girl who worked on a farm. Kim took a deep breath and followed Nat inside.

'Oh my gosh, look at all the people,' said Kim as she peeked out the window into the backyard. People had been turning up and filling the yard over the last half-hour. Searching the crowd, she tried to find Charlie but couldn't. Was that a good thing? Had he changed his mind about coming?

'It's nearly time, girls,' said Alisha.

Kim joined Alisha, Nat, Nat's parents and her uncle Kent, who Kim found she liked the most. Kent loved sharing his own stories as well as listening to others.

'You all look amazing,' said Kent. 'Smile for me?' He took a few last-minute photos.

Kim went to stand by the full-length mirror as they waited. The make-up artist had done wonders with her, even using some fake tan to hide her sock lines. Kim didn't recognise the girl in the mirror. She so wanted Charlie to see her, and yet she didn't. She wanted another kiss, yet she was scared. Her heart was a see-saw of emotion.

'You okay, Kim?' said Nat as she glided over in her dress. It had a fitted bodice with lace overlay sleeves and an elegant drop to the floor. Of course she looked amazing. The small veil and diamond jewellery completed a perfect look.

'I'm fine. A bit nervous, maybe. You?'

'Shitting myself,' she said with a smile. 'But I can't wait to marry Drew. I'd marry him tomorrow in my work clothes and still be happy.'

That was all Kim needed to hear. She smiled. 'You are both going to be so happy. Thanks for letting me be a part of your day.'

'We wouldn't have it any other way.'

'The boys are here. You're up, ladies,' said Loz from the back door.

'Right. Out the front door, around the side and just follow the path,' said Nat.

Kim was going first – nothing like added pressure – followed by Alisha, then Nat and her dad.

Outside it was warm, but the sky was a little overcast and a slight breeze made the skirt of Kim's dress move gently against her leg. Kim was scared of a great gust coming past and lifting her hem, showing everyone her tiny pink G-string. And she couldn't wear a bra with this dress, so she was far too close to naked for her liking.

As the back lawn came into view she saw the eighty guests all turning around as she appeared. She clutched tightly at the white and pink rose bouquet in her hands. So many eyes watching her. Holy shit!

Don't fall over, don't fall over, she repeated in her mind as she took careful steps in the fancy shoes. It was hard on the uneven path. She couldn't wait to make the red carpet. Up the aisle she stepped, past Doris, who looked great and waved at her like a little kid, and then past more locals. She couldn't divert her eyes too far from where she was headed in case she fell over, but the desire to find Charlie was growing by the second.

Up front Drew stood with Matt and Jason, all three in black suits with white shirts and dusky-pink ties. And Billy stood beside Drew, holding his hand and looking so cute in a matching suit.

'Hi, Kimmy,' Billy said loudly, causing a few chuckles in the crowd. He waved energetically.

She almost laughed at the sight of Matt in a suit, clearly as uncomfortable as she was in a dress. He pulled a face at her.

Drew was grinning, enjoying Kim's discomfort. She rolled her eyes at him as she took her place off to his side. 'Hey you,' she said.

'And who are you?' he teased. 'I don't recognise my friend. Oh, and by the way, this is amazing!' Drew raised his eyes to the archway.

Alisha followed Kim, and then it was Natalie's turn. Drew's focus stayed on his future wife and didn't waver.

Kim turned to scan the crowd and spotted Loz in the first row beside Drew's sister and her husband. Next to Loz was Charlie. Kim should have known Loz would take good care of him.

Charlie was the only person not watching Nat walk down the aisle. Instead his eyes were on Kim. His gaze brought a wave of tingles across her skin and a skip to her heart. He was sexy as ever in a grey suit, a black shirt and a tie.

He smiled, those dimples appearing, and then he winked. Kim half smiled back, but inside she was a mess of knotted-up string.

As Nat came closer Kim watched Drew's face. She revelled in his happiness. Billy was no different; he gazed up at Natalie as if she was a fairy princess. He reached out to touch her dress as she came close. She bent down to Billy and hugged him.

Together all three stood together as the celebrant began the vows.

Throughout the ceremony Kim sneaked glances at Charlie and found him watching her every time. His gaze felt charged with electricity and it made her tremble.

'I now pronounce you husband and wife. You may kiss the bride,' said the celebrant.

As Drew and Natalie kissed, Billy watched for a moment before screwing up his face and turning away. Kim hoped the photographer captured that moment. It was classic.

Before she knew it the celebrant was announcing Mr and Mrs Drew Saddler, and everyone was clapping.

Kim took Billy's hand while the guests rushed forward to hug the newly married couple.

'What do you think, Billy? What's it like being married?'

He shrugged. 'It's okay, I guess. When can I get out of this suit?' he asked. 'Can I go and let Turbo out yet?'

'Not today, buddy. He's too boisterous for this crowd. But you can go and play with Seth and Mallory now. They're up the back with Doris.'

'Cool,' he said pulling out of her grasp and running off through the crowd.

'You look absolutely edible.' The words were whispered behind her.

Kim didn't have to turn to know it was Charlie. His words did delicious things to her. She wanted to fall into his arms, with their familiar scent of earthy crispness, but she didn't.

'I've gotta go check some stuff before the photos,' she said, and then walked off quickly into the crowd. Kim knew sooner or later she'd have to bring up Laura – just not now. Not here.

Chapter 25

KIM stood at the doorway of the town hall. The reception was underway, and the bridal party had to walk into the hall, in front of the crowd again. Once more, Kim was trying not to sprain an ankle. Welding that archway was child's play compared to this. To make matters worse, the wine and beer had been flowing while the bridal party had their photos taken, leaving Kim buzzing with a warmth that made it hard to concentrate on walking properly. Or at all. At least this time she could grip Matt's arm, as he was her partner.

'Going all right, sis?' he asked as they began their walk.

'Yeah, I am. It's been a great day.' And she meant that.

Her brother nodded and smiled. 'Feel like an arse in this suit, but it's worth it to see the look on Lozzie's face. Reckon I might get a leg over tonight,' he said with a wink.

Kim pulled a face. 'Too much information.'

Matt threw his head back and chuckled. He was in a very merry state. A few more beers and he wouldn't be getting a leg over anything.

The town hall had been made over with white and pink sashes draped from the ceiling and pink balloons in a heart shape hanging in the middle. Circular tables were set out around the bridal table at one end, and beautiful pink and white bouquets adorned every table. Waiters ran around filling up people's glasses.

'Man, I'm starving,' said Matt as he sat down beside Kim.

Billy was sitting with Seth and Mallory at a table close to the bridal table, a special one just for them. He was looking pretty proud.

'You're always starving,' Kim said, nudging her brother in the gut.

'Bloody Doris scrubbed up all right. She might get lucky,' Matt said.

'Oh my god,' mumbled Kim. 'Sex and food, I swear that's all you think about.'

Matt smiled and didn't deny it. 'You might get lucky. I've seen a few blokes checking you out. Go dust off those cobwebs!'

Kim put her hand out as a waiter offered a beer to Matt. 'No, he needs food, not more beer.'

Matt wasn't too happy. 'Cruel, sis – punch a man where it hurts.'

Kim ignored her brother while she searched for Charlie, and found him on a table with Loz. They were deep in conversation, Lozzie laughing loudly from time to time. Kim wished she knew what they were talking about.

Dinner came and went, and then it was time for the all-important cutting of the cake.

Natalie took the microphone and the crowd hushed down to hear her speech.

'Thanks. I won't be long, I just wanted to say a huge thank you all for coming to celebrate our important day.' Nat glanced at Drew. 'I am marrying the most amazing man, and he has my whole heart. And the icing on the cake is that I get two for the price of one,' she said, reaching out to Billy as he ran to join them. 'I am so honoured to have Billy call me Mum and —' her voice wavered as she sniffed back fresh tears —'I love him so much. Billy, you will always be my son, never doubt that.' She bent down to hug him as tears rolled down her face.

Kim sniffed back her own tears and tried to discreetly mop at her face. She looked around and saw she wasn't the only one. Doris was blowing her nose loudly into an old hanky.

Nat took the tissue Drew offered. He kissed her forehead, and the whole room sighed. Nat smiled and brought the microphone back up. 'Family, I have realised, is more than just blood. It's a community, it's friends. I have all of those things, and I feel like the luckiest girl in the world. Thank you for making my life full and wonderful.' Nat handed the microphone to Drew.

'Well, I'm not sure there's much left to say, except that I agree wholeheartedly. Natalie has given me – us – something I thought we'd never have, and that is a family. After my mum passed away, I thought it would just be me and Billy, tackling the world together. I didn't think there was a chance I'd find love *and* a perfect mother for Billy. I sometimes feel that Mum was up there orchestrating the whole thing.' Drew's voice cracked and he dipped his head for a moment. 'I only wish she was here today to see how happy we are. But she's with Dad, and we have all of you, our amazing friends, here to witness this day. We couldn't have done it without you guys. Anyway, let's cut this cake before Billy helps himself,' he finished as Billy reached out a finger to poke the icing.

The crowd laughed, then clapped and cheered while the newly-weds prepared to cut the cake. It was a big three-tiered creation, with a toy tractor and a Matchbox car like Nat's on top. It was a nice personal touch.

Music filled the hall and Kent, the MC for the night, took the microphone. 'It's time for the bridal waltz. Drew and Nat, can you please take the floor?' he said.

Kim only got to watch for a minute before her brother was dragging her out onto the dance floor. 'We have to join in now, sis,' he said enthusiastically.

'It's like dancing with a tree trunk,' said Kim as she tried to avoid his heavy, stomping feet.

When she stopped for a drink, Alisha leant over towards her at the bar and asked, 'Who is that handsome suit with your sister-in-law?' She held a large glass of wine and was watching Charlie with hungry lioness eyes.

'Some married man,' Kim said bluntly and walked away. If Kim couldn't have him, no one else could either.

'Hey Kim, wanna dance?'

She turned to see one of the single local lads, Marty. He'd never been interested in her before, nor had he ever given her the time of day at any of the farming talks they'd been at together. Now he was looking at her like they were pals. Kim cynically thought he'd probably try to sleep with her only to discard her again tomorrow. She was done with those sorts. He reached out to hold her arm but it was brushed off by another hand.

'Sorry, her dance card is full.'

Charlie pulled Kim into his arms and spun her towards the dance floor. She didn't have time to stop him.

'If I have to watch you from the other side of the room any longer I'm going to snap,' he said gruffly.

Kim couldn't meet his eyes. She held her body stiffly, trying to resist the magnetic pull that Charlie had over her.

'Are you okay, Kim?' he asked.

Denny's words burned in her brain. Communication was the key, after all. Gathering up her courage, she turned to face him. His steps slowed as he realised something was going on.

'Not really. I'm worried I'm being lied to, Charlie. I overheard your sister talking to Laura at the coffee shop. It sounds like you're still close to your wife.'

Charlie's eyes softened and he nodded. 'Yes, I won't lie. Laura is still close to our family. We may be separated, but we can't ignore the years we've spent together. It was an amicable separation, so there's still a lot of love there.'

'Do you think you'll get back together?'

Charlie smiled and she wondered what was so funny.

'No, Kim, we'll never get back together. But Laura is my mate. She was my best friend before we married. Some days I think we were both scared of being alone so we got married. It turned out to be a big mistake. We were always better off as friends. You do believe me, don't you?'

Kim gazed into his eyes, trying to sniff out the truth. She should be good at it after Travis and Chris. Despite herself, she believed him. He didn't seem to stumble over his words or look away. His gaze was intense and direct. 'I want to,' she said, and leant against his chest. She wanted so badly for him to be the one.

Charlie groaned and she felt his body relax. 'Good. I care about you a lot, Kim. I don't want to ruin that.'

'I feel the same way. It's just scary,' she mumbled against his shirt. 'I've been hurt before.'

'I never want to hurt you,' he said.

And in that moment she knew he spoke the truth.

Charlie bent his head, nuzzling her ear. 'I want to kiss you so badly.'

His hand slipped down her back, very close to her backside.

Kim whispered to him, making sure her lips grazed his earlobe. 'I'd like that too.'

She felt a low growl vibrate through his body. 'Hey, are you worried about what people will think? About us?' he asked.

Kim looked into his grey-blue eyes, which were dancing from the fairy lights. 'Is there an us?' Her whole body froze as she waited for his reply. They stood still on the dance floor while others moved around them.

'I'm keen if you are,' he said with a smile.

'In that case, no, I don't care what anyone thinks.'

'I was hoping you'd say that.' Charlie let go of her, cupped her face and dropped the sweetest kiss on her lips. 'I just had to do that.'

His grin was full of mischief as he held her back to dance. Kim reached her hand up to feel his smooth jaw, her thumb brushing over a dimple. Then she kissed him back, only she didn't reciprocate his sweet one, no. She went for the full experience, threading her hand into the hair at the back of his neck and pulling him closer. She didn't want the feeling to end but she remembered where they were.

'Wowee,' said Charlie in a low voice as they hugged each other tightly.

She could feel his heart racing – or was that hers? She could also feel something else. Kim pressed against him and wiggled a little.

'That's not fair,' he moaned in a mix of agony and pleasure.

'Shall I go get us some drinks then?' said Kim, pulling away. A teasing smile was on her lips.

Charlie gripped her arm and pulled her back against him. 'Don't you dare wander off and leave me like this.' He whisked her around the dance floor, further away from the speakers. 'You can't leave until this goes down. You created it,' he said, kissing her forehead. 'Quick, start talking to me about something, anything. Tell me about how you made the archway, or talk about Doris's favourite hobbies.'

Kim rocked back and forth in his embrace as her heart swelled. Just knowing she was capable of making him hard had her floating on air. She felt as if she had some magic power simply by being herself. It was ego-boosting in every way.

'So I shouldn't tell you about the tiny pink thong I have on under—'

Charlie pressed a finger against her mouth before she could finish. 'You are trouble, young lady. Keep that up and you'll never get off this dance floor!'

237

Kim chuckled. 'I don't mind,' she said, resting her head back on his shoulder.

'I don't know what's going on. I thought I was too old to feel like this. When I'm with you I feel rejuvenated, inspired —'

'Turned on?' said Kim with laugh.

'Yeah, that too.'

'It's a good thing though?'

'Oh yeah, it's a good thing. If you don't mind being with an old fart.'

'Charlie, I don't see you as old at all. You're as sexy as hell, you're fit and you have years ahead of you.'

'Careful, all this praise will go to my head. I'm trying to deflate it already,' he said jokingly. 'How soon can we leave the wedding?'

'Hmm, I've been trying to work out the same thing. An hour or two?'

'More dancing it is then.' Charlie spun her around, dipped her back and then hugged her tightly again.

An hour later Charlie whispered in her ear, 'The bride and groom have gone home. Can we?'

Kim's heart skipped a beat. She was nervous, but her desire to be with Charlie outweighed everything else. 'Yes, most definitely.'

Holding hands, they carefully sneaked out of the hall and walked the two blocks to his house, Kim's shoes dangling from her free hand. There was no talking on the walk home. Kim was too excited to think straight.

It wasn't until Charlie unlocked the front door that he spoke. 'It's rather bare. I wasn't sure how long I was going to stay in

Lake Grace for,' he said as he turned a light on and led her through an open lounge–dining area past the kitchen.

'What do you mean by that? You thinking of leaving already?' She felt a sudden panic.

Charlie stopped in the dim passageway. He held her hands. 'No. I'm not leaving yet. It's a bit complicated.' He brushed a strand of hair back from her face. 'Even more so now. I didn't see you coming, Kim, but you've knocked me flat on my arse. Bewitched me with those dark eyes . . .'

He watched her lips longingly, and it seemed like forever until he finally claimed them. Kim thought she'd die from the anticipation. Charlie put his hands on her bum and lifted her up, and Kim automatically wrapped her legs and arms around him as her shoes dropped to the floor with a clunk. He carried her into his room, faint light showing the way to his bed. He lowered her feet to the floor but his hands remained on her arse while he kissed her. She wanted his hands all over her body, and decided to speed things up. She pushed off his jacket and began to unbutton his shirt. His tie was already screwed up in his jacket pocket.

As his shirt fell to the floor she ran her hands up his chest, through the light hair and over his nipples. It had been so long since she'd touched a man like this, but it had been worth the wait. She kissed along his jaw and down his neck while his hands found her thighs and slowly moved up under her dress to her naked skin. His fingers found the lacy top of her underwear, tracing it slowly. His body trembled as his breath quickened.

'Jesus,' he mumbled. 'I don't have anything . . . you know.'

Kim pressed against his erection. She had to get him out of those pants now.

'I do. I mean I don't, but I'm on the pill.' Her brain had turned to mush and she knew she wasn't thinking straight. Quickly she undid his belt, her fingers shaking with desire. It took a few goes to get his button undone. As he kicked off his pants Kim unzipped her dress.

She could feel the heat from Charlie's gaze as he watched the dress fall to the floor.

'Wow.'

They stood still for a moment, breathing heavily. Then Charlie reached out and cupped her breasts tenderly. At the same time she reached down and felt the length of him through his boxers, running up and down it a few times. Charlie hardly needed further invitation to pull his boxers off. She reached for him again but his hand stopped hers.

'Just wait a moment . . . It's been a while.'

She understood. Instead she focused on kissing him while his hands explored her body. One hand slid underneath the pink lace of her G-string, causing a moan of pleasure to escape her lips. Her hips jutted forwards as he explored further. As her panting grew deeper she realised she was close. Charlie must have realised also, as he paused. Carefully he tugged the tiny scrap of underwear down and she shimmied out of it.

Kim lay back on his bed and he followed her, sinking down to kiss her breasts. She could feel him hot and hard against her leg. Charlie licked her erect nipples until she thought she was going to lose all control – and then he moved his lips and trailed them up her skin, along her neck and to her mouth. Kim wrapped her arms around his back, holding him to her as their bodies melded.

'I can't wait any longer,' he said urgently.

'Neither can I,' she moaned.

Gently, he entered her. But as their kisses grew fast and deep, so did the rhythm. Kim wrapped her legs around Charlie as he arched back, and together they built up to an explosive climax.

After catching their breath, Charlie apologised.

'I'm sorry. Like I said, it's been a long time and I couldn't make it last.'

'Don't be sorry. I wasn't any better myself.' Kim rolled onto her side. 'Besides, we have all night,' she said. Her fingers danced along his chest.

'Remember, I'm old. I may not cope.'

'Only one way to find out, Charlie.'

He pulled her in closer and kissed her forehead. 'Boy, are you trouble.' He trailed a finger along her side. 'But I like your kind of trouble.'

Kim smiled as she snuggled up to Charlie, listening to his breathing, to the beating of his heart, savouring the skin-on-skin contact. It felt so perfect.

Chapter 26

KIM woke up. It took only a second before the warmth of Charlie's arms made her smile. How much had she longed for a moment like this: a night of lovemaking and then waking up in his strong arms. She sighed and snuggled closer to him.

'Morning, Miss Kim.'

His voice was bright, as if he'd been awake for a while. Had he been watching her sleep? Hopefully she didn't snore.

'Morning, Charlie,' she said.

Charlie moved so he could lean over her and kiss her. 'I've been waiting half an hour for you to wake up so I could do that.'

'Hmm. What time is it?' she asked, looking for a clock of some sort. But Charlie's walls were bare and there was nothing on his bedside table except an envelope.

'About seven-thirty. I thought I'd sleep in after all that exercise last night.'

'Ha, this is a sleep-in for me,' she said. 'I don't have to be at the hall until ten for clean-up, so there's no rush.'

Charlie reached for her hand and entwined his fingers with hers. 'You know, as amazing as you looked in that dress, the thought of you welding in your singlet and torn work jeans turns me on just as much, if not more. There's something very sexy about a woman who can wield tools.'

Kim smiled as she gazed at his blank wall. She realised she didn't know much about Charlie. For example, what did his ex-wife look like? What was their home like? What did she do for a job? She was curious as to what type of person he'd married. But that might kill the moment. She went with something safer. 'Charlie, tell me something personal about yourself. Something not many people know.'

'You want to know if I have any dark secrets? Bit late now, don't you think?' he said with a chuckle as he kissed her naked shoulder.

But she'd felt his body tense and she knew she'd touched a nerve. Just what was he hiding? she wondered. He was quiet for a while. 'You don't have to,' she said, moving to face him. 'I mean I just want to know more about you.'

Charlie touched her face, as if checking she was real, and then he smiled. 'I do have a few things that are hanging over me at the moment, stuff I haven't told anyone. Mainly because they're too complicated and I really don't know much myself yet.'

Kim raised her eyebrows but didn't say anything. She didn't want to push the issue. 'I understand.' Was this the thing his sister had been talking about with Laura?

'I feel like I could tell you anything.' His eyes were glued to hers as he spoke. 'You remember I told you my mum had passed away recently?'

243

She nodded and pressed her hand against his chest.

'Well, when Sarah and I were sorting through her house we came across that envelope there. It was in her bedroom, hidden away.'

He gestured to his bedside table and nodded at her to pick the envelope up. Kim did so, and tentatively opened it.

'It's a birthday card to you from your dad,' she said after reading it. 'It's sweet.'

'Yep, but look at the back of the envelope. J Parson is not my father. Robert Macnamara was – or so I thought.'

Kim cocked her head as she tried to understand what this all meant. 'So, your mum had an affair? Or was pregnant with you when she married?' It could be many things.

Charlie shrugged. 'Truthfully, I have no clue. There's just this card. Why would Mum hold on to it all these years? I don't really know what to think. Maybe he was an old flame. But he knew I existed. Is this the only contact he tried to make? It seems like he knew where I was and was happy he had a son. I'm just not sure about any of it.' Charlie pressed his lips together, a frown creasing his forehead.

'What about your sister?'

'Do you mean, is she my real sister? I remember Mum being pregnant and coming home from the hospital with Sarah. There are lots of baby photos of Sarah. We went back through all the albums after we found this card, and there are none of me until I'm about one. I'm walking in all the photos.'

'Your parents might not have had a camera then.'

Charlie frowned. 'That's what Sarah said, but something just doesn't sit right. My birth certificate doesn't list anything out of the ordinary. So the only clue I have is that card. At first I assumed it just meant I had a different father to Sarah, but when I couldn't find any baby photos, I started to wonder. Maybe my mum wasn't my mum either? Something isn't quite right, but if I find J Parson I might find the answer.'

He flipped the envelope over and pointed to the postmark on the front.

'Lake Grace,' Kim read out loud. 'That's what brought you here?'

'Yep.'

Kim wasn't sure if she liked that. If he found J Parson, would he leave? She didn't want Charlie to go back to Perth.

'Have you had any luck?' she asked. 'Finding him?'

'I've been asking around, and there was a Parson family who farmed in the southern Lake Grace area. They had a son called John Parson. I'll keep looking for him, but I'm in no rush,' he said as he rubbed her arm. 'I'm quite happy to take my time.' He kissed her.

'I hope so. I like you hanging around,' she said. 'How are you feeling about finding all this out?' Something this big would have to have an impact. She couldn't imagine what it would be like to discover something that made you question your whole identity.

'Honestly, I'm trying not to dwell on it. Some days, though, I wonder if that's why I was so different to my family, why I've taken to the country so much. If this guy was a farmer, maybe that's where it comes from. I don't know. My brain goes all over the place. I looked at old family photos and tried to see resemblances. It started to mess with my head so now I stick to the facts.'

Kim nuzzled her body against Charlie's, holding him tightly. After a while her belly grumbled, causing Charlie to laugh.

'I guess you would normally have eaten hours ago,' he said.

'Yep, or at least had a cuppa by now. I'll go make us one. Coffee?'

'Yes, please. White with one. I'll go have a quick shower and then I'll make you breakfast.'

'I like the sound of that.'

She climbed out of bed, Charlie watching her with hungry eyes. Quickly she reached for his black shirt from last night and slipped it on before heading to his kitchen. It was easy enough to find everything in the tidy cupboards. Charlie was neat – maybe he'd been trained by his wife, or maybe he just knew how to look after himself. She heard the shower start up and smiled as she flicked the kettle on. Maybe she should slip in there with him.

The phone rang as she was putting sugar in his coffee but she ignored it. Her eyes scanned for anything that might give her a clue about Charlie – photos, magazines – but there was nothing except the local *Lakes Link* on the table and nice blue and white tea towels.

'Charlie, pick up the phone. Come on, darling, I'm worried about you.'

Kim paused as a woman's voice on the answering machine caught her attention.

'Charlie?' A big sigh. 'Please call your wife. I miss you. I need to see you. We can work this out. I love you. Bye.' Then the call disconnected.

Kim stood there with the spoon full of sugar hanging over

the cup. She stared at the answering machine, its red light blinking. Had she just heard that right? Her heart refused the reality but her head told her she'd been deceived. She could tell by the woman's voice that she still cared deeply for Charlie. His wife Laura. He'd said they were separated, over. Was that just wishful thinking? The sincerity in the woman's voice was real. He had said they were still best friends. But what if down the track they got back together, with all that history? Kim didn't want a relationship with an ex always around. She'd been down this road before, with Travis.

With trembling fingers she dropped the spoon and darted back to Charlie's room. She needed space to think. Quickly she pulled off his shirt and climbed into her dress, grabbed her underwear and found her shoes just as Charlie was getting out of the shower.

'Everything okay?' he asked.

'Yeah, sorry, gotta go. Just had a call. I'll catch you later,' she said, practically running from his house. The fact that she'd managed to speak to him normally was a miracle. He'd been standing there naked, dripping with water, like some hot firefighter from a calendar. The sight was almost too bittersweet to bear.

Kim power-walked barefoot back to the hall, hoping nobody would see her, got in her ute and drove home. She needed a shower and some comfortable clothes. The whole drive back she tried to figure out why Charlie might be lying to her. It was clear he and his wife weren't over. Maybe the card from his supposed dad had created an issue? Something that huge could have put a strain on his marriage. But why start up with Kim? Did she make him feel better, help him forget his problems?

The road blurred as tears obscured her eyes. Quickly she tried to blink them away but more came. *Why?* Why did this always seem to happen to her? Why did she end up being the one used? It had taken her almost four years to trust someone again, and now it seemed history was repeating.

Chapter 27

1969–70

Dear Beth,

272 and a wakey! (I'm not really a reo any more.)

*Sorry my letters are so few and far between, my love.
I have to wait until I'm back from operations to be able to
write and post them. I do love getting back to your piles of
letters. The boys are so jealous – only Harry can match me
in mail from his wife. Plus he gets scribbled drawings from
his kid. Macca tries to take the mickey out of him but Harry
doesn't care, you can see he's proud as punch.*

*I've finally read all your letters and caught up on your
news. I'm so glad you got a job helping Dad. Who knew his
business would grow so big that he'd need someone to keep
him organised? It's a great venture for you both. I love those
new flares – thanks for the photo. Wish I were there to show
my appreciation in person. Judy saw your photo and reckons
you are gorgeous. He actually had the nerve to ask if he could
use you as his pin-up girl. I nearly throttled him. Judy's not*

249

happy unless he's yanking someone's chain.

I'll head down to the post office after writing this letter and send you some more money home, seeing as I was paid yesterday.

I went into town the other day and bought you some silks, which I'll post with this letter and some souvenirs. The silk cost sixty-six piastres per metre, which works out quite cheap. You'd like it here, I think. The wildlife is incredible: monkeys in the trees and wild peacocks roaming. And there are so many strange sights. It's so different to back home. Even the shops are full of different things, like kero lanterns, dragon fruit and lychees, and preserved bits and pieces.

We just got back from a company operation where we patrolled an area within the Phuoc Tuy provincial boundary in hot and humid conditions. We were mainly in the jungle, where the undergrowth was thick and matted thanks to the months of monsoonal rain we've had. Luckily contact with the enemy was limited to six clashes – two Viet Cong were killed and another wounded. I'd kill for some hot Aussie sunshine to be able to dry my feet for once.

One of the lads from another platoon went to sleep on picket duty and got charged. The major said that he would be pretty lenient and gave him fourteen days CB (Confined to Barracks) and seven extra pickets. I'm not sure he understands the word 'lenient'! It didn't take long for the story to do the rounds. I reckon everyone will be careful now.

Got to have a good look at the MPs' prisoner of war compound, which they call the Playboy Club. They have

*a big sign stating it too. There wasn't anyone in there but
I've heard a few stories of fellas ending up in there. The boys
thought it was funny when I told them how I was met by the
MPs when I first went to training. They started calling me
AWOL for a while – well, Judy did.*

*The propaganda plane has started broadcasting as
I write. It has a set of speakers and broadcasts a lot of stuff
in Vietnamese to convince the VC to chieu hoi (surrender).
The plane flies low and you can hear the words for miles.
It interrupts a perfectly good night.*

*Judy is now upset and wants to play a game. He's been
collecting spiders and painted them to start up a betting ring.
I don't participate but it can be funny to watch. Sometimes Judy's
ideas aren't so great, but this one has been a big hit so far.*

*Harry and I are drawing scales of our farms, well as much
as we can remember them. Keeps us connected to home.*

I'll write more soon, Bethy. I love you.

Lots of love, John xxx

John just finished marking his 212 and a wakey on his calendar
when Macca walked in.

'Next lot of ration boxes are here.' Macca threw them their packs.

The boxes came about every three weeks and usually contained
American sweets, chewing tobacco, cigarettes, comic books and
the like. The cigarettes were menthol and no one ever wanted them.

'Chuck 'em here, boys,' said Judy as he collected up the smokes.
'I think it's your turn on the pie cart run today, Johnny.'

'Everyone has to take their turn,' said Harry. 'Can I get a pon-cho liner, please?' he asked as he threw his pack of cigarettes to John.

Harry lifted the photos he had in his hand and gazed at them, as he often did. John understood Harry's longing to see his wife Clarissa, but he didn't or couldn't truly understand what it would be like to miss your only child. Harry had told him at length about his daughter's arrival, the sounds Megan made, the way she'd grab his little finger and the way she laughed. John could see the joy it brought Harry to speak about her, and that was enough. Sometimes Harry'd get choked up, but only with John. He hid it well from the other lads. They had a close bond, and John knew they would be mates long after the war.

'A new photo?' he asked.

Harry nodded and held it out. 'Megan's running around the place and getting into everything. No cupboard is safe,' he said with a chuckle.

John gazed at the curly-haired child with chubby legs in a white lace dress. 'Cute,' he said, handing it back.

'That will be you soon, mate. I thought I was tough but this little girl, well, she just melts my heart.'

John couldn't help but smile at the expression on Harry's face. He was totally smitten.

'Righto, I better go get this job done then,' John said. 'See you when I get back.'

'Roger.' Harry gave him a wave.

John knew the drill from watching the other lads in the pla-toon take their turn. Nearly every day the laundry went to Ba

Ria to be washed by a local contractor. The boys could hitch a ride with the truck. One of them would put all the menthol fags into an empty sandbag to take to the black market to sell, and then buy other things with the proceeds. Within fifteen minutes John had a list and was off to catch the pie cart, as they called it.

'G'day mate. Mind if I catch a ride?' he asked the driver, who was standing at the back of the truck getting the last of the washing.

'No worries, jump aboard.'

John headed to the passenger side and put the bag of cigs under the seat. The driver jumped in and they headed off down the right hand side of the road, something John was now used to. As they approached the main Nui Dat checkpoint, John noticed there was an MP ute parked at the exit. A soldier was inspecting the vehicle in front of them all over.

'What's going on?' asked John curiously.

'That's just the MPs. They're trying to cull some of the black-market profiteering. Nothing to worry about,' the driver said, changing down a gear to slow the car and puffing on his cigarette.

Oh shit, thought John. What the heck was he going to do?

When it was their turn to be inspected by the MPs, John was feeling sick in the stomach.

'Morning, lads. We're just going to do a quick search for —'

John held up the bag full of cigarettes. The MP paused, nodded his head and then opened the door.

'This way, please, sir.'

Half an hour later, as he stood inside a cell in the Playboy Club, John couldn't help thinking just how much Judy was going to split his sides laughing.

Dear Beth,

182 and a wakey!

I can't believe Christmas is nearly here. Yesterday we received Christmas parcels from the Australian Forces Overseas Fund. I ended up with a pen and some writing paper, which was great, as I was getting low. There was also some soap, a book, a bottle of cordial, some shaving cream and a razor, a polishing cloth, some peanuts and some sweets. It's the little things that count, and the fellas feel great knowing that the folks back home really do care.

I got a Christmas card from your parents as well. Macca and Judy have a bet on which of them will get the most Christmas cards. Judy has also been burying cans of grog in as many hiding places as he can so there will be enough for Christmas. There's a bit of a supply problem at the moment.

172 and a wakey! Those planes that usually fly around broadcasting to the VC have been playing Christmas carols. Makes a nice change. And the radio stations are playing carols too. It's starting to feel a lot like Christmas. Tonight Harry and I are going to the Luscombe Bowl for midnight mass. It's only a short walk through the rubber trees.

171 and a wakey! Merry Christmas, my love. I hope you have a great day with the family. I'm thinking of you always. We were woken up at seven with the sergeant giving us a cup of rum-laced coffee in bed – not a bad way to start the day. Judy was cheeky enough to ask for seconds. At about eight Father Christmas arrived by Land Rover, ringing a bell and waving to us. The day got better: the officers served our lunch, which was prawn cocktail and roast turkey with all the vegetables. Dessert was Christmas pudding. What a meal.

We have the afternoon off as there is a ceasefire with the VC, so Harry and I are writing letters to home while Macca and Judy relax. The brigadier just came around the base wishing us all a merry Christmas. He's a seriously big fish, as head of the brigade. The lowest level is a platoon, and three platoons make up one infantry company. Next level up is a battalion, with at least four companies – anywhere up to nine hundred men. Three battalions make up an infantry brigade. So to have the brigadier come around and chat to us was pretty special.

As I write this letter to you I'm feeling incredibly homesick. I can see Harry is too. He's missing his kid and wife. I think we'll have to try to cheer each other up before Judy picks on us for being sooks. But what would Judy know? He doesn't have a wife like mine back home. I miss you like crazy. Can't wait for your next letter and hopefully some photos of you all enjoying Christmas.

Not long to go now, my love. Halfway.

Love you lots, John xxx

Chapter 28

CHARLIE pulled on some jeans and a white T-shirt and thought about Kim's rapid departure. He hoped her phone call wasn't anything too serious. He'd been looking forward to making her breakfast and having a chat. Any time together with Kim was great.

He got to the kitchen and saw the half-made cups of coffee. She really had left in a hurry, he thought, as he cleaned up some spilt coffee and then put the kettle on.

It wasn't until he'd made his drink and was walking over to the table that he saw his answering machine blinking. He pressed play on the way past.

'Charlie, pick up the phone. Come on, darling, I'm worried about you.'

Charlie smiled at the sound of Laura's voice. He had to admit he had missed her. It was hard to live with someone for years and then not see them for months.

'Charlie? Please call your wife. I miss you. I need to see you.

We can work this out. I love you, bye.'

He probably should call her, but he'd been avoiding the conversation. He didn't want to talk about his search for John.

It wasn't until the machine announced the time of the phone call that he finally put two and two together.

'Shit.' He ran to grab his mobile phone off the bedroom floor and call Kim. Her phone went to voicemail. She could just be in a black spot, he thought. There was bad phone reception on the way to her place.

But she'd be back to help clean the hall, surely? Yes, he'd go help clean up and talk to her then, and make sure they were still okay.

He downed his coffee and decided he couldn't wait until ten. Maybe she'd be there early.

Chucking on his thongs, he locked up and walked back to the hall. The door was open and Loz and Matt were already there. Inside it wasn't too bad – much how they'd left it but with a few more glasses and empty beer bottles. Popped balloons and streamers were scattered about.

Loz was in the far corner picking up bottles and putting them into a bin Matt was holding. Both of them cringed each time a bottle clinked loudly into the bin.

'Hey there,' Charlie called and walked over.

'That's it, I can't take any more of this noise,' said Matt, nodding hello to Charlie. 'I'm going to get a coffee and a bacon and egg burger for my hangover. Want one?' His eyes were bloodshot and his hair stuck up at funny angles.

'Nah, I'm right,' said Charlie.

'Oh, yes, please,' said Loz with a groan. 'Even though the sound of it makes me want to throw up.' She sat down in a nearby chair. 'Hey, Charlie. How are you feeling?'

'Want a coffee, mate?' asked Matt as he started to leave.

'No, just had one. Thanks anyway, Matt.'

Matt gave him a wave and headed out of the hall.

'Argh, they are so loud!' cringed Loz as a clang came from the kitchen at the side of the hall. The catering people were cleaning and picking up the last of their stuff.

Charlie glanced around the hall and sat down. 'Just us two here so far?'

'Just us. There'll be a few more later, but we thought we'd come do our bit early before we have to get the kids from their friends' house.' Loz frowned at him. 'You look too good to be hungover. Or do you have a secret remedy?' Then her eyes flew open as if she'd only just remembered who he'd spent the night dancing with. 'Is Kim the reason you're looking fresh?' she asked with a goofy grin.

'Maybe,' he said sheepishly.

'You two were so cute last night. A perfect match. She deserves someone special in her life. Does this mean you two are officially together now?' she said with a grin. 'How come she's not here with you?'

'Well, that's the thing,' said Charlie. 'She rushed off in a hurry this morning and I can't get hold of her.'

'Oh. What happened? Get too serious too fast? Or do you have some weird habit?' said Loz, cracking a smile.

Charlie shrugged, pulled out his phone and tried to call Kim again. 'I think she's screening my calls.'

'Huh. Let me try.' Loz pulled out her phone and called Kim. She pulled a face when Kim answered. 'Hiya. Just wondering what time you're coming in to clean?'

Charlie watched them talk with a bad feeling. She *was* screening his calls.

'Charlie's here helping, wanna say hi?' said Loz. 'Oh, okay. . . Righto. See you later.'

'Is she coming?' he said the moment Loz hung up.

'Maybe. Said she might go see Harry instead. She didn't want to talk to you.' Loz raised her eyebrows.

'Dammit, she must have heard the message from Laura.'

'Laura?'

'My ex-wife. She's worried about me, and left me a message that could be taken the wrong way. Kim probably thinks I lied to her about our separation.'

Loz shot up from her chair. 'You idiot!' Then she held her head and wobbled on her feet a bit. 'Ugh.' She sat back down. 'Let me say that sitting down. *You idiot.* Did she not tell you about Travis?'

Charlie screwed his face up. 'No. Who's Travis?'

'Travis was her boyfriend a while back. Only problem was he neglected to tell her he was married. Stupid fool lied to her, and killed whatever trust she had in men. Took her years to get over that, and, quite frankly, I'm not sure she actually is over it.'

'Oh shit.' Charlie buried his face in his hand.

'Please tell me you're not still married?' Loz groaned. 'Tell me I don't have to worry about this with a hangover!' Her blood-shot eyes narrowed.

'Officially I'm still married but we've been separated for ages. I told Kim that. I just didn't go into the details because it's a bit embarrassing.'

Loz shook her head. 'If she thinks you've lied to her about your separation, then you're not going to win her back with words, buddy. Travis lied to her for ages. You telling her that you're separated won't be enough. She'll need to see the divorce papers or something concrete. And it better be good, bucko. She won't be made a fool of twice.'

'I swear, Loz, I'll fix this. I care too much for her.'

Loz squinted, trying to read him. 'That's what Travis said too. Then he had the nerve to ask her to continue the affair after she found out about his wife.' Loz stood up, slowly and carefully this time, and reached for the bin. 'What are you waiting here for? Go fix this now. You mess with Kim, you mess with us all.' She walked off to the next table to clear it and mumbled, 'And I really liked you, Charlie.'

With his elbows on his knees and his head in his hands, Charlie tried to think. Loz was right, Kim deserved to know everything. He had to go speak with her.

He went home for his car and drove straight out to the farm, but she wasn't home. Then he remembered that she'd said something about visiting Harry. Charlie had an idea where he lived. He knew how to get to Tom's place. He hoped Tom could direct him the rest of the way. He couldn't sit around and wait for her to get back. Charlie couldn't handle the thought of Kim thinking he'd lied to her. Not even for a few hours.

Chapter 29

KIM sat on her bed naked, pink dress dumped on the floor, and stared at her phone. She'd ignored all of Charlie's calls. She just didn't know what to say, or how to say it. Had he realised what she'd heard, or was he just concerned about the way she'd left? He couldn't have been that concerned, because Loz just said he was at the hall helping to clean up. Was he just happily going about his day? While she felt used, stupid, gutted?

Damn it. There was no way she was going to clean up the hall if Charlie was there. First she needed a long, hot shower and then a coffee.

But the coffee didn't really help, because it just reminded her of the coffee she should have been having with Charlie. Her mind kept going back and forth, raking over the reasons why Charlie would lie to her, and then back to how gullible she was for letting it happen all over again. She'd so badly wanted to believe there was some explanation for his wife, but she wasn't about to offer her blind faith a second time around.

It was best just to keep her distance until she could figure out what to do. The perfect place to get some headspace was at Harry's. She loaded the ute with another gift she'd been working on and headed off.

Harry's place was surrounded by dozens of wattle trees, which had inspired the gift. She didn't know if he liked the trees or if they had been there long before he arrived, but someone had definitely made a feature out of all the wattles. When in flower the trees must look amazing, with hundreds of yellow blossoms floating in the breeze and the smell of wattle in the air.

The sculpture had taken a while, but the effort was worth it. From a roll of barbed wire, Kim had used pliers to make heaps of small balls, trying to recreate the pompom-like wattle flower. Then she'd welded some steel into a branch shape, attaching long thin leaves, which she'd cut out of sheet metal. Next she'd painstakingly attached the wire balls. The combination of the flowers and the leaves left no question as to what it was. She just hoped Harry liked it. She had thought about painting it, but there was something about the natural beauty of the metal and the rusty parts that she loved. If Harry wanted to paint it later, she'd leave that up to him.

As she approached Harry's she came across Tom's wife, Marie, walking down the road with a little Jack Russell by her side. The morning sun was bright, making the grass glitter gold.

Marie was wearing walking shoes and swung her arms briskly. Tom wasn't wrong when he said she was into health and fitness.

Kim slowed down to say hello. 'Hi, Mrs Murphy,' she said, winding down her window.

'Oh, call me Marie,' she said, breathing heavily. 'You back visiting Harry?' Her eyes narrowed and there was an edge to her voice.

'Yep. Just thought he could use some company,' said Kim. 'Well, actually it's me who needs it today.' Kim grinned but soon stopped, thanks to the scowl on Marie's face.

Marie put her hands on Kim's door and leant in. 'I don't know much about Harry. Only snippets Tom's mentioned, and Tom doesn't say a lot. I think he's careful with what he tells me. But I feel I need to warn you to just be careful out there.'

'Harry's okay. He's told me he's suffering from PTSD.'

'It's not just that, Kim. When he first came here Tom told me I was to steer clear of Harry because he'd just come out of jail. I wasn't supposed to tell anyone because he didn't want people sticking their nose in where it didn't belong. Plus Harry never leaves the farm. But I feel I need to tell you anyway. He's not put a foot wrong, all these years, and Tom has a great affection for him. But you never know what might cause a man to snap.'

Kim found it really hard to believe what Marie was saying, but the truth was she didn't really know anything about Harry's past.

'Just be careful, that's all I'm saying. Besides, a young girl like you should be out with your friends, not hanging around old folks.'

Kim quite liked old folks. But she bit her tongue and smiled. 'Thanks, Marie, I'll be careful.' Best just to placate the poor woman.

Marie went to move off but then paused. 'Tom did say that

lately Harry's the happiest he's seen him. He's been more communicative. Tom thinks that's thanks to you.' Marie smiled, patted her arm and then stepped back. 'See you later, Kim.'

'Bye, Marie.'

As Kim pulled up at Harry's place, all the dogs greeted her and then raced off around the house. Following them, she found Harry weeding his vegetable plot.

'Wow, Harry, that's some vegie garden,' she said.

Harry stood up and stretched his back before he turned and smiled at Kim.

'Hello, Kim. I thought it was your ute that I heard.' He turned back to his garden and put his hands on his hips. 'I try. It's cheaper to grow your own, plus so much better for you when it's fresh. And I have plenty of time on my hands.'

'I wish I could devote more time to mine. The weeds are running rife.'

'You put your talents elsewhere, love. It's hard to try to fit everything in sometimes.'

'I agree. Time for a cuppa?' she asked, giving him a smile.

'For you, always. Do you mind putting the kettle on while I wash up?'

'No probs.' She followed him to the back verandah and went inside while he washed his hands. He joined her soon after and finished making their cuppas. Together they went back to sit on the verandah's edge, their favourite spot. Harry was an outdoors person, and Kim didn't mind that one bit. Most of his dogs found places to lie nearby.

Kim put down her coffee and jogged to her ute. 'Hey, Harry,

I made you something else. I needed a project and this came to mind.'

'What ya got there?' His voice faded away as he recognised what she was carrying. He reached out a finger to touch a prickly blossom. 'A wattle?'

'Yep. I saw how many were around your place and thought it was fitting.'

Kim put the small sculpture down between them and Harry inspected it. 'It's magnificent. So lifelike. Gosh, you have an eye for detail.'

'Did you plant all these trees, Harry, or were they here before you arrived?' she asked.

'Most were here already, and someone else added a few extra. I just get the benefit of the floral display. Mind you, it's crazy with bees. I did think about setting up my own beehive and getting fresh honey.'

'Oh, that would be fantastic. I'd gladly help you in return for some honey,' she said. Yes, coming to Harry's had been the best idea she'd had all day. And she'd left her phone at home. No distractions. This was what she needed, an escape.

They chatted for a while and then Kim asked, 'Have you ever been married, Harry?' She almost covered her mouth after the words were spoken. Shit, she wasn't supposed to ask personal things, but their conversation was flowing so easily she'd forgotten. 'Sorry, Harry. I said that without thinking.'

He sat there quietly and she wondered what memories she'd churned up. But he surprised her when he replied, 'Yeah, I was married.'

Kim straight away thought of the pretty girl in the photo in the spare room.

'Had a kid too,' he eventually added.

She actually saw him smile. These were good memories.

'I used to have my own farm before the war.'

Kim wasn't sure how long he'd keep talking, but she was dying to know what happened to his family. Did she dare ask? 'What happened to them, Harry?'

His bottom lip trembled and that smile disappeared. He didn't close down completely, though: instead, he turned to her with big sad eyes.

'PTSD happened.'

Kim ran over the words in her head. *Post-traumatic stress disorder*.

Harry shook his head. 'They thought losing men during the Vietnam War was bad enough, but they didn't count on the men they'd keep losing after it, even years later.'

Kim sat silently, hoping Harry would keep talking.

'It was a hard transition for me to make, from a farmer to a soldier. I learnt the true meaning of mateship in the army, but I also felt betrayed and rejected by the anti-war movement. Yet far and away, the biggest cost of the war was living with PTSD. It didn't do any of us any good, lass. It tore up families, made strong men feel weak, and sent them into such despair that they killed themselves to be free from it all. There wasn't even a diagnosis for it for many years after the war, and then when there was most blokes would say, "There's nothing wrong with me,"' said Harry, his voice cracking.

The dogs all sat still, their eyes focused on Harry. Kim was no different. She'd come to respect and like Harry a lot, and she knew that sharing this wasn't easy for him. It brought a lump to her throat, and she could only nod for fear of crying.

'Sorry to bring all that up.'

'No, don't apologise, Harry. If you want to talk I'll gladly listen. It's nice to get an understanding of what you went through. I know I'll never fully understand just how difficult it was.'

'This place and my dogs are all I have left, and yet I'm lucky to have this. I probably don't deserve it,' he finished. Then he picked up his cup and finished his tea. 'Well, where shall we put this wattle? Any ideas?'

'Up to you, Harry.' She was sad the candid conversation was over, but maybe in time Harry would open up to her again. She felt he needed someone to listen and to care about what he'd been through.

'I think I might put it inside so I can see it all the time. You spoil me too much.'

'I like coming to see you. I have another friend, Doris, who's about the same age as you. She's a bloody wild chick and an amazing woman. You'd probably like her.' Kim felt it was important to spend time with people like Doris and Harry. They had so many stories to tell, and funny sayings from the old days, things you wouldn't hear from anyone else. Kim wanted to witness and to remember, before the old ways disappeared from memory.

'As long as you don't try to set us up! We're too bloody old for any of that.'

Kim laughed. 'I promise, Harry.'

'Who's this?' he said, pointing down his driveway.

Kim saw the vehicle coming towards them and it wasn't until it began to slow down that she recognised Charlie's car.

Chapter 30

1970

'HEY, Macca, when we get back, can I get a copy of your tape, mate?'

'Which one?' said Macca as he shifted his gun to his other arm.

'The one you taped off the radio on New Year's Eve, with the top hundred hits. From the American Forces Radio. I really liked that song "Sugar, Sugar" and it's driving me nuts. I need to hear the rest of it,' said John.

'I preferred "Aquarius",' said another soldier walking past.

'You would, ya pansy,' said Macca, who clearly knew the bloke.

The soldier gave him the finger and Macca blew him a kiss back.

'Yeah, Johnno, that's no problem. Just remind me when we get back from this shitty-arse jungle.' Macca took a swipe at a branch, which flicked him in the face after he let it go.

'At least it's not the wet,' said John. The dry season had arrived and the rubber trees had started losing their leaves.

'Can you believe they are still going on about the My Lai massacre in all the hoo-ha they're making back home?' said Harry, who was only a step behind them. 'Be nice if the media could perhaps focus on how the Viet Cong torture people as well,' he said lowering his voice as he got closer.

They were behind the first platoon so they didn't have to be super quiet but still they liked to be half-alert.

'Not long to go now,' said Macca. 'We'll be out of here soon, and about bloody time. I'm getting tired of reading in the papers that we have no right to be here. What choice do we have as national servicemen? It's shit.'

John nodded. It was hard not to take the anti-war criticism on board, as they were all stuck in this war, regardless of whether they wanted to be. They had to do the best they could, trusting those further up the chain of command and praying that their hard work was worth it.

Macca, Harry and John caught up with the platoon in front and were told to make camp for the night. Watch duty was assigned. The VC were close – there had been some contact in a few places, but nothing serious yet. The VC were incredible at surveillance. This was their land, their country, and they knew all sorts of ways of making things easier for themselves out here.

Harry was in a good mood. He was short on time now, and would be going home within the month, much to John's dismay. He couldn't imagine Vietnam without Harry. Being stuck with Macca and Judy and some reo didn't sound like much fun.

'I'll call in and see your wife, John, before I head home. Do you think she'd like that?' Harry asked as they pulled off their webbing and looked for a spot to camp.

'Yeah, I reckon she would.' John was a little jealous that Harry would get to see Beth before he did.

Harry paused for a moment, scratched his chin and looked about. 'Duty calls,' he said, reaching for his gun.

'I'll come with you,' said John, reaching for his own gun. It was hard to crap in peace out in the jungle, with platoons of men and VC about. Best he went and kept watch.

Harry picked a spot that was far enough away to have some privacy but where they could still hear the platoon chatting quietly. As Harry went behind a tree, John decided to have a quick leak while he was alone. He put his gun against the tree trunk next to him and undid his pants. He could hear Harry using his boot to kick a hole into the ground.

John tried not to pee on the dead leaves, as the sound it made seemed to echo around the bush. As he finished he asked, 'Hey, Harry, how many days you got left exactly?'

There was no reply. He heard a strange, muffled noise and the rustling of leaves. 'Harry?'

John did up his fly and stepped cautiously to peer around the tree. He spotted Harry down near the ground, and suddenly realised his friend wasn't alone. An arm was wrapped around Harry's neck. Automatically he stepped closer to investigate.

Harry was locked in a tussle with a skinny dark-skinned bloke in a uniform of sorts. The VC had his hand clamped over Harry's mouth, but it wasn't until John saw the splash of red over Harry's uniform that he leapt into action.

Launching himself, he landed on the back of the VC, wrapping his arms around the man's throat. The man tried to wriggle free, his hands releasing Harry's mouth and the knife in his guts. But Harry didn't call out for help. John knew he should stop to help his friend, but instead he squeezed harder and harder, holding on to the VC with all his might, as the man squirmed and tried to fight back. But John could only see Harry, watching him as red gushed out of his body.

John wanted to say something, like 'Hang on, Harry', or 'You'll be okay, mate', but nothing would come out of his mouth. There was a loud rumbling, groaning sound and John felt the bones in the VC's neck and watched him struggle for air. He kept squeezing as a rage built up inside him. This man would pay for hurting Harry. He was going to kill him.

The VC's body began to go limp, but John gripped the bastard just as hard. Soon he saw boots beside him, men calling out, people talking to him, pulling him back. 'No!' he cried out, and that's when he realised the groaning sound he'd heard was himself. John eventually let go of the VC and a soldier dragged him away while others looked down the tiny tunnel the VC had appeared from. John crawled to Harry, pulling him into his arms. Soldiers were calling for the medic.

John held Harry's head and almost shook him. 'Harry! Harry, look at me,' he begged.

Harry's eyes opened a crack.

'Hang on, you hear me? You're gonna make it. Hang on, buddy.'

'Come on, Harry!' yelled a voice beside him.

John didn't take his eyes from Harry's face but he knew that it was Macca, with Judy probably somewhere close too.

Harry's lips moved but nothing came out. John bent down closer and felt his friend's breath on his cheek.

'It's no good,' said a faraway voice. The medic. 'The bastard has sliced him wide open and jabbed . . .' The medic's voice faded away.

'Fix him, he's strong, he'll recover. Please, you have to try. He can make it. I know he can,' begged John, who realised he was crying. It was all too much: the blood, Harry's face, the fear that he was about to lose his best mate.

John stared into Harry's eyes. He wanted to be strong for him, but he felt so helpless. 'I'm sorry, Harry. I'm sorry I didn't get him sooner.'

Harry moved his hand and latched on to John's arm. He squeezed it weakly and then gave a faint half-smile. Then he closed his eyes and his hand fell away.

John could feel the moment Harry breathed his last, the moment his lungs no longer expanded; the weight of his body was suddenly still.

John wanted to scream. He wanted to hit something – no, he wanted to kill something. He wanted to kill all the VC bastards.

He wasn't sure how long he sat there with Harry, nor how many soldiers came and went. He watched the body of the VC being dragged away and searched. He hated him, a man doing the same job as him. He did not regret killing him.

'Come on, Parson,' said the company commander.

John didn't realise the company commander even knew his name. He didn't want to leave Harry, but he knew he'd be brought back to base. Harry needed to go home to his family.

John stood up with help. He looked at his hands and they trembled something fierce. Some of Harry's blood had ended up on him and he stared at it strangely. It just didn't seem real.

His life had changed course, John knew. He felt the shift in him. Nothing would ever be the same again. He'd lost Harry and killed a man with his bare hands.

Dear Beth,

I'm sorry I haven't written in a while. I haven't been able to. On our last mission Harry was killed. We are still in shock here.

Love, John xxx

Dear Beth,

Thank you for your letters and for trying to cheer me up. I wish you were here to hold me. I've stopped counting my days till home and Macca has shaved off his precious moustache. Judy no longer pranks anyone, not even the reo who came today. He was to replace Harry after his time was up, but he's come early.

We packed up Harry's things, putting them in his trunk to go home to his family. We are a sorry state. I just want to get through these last few months and get home. I can't seem to distract myself, not even with movies or music. I just lie in my cot. I don't know what to write to you any more. I'm sorry.

Love, John xxx

Dear Beth,

*Your hand must be sore from writing all your letters.
I really appreciate it, the normalcy of your lives is nice to hear.
It's about the only thing that can put a smile on my face lately.*

*I know I said I'd stopped counting but it brings me closer
to you. So 102 and a wakey!*

*I just came back from rest and care leave in Vung
Tau, down south. The R&C centre is a villa rented by the
government, and it's a bit like a holiday camp. The 'mama
san' cleans the rooms and does our washing. We wear civvies
there and the food is topnotch. I did lots of walking, took
some photos and bought some things to send home. My
roommate and I jumped on a Lambretta and we did some
sightseeing. It took my mind off things.*

*We are off on another operation soon. I'm not sure how
we'll go. Judy has asked to take on Harry's job as machine
gunner. I'm not looking forward to it at all. I just want my
tour over with. I miss you. Love you heaps.*

Love, John xxx

Dear Beth,

40 and a wakey!

*So close to home I can almost taste it. Today I found out
the name of my reo replacement. He should be here in the
next month. Judy is leaving next week with Macca, and I will
be in a sorry state without them. At least Judy has survived
being machine gunner. I think he's actually a bit disappointed*

he hasn't had a chance to find some VC. He's still looking to avenge Harry's death. I think we all are. Not a day goes by that I don't think of Harry.

Love you. Soon, my love, soon I'll be home.

Love, John xxx

Dear Beth,

32 and a wakey!

I started my happy pills today: good old primaquine and chloroquine to help clear up any malaria bugs before I go home. Home. I love writing that word. Home. Australia! That's another word I love to write. And Beth. Beth is my favourite word.

The wet is starting to come again, and the monsoon flies are out in force tonight. Makes me think about the crazy flies at home during the summer. For once I'd welcome those pesky flies. I've gotta go – we have to clean up the lines before inspection. Later, my love.

Love, John xxx

Dear Beth,

A wakey!

Yesterday I got my leave and payments sorted out. The boys had a going-home party for me and it felt weird – maybe even more so for my reo, who has a whole year to go. I know how he must have felt, sitting in the corner, unsure of all the blokes I now call mates. I can't believe that was once me. Saying goodbye to everyone is hard. We share a closeness, a common link that this place seems to create, and they've become like family. But I'm also excited and nervous to be going home.

I'm getting on the Freedom Bird this morning, destination Australia. I may even beat this last letter home. I just keep picturing you. Soon I will hold you tightly in my arms. Soon.

Love, John xxx

Chapter 31

1970

THERE she was. As beautiful as the day he'd left her.

'John! John,' yelled Beth, waving to him. She was standing beside his parents, but not for long: she ran through the airport towards him.

She hit him hard, with a welcome impact. He'd missed her so much: her body, her soft fragrant hair and, as his hand slipped under her blouse along her back, the silkiness of her skin.

'Oh my god,' he groaned. They hugged tightly, Beth sobbing against his chest.

'You're home, I can't believe it. Finally . . .' Beth leant back and wiped away her tears. 'Sorry I'm such a mess.'

John took her face gently in his hands and studied her. 'No, love, you're a sight for sore eyes.' He brushed a tear away with his thumb. 'I don't want to let you go again,' he said, kissing her.

Someone cleared their throat and they pulled apart.

'Sorry to interrupt, son, but we can't wait any longer,' said his dad.

John smiled and launched into his mum's waiting arms. She was crying, but the sparkle in her eye and the grin on her lips showed her true emotion. Next he hugged his dad.

'Finally we have our boy home. Finally!' said Norma.

'Let's all go home and have a beer or two,' said James with a wink.

He drove them back through the city to John's house in a new Ford Fairlane ZD with a vinyl roof. John didn't want his parents to come home with them, he wanted Beth to himself, but he knew he had the rest of their lives for that.

'Nice wheels, Dad. Business must be going well?'

'Sure is, son. Who knew? A job I can actually do with my crook back, and if it plays up – well then, I just don't book any work. Simple. Beth has been great too. I couldn't have done it without her.'

'We were thinking of having a welcome-home party, John,' began his mum.

'No, please. I don't want any parties,' he said quickly. Beth's brow creased and his mum's head turned quickly in his direction.

'Are you sure, love? The rest of the family would like to catch up.'

'They can when they want to. I just don't want a party. I want to settle in back home and acclimatise. I need time, Mum. Not heaps of people all at once.'

'Oh, okay. If that's what you want, dear.'

'It is. I just want to go home.' His voice cracked on the last word. He still pictured the house on the farm as home.

When they arrived at the house they had a beer as they sat

on the new patio under the pergola. Only it didn't look brand-new any more, with plants hanging from the pergola in pots and some growing up the sides. It looked as if it belonged here. To Beth, it probably felt like it had been there forever. He watched her move around the house with ease. This had been her home for over a year now, but to John it was still new and uncomfortable. The farm was what he'd dreamt of while he was stuck in the foreign jungle.

Sitting here with his family in Australia was surreal. Different smells, different colours . . . it would take time to adjust. And he knew he was swearing too much – he'd spent too long with the lads. His mother grimaced each time and he apologised, but he knew it was upsetting her. John would try to make an effort to think before he spoke, but it was hard.

His parents asked him many questions, but in the end he grew tired of war talk and yawned. It was too much. 'I'm sorry, Mum, Dad, but I'm just worn out. I need to sleep off the jet lag.'

'We understand,' said his mum. His parents rose and said their goodbyes.

John smiled at Beth after they'd left.

'What would you like now, John?' she asked carefully. 'Anything I can get you? Are you hungry? Thirsty?' She sucked her bottom lip.

'I'd like a nice hot shower before lying down with you beside me. Think that can be arranged?'

She smiled, blushing.

He reached out and pulled her close to him. 'Don't go all shy, my love. It's still me.' He breathed in the scent of her hair. 'I just want to hold you all night long.'

'I like the sound of that,' she said.

It didn't take long for them to get reacquainted with each other. In the following weeks they made up for their time apart. John spent his first month at home relaxing and doing things around the house, like repairing a hole in the fence or a sticky window that wouldn't shut. He helped carry out rugs to be cleaned and spent time fixing his dad's broken rakes. Some days he'd do nothing but read the paper and annoy Beth as she went about the housework. On occasion he'd go out and help his dad do some gardening if he had a heap of work lined up. His dad even offered him a partnership, but what John really wanted was a farm, to get back to the country.

John found himself looking through the paper for land sales and jobs out in farming areas. 'There's some land out near York for sale,' he said optimistically one morning.

'That sounds great,' said Beth. She peered over his shoulder at the ad in the paper. 'Shame it's so expensive. I wish we could afford it.' Her expression tugged at his heart. 'We'd have to work hard for a few more years, John. And if we sell the house we might have enough for a loan to afford one of those smaller farms.'

He knew she was right, but he felt like they were just killing time.

'Why don't you work with your dad? It's better than any of the jobs you've looked at so far,' she said. 'Help build up the bank account for the farm – if you want to.'

John nodded, but he wasn't so keen. 'I don't really like going out much,' he admitted.

'I've noticed.' She sat beside him and ran her hand through his hair. 'Why?'

He chewed his lip. He didn't want to burden Beth, but he knew she'd just keep at it until he told her. 'Last time I went to the shops I was spat on by an older lady.'

Beth drew in a sharp breath but remained silent.

'And the shop owner refused to talk to me.'

'Dudley? Not a word? I would never have expected that from him. Well, that's the last time we'll shop with him.' Her voice was raised.

John could feel her tremble with rage beside him and it was comforting to know he had her support. 'I didn't realise how much the people back home were being fed all sorts of things through the media. When people see me, they see a soldier who's been killing innocent people in Vietnam.' At one point he'd got into a heated discussion with a bloke whose lawns he'd been mowing, a client of his dad's, about what he'd been doing over there.

'I was doing my national service,' John had said. 'Doing what I was told to do. I had no choice.' The grumpy bloke had told him to pack up and nick off as he didn't want a 'kid killer' on his property.

It had stung. Even though John knew it wasn't true. That bloke had no clue what it was like over there, yet nothing John could say would change his mind. It churned up his stomach, and made him afraid to go outside. And he hadn't been able to tell Beth, as he knew she'd only worry. He was sure she'd noticed anyway – he'd realised some friends of hers hadn't visited like they used to.

'Yeah,' he mumbled to Beth. 'I just need a bit more time to hang out here. I'm sure there's some painting I can do.' He looked up at his wife and his body grew warm with desire. 'Or I can think of a few other things,' he said, winking.

Beth sat down in his lap and put her arms around his neck. 'Well, actually, John, you might need to paint the spare room soon.' She watched him carefully.

'Yeah, that's fine. I don't mind. Some snazzy wallpaper might look good,' he suggested, trying to sound upbeat.

'I don't know whether blue or pink would be best, so it might be safer to go with yellow.'

John frowned. What was he missing here?

Beth grabbed his hand and put it against her belly. 'I saw the doctor yesterday,' she said with a nervous grin. 'We're having a baby.' Her lips pressed together as she breathed in deeply through her nose. 'Well? What do you think?'

John's eyes widened. 'I'm going to be a dad?'

Beth nodded. 'That's right.'

'Holy crap. We're gonna have a kid?'

She nodded again. 'Good news?' she asked slowly.

'Oh, baby, the best.' He stood up, taking her with him, and swung her around in his arms. Then he put her down and hugged her tightly before hunkering down to talk to her belly. 'Hello, little one.'

As he rested his head against her abdomen he couldn't help but think of Harry. His mate had been a proud dad, which had made John eager to get home and start his own family. Sometime soon he should go through all his photos and get copies of the ones with Harry so he could visit his widow and pass them on. Yes, he really needed to go visit Clarissa. But not just yet. He wasn't ready to open that wound.

Besides, now he had a baby to get ready for.

He stood up again and kissed Beth. 'Do you want a girl or a boy?' he asked.

'I'm happy with either. We'll have to think of names,' she said.

'And get paint,' he added. 'Let's get a beer to celebrate.'

'Just a small one for me.'

'You got it. I'll have your leftovers.' John went through to the kitchen and stopped dead, his face alight. 'A dad. I'm gonna be a bloody dad!' He heard Beth laughing. Today was a good day. Today he felt on top of the world.

Chapter 32

'OH, no. I'm sorry, Harry.' Kim watched Charlie's car pull up. She had no idea what would happen.

'Who is it, lass?'

'It's a guy I'm seeing, kind of.'

'Kind of?' Harry's brow creased.

'Yeah, long story.'

'Hi,' said Charlie as he headed towards them. He held out his hand to Harry. 'I'm Charlie. Kim's told me lots about you. It's great to finally meet.'

Harry shot Kim a sly glance.

'I hope you don't mind me dropping by, but I had to see Kim.'

'Not at all, Charlie. It's nice to meet some of Kim's friends,' Harry said. 'Please join us.'

Charlie's gaze found her. 'Can I sit?' He gestured to the spot beside her.

Kim nodded. She was still in shock. She never imagined Charlie would come and find her all the way out here.

'I'm sorry to interrupt, but I really do have something important to sort out with Kim. It couldn't wait,' Charlie said to Harry.

'No, by all means, stay. I'm just going to pick some vegies for dinner.' He winked at Kim, who suddenly felt uneasy.

'I think I know why you left,' Charlie began as Harry headed into his garden. 'You heard Laura's message, didn't you?'

Kim could only nod as she stared at Harry's dogs, who watched their master, ready to go if he called them.

'Loz told me about Travis, so I get it.'

Kim's head jerked up. 'She did? You do?'

'I wish you'd told me. I'd have been more up-front with you. I left out a little detail about my marriage with Laura.' Charlie paused to take a breath. He reached for her hand and squeezed it. 'Kim, Laura is gay. And when she first told me I thought it was all because of me, that I'd done something to put her off men. Of course she tore me to pieces for even thinking it. Fact was, she had an inkling when we first married. Because we were best friends she figured I could make her happy enough. We've been separated for a few years now. It's not something I like to tell everyone I meet, but I see now I should have told you from the beginning and saved you all this grief.' He let go of her hand and pulled out his phone. 'Here are some photos of Laura and her new partner, Emily. Laura's already put our divorce in motion so she can marry Emily when it becomes possible. Laura still loves me and I do love her, but not in a way that will ever affect your relationship with me.'

Kim took his phone and flicked through the photos and text messages from Laura. She felt a wave of emotion crash down as the words grew blurry. 'I really wanted to believe you, Charlie, I did —'

'You don't have to explain. I get it. I would be suspicious too if I'd been through the wringer like you. I'm sorry you had to put up with those jerks.'

Kim smiled and blinked tears away. 'I'm just glad you're not one of them. Thank you.' She hadn't seen this coming. No wonder Charlie spoke wistfully of children. Maybe they still had a chance together.

'Everything okay, lass?' asked Harry, who'd wandered back. Perhaps he'd heard her sniffling.

'I'm fine, Harry.' Kim smiled and saw him relax.

'I'm sorry to barge in, Harry, but this had to be said,' explained Charlie. 'You see, I've become rather fond of this amazing lady. I couldn't bear to have her think poorly of me.'

'Not at all. It's nice to see Kim happy. She's become a bit of a treasure of mine too. She's a rather special person.'

'I couldn't agree with you more,' said Charlie.

Kim smiled at Harry. 'Aw, Harry, you're special to me too. You don't mind Charlie hanging out here?'

'Not at all. I thought I liked being a hermit, but your visits have proved me wrong. I'm glad you drop by, and Charlie is welcome too. Would you two like to stay for lunch? I have some silverside and salad, and there's enough to go around.' Harry glanced at his watch.

Kim looked to Charlie and then back to Harry. 'Actually we might take a raincheck, Harry, but we'd love to come back for a meal. I've told Charlie all about your amazing stew.'

Harry chuckled. 'I hear ya. You two have a bit to sort out, I'd say. But dinner is always on offer. I'll jot down my number, Kim, so we can work out a time.'

They stood up as Harry went inside. While he was gone, Charlie pulled her into a hug. 'Is this okay?'

'Yeah, it's more than okay.' She rested her head on his shoulder and breathed in his scent. 'I still can't believe you came here.'

'I'd go to the end of the earth for you, Kim.'

His words melted her heart. She pressed a kiss against his lips just before the door opened again. Harry came out with a notepad and pen, and gave Kim a bit of paper with his number on it.

'Can't say I've ever given this number out. Only Tom and Marie call me,' said Harry.

'Well, look out, Harry. You might regret this,' she said, and he chuckled.

Kim and Charlie wrote down their numbers for him and Harry put the notepad and pen back inside the door.

'Hey, Charlie, did you see what Kim made me?' Proudly Harry walked over to her latest creation and picked it up.

'Oh, nice. I haven't seen this one before. A wattle. It's beautiful.'

Kim screwed her face up. She felt embarrassed by their praise. 'It's just a bit of fun. I can make you anything you like, Harry. Are there any things related to the war you'd like me to do? I'm pretty good at cutting out pictures and words in metal. Did you have a regiment you were with? Or . . .' she realised she was rambling on a bit. 'Would you prefer not to have the reminder? Sorry.'

'It's okay, love, I know you mean well. I was with 5 RAR, A Company, 2 Platoon. I do try to leave it in the past, but I'm not sure that does anyone much good. I'll think about it. There is something that comes to mind, but I'm not sure if I'm ready yet.'

'Cheers, Harry. Anyway, we best be off to let you enjoy your Sunday afternoon,' Kim said. She was eager to get Charlie back home.

'Thanks, Harry, it's been a pleasure.' Charlie shook his hand before taking Kim's. Together they walked towards their cars.

Harry waved them off. 'See you both next time. Molly, come back,' he said, whistling to his dog.

It was hard to let go of Charlie's hand. 'Follow me back to my place,' she said quietly, before letting him go.

'For sure.' Charlie kissed her forehead and got into his car.

'Would you like a beer?' Kim asked, feeling a little nervous.

Charlie put his hand out to close the fridge door. 'No. Not right now.' He tucked a strand of hair back from her face. 'Are we okay?'

Kim had trouble finding a reply. The fact that she was now a foot from Charlie was making her senses go crazy. He did things to her body that she couldn't seem to control. She put her hands onto his chest, feeling the beat of his heart. Then she met his eyes. His lips taunted her, and she ached to kiss them as the memories of their lovemaking came instantly to mind.

Kim moved her hands up to his face, cupping his strong jaw. 'We're fine, Charlie. I do feel a little stupid though.'

'Don't,' he said as his arms wrapped around her. 'You had every right to react the way you did. I'm just sorry you had to go through that, feeling like you'd been deceived again.' His grey-blue eyes grew serious. 'I never want to put you through anything like that again. Never.'

Kim smiled. 'Then you better hurry up and kiss me.'

Flames of desire flashed across his eyes and he wasted no time claiming her lips. Kim groaned softly as she pressed against him.

'Do you wanna stay?' she managed to get out between kisses.

'Hmm, sounds nice. Sure, why not?' he said teasingly. He chuckled and cupped her bum in his hand, lifting her up against him. 'Now . . . where were we?'

Kim pointed her finger to her lips. 'You were right here.'

Chapter 33

1971

THE midwife took John through the hospital ward, guiding him to where Beth lay on a bed. In her arms was a tiny bundle.

He couldn't stop the tears that welled up as he looked at his amazing wife, holding their child. 'Hello,' he said as he practically tiptoed in and sat by her bed. 'How are you feeling?'

'Better now.' Beth smiled, her face radiant despite her fatigue, her hair damp with sweat. Her eyes didn't stray from the baby. 'Look at him, John. He's so perfect. We made him.' She looked up at John to say, 'We have a baby boy.'

The little tyke squirmed a bit in her arms, opening up his tiny hand. John couldn't help but stick his finger out for the baby to wrap his fingers around. 'He's so small.'

'Do you want to hold him?' she said.

'No. I might drop him. He's too delicate.'

Beth grinned. 'John, you'll be fine. Here, take him from me. Just make sure his head is supported.'

John felt nervous and excited at the same time. 'Oh, wow,

look at him.'

'What do you want to call him?' asked Beth softly.

'We had some good names on the list for boys, didn't we? I'm happy with any of them,' said John as he watched the little lad sleeping. He sat down with him and the slight movement made the baby open his eyes. 'He's going to have your blue eyes.'

'Yes, looks like it. But that is definitely your nose and your lips. I'd recognise them anywhere.'

John wasn't so sure he could pick it. It was too soon to tell. 'I hope when we have a girl she takes after you in every way.' Already he couldn't wait to have more.

'Hey, we haven't even tried to get this fella to sleep, or fed him or toilet trained him yet. Don't scare me with the idea of more kids already,' said Beth, laughing. 'Johnny?'

He looked up and couldn't read the expression on Beth's face.

'I think I've got a name for him. I really like it and hope you do too.' She took a deep breath and continued, 'I'd like to call him Harrison Charles Parson. Charles after my father, and Harrison for Harry.'

John felt the breath squeezed out of him. 'Harry?' As he said the name, his sight went blurry with tears and his bottom lip trembled. Holding this new baby was emotional enough, but now Beth wanted to name their son Harry? There were no words for how much this affected him. Quickly he got up and handed the baby back. When the little one was safely in his mum's arms, John pressed his fists into his eyes as sobs threatened.

'I didn't mean to upset you. I'm sorry,' said Beth, her voice cracking.

He could see tears running down her face and it gutted him. John sank down on her bed and put his face against her shoulder. He wrapped an arm gently around her and the baby. 'It's not that. I love it. I love that you thought of it, and I'm honoured. I think Harry would be too,' he managed to say before he broke down.

The two of them huddled together, crying. It was only when their son, Harrison Charles, began to cry too that they ended up laughing and wiping away their tears.

'I think he's hungry,' she said.

'That might be my cue to leave. I'll go and tell our parents the news,' he said. He stood up and brushed Beth's cheek with his fingers. 'You are truly amazing and beautiful. I didn't think I could possibly love you any more, but I do. You are my world, Beth. I love you.'

Beth reached for his hand and squeezed it. 'I love you too, John. Forever.'

The baby was giving his lungs a good workout now and John chuckled. 'Love you too, Harry,' he said softly, trying out the name that had once been so familiar on his tongue. Then he turned and left, his heart full of joy and yet heavy. He only wished Harry was here to meet his namesake.

A month later and John realised Beth's hesitancy about talk of another baby was well-founded. John watched Beth endlessly feeding, changing, and trying to get Harry to sleep. Who knew a baby could poo and cry so much and take up so much of Beth's time? John, not wanting to venture outside much these days, had learnt how to change nappies and look after the little fella to help Beth out. And it was one day while he was bathing Harry and the child looked up and smiled that John truly understood what his mate had said about being a father, and how much joy a child could bring. John thought about Harry's girl Megan and wondered how she was coping without her father. How was his wife going? John's guilt at not visiting burned in his gut, but he couldn't go now. Not with a new bub, and the fact he didn't like going out. But he promised himself that one day he would.

They were lucky to have both sets of grandparents around to help out. Both grandmothers liked to come over when they could, although some days they were too much and Beth had to send them home. John did try to work more with his dad, as it meant he could pick and choose when he worked, and it didn't matter so much if he was sleep-deprived. Sleep was probably the hardest part.

Somehow they managed, and the months flew by with little Harry keeping them very busy. He was a brilliant kid. John would take him out onto the back lawn, set him down on a blanket and just lie with him while Beth tried to catch up on sleep. Together they'd stretch out and watch the clouds go past. Harry's eyes perfectly matched Beth's, and it was such a strange sensation to look at him and see her there. Beth had also been right about Harry having John's nose and mouth. John had stood staring at himself in a mirror only to look at Harry and realise just how right she was.

John made sure his son had a farm playset, and his dad made

Harry wooden trucks and tractors. When they played together, John would show Harry how the dogs rounded up the sheep and tell him about the tractor and how it pulled a plough. As Harry grew, John added to the farm toys and would set out a whole farm for him with yards and paddocks.

'Sometimes I wonder if that's for you or him,' said Beth one day as she was hanging out the washing. Harry had just picked up a tractor and crawled off with it.

'Harry, we need to finish planning the crop,' he said as his son crawled along the lawn to Beth's feet. The little fella held up the red tractor for her in his plump hand.

'Thanks, darling, but Mummy doesn't need a tractor to hang out washing. You give it back to Daddy. I think he wants it more,' she said, shooting a smile John's way.

'Look, the rams are in with the ewes – everyone's getting frisky.' He showed Beth just how the plastic sheep did it and laughed before rolling onto his back.

'You're trouble,' she said with a grin, pushing the washing trolley back to the house. 'John Parson, don't you teach your son any bad habits,' she called sternly, but her eyes were smiling.

Beth left the trolley on the patio and came back to join John on the lawn, sitting down beside him but watching her son. 'I can't believe he'll be walking soon. I was an early walker,' she said.

John rolled his eyes. 'I know. Your mum loves to remind me. Just because I was eighteen months before I walked.'

Beth laughed and then stopped, turning her head. 'I think someone's at our door. Can you go see? I'll sort Harry out for his bath.'

'Righto,' said John, kissing Beth before he got up.

He heard the knocking as he got inside. 'Hello?' said John, opening the door.

There was a woman standing there, dressed up in a yellow skirt and blouse with matching shoes. Her hair was in a blond bob. Holding her hand was a little girl with a spotted yellow dress and ribbons in her pigtailed hair.

'Hello. Are you John?'

'Yes. That's me.' John assumed this was a friend of Beth's he hadn't met.

She smiled sadly and John suddenly didn't feel so sure.

'I'm really sorry to turn up uninvited, but I saw your birth notice in the paper a while back and I've been working up the courage to come and visit. Congratulations on the baby, by the way.'

'Ah, thanks,' said John, wondering who this could be.

'I'm sorry, I forgot to introduce myself. I'm a bit nervous.' The woman held out her hand, a big white handbag hanging from her arm. 'I'm Clarissa. I'm Harry's wife.'

John froze.

'Harry wrote that you were best mates in Vietnam?' she queried worriedly when John didn't say anything.

'Yes, yes, we were. Sorry,' he said, rubbing his forehead. 'You've just blown me away.' John glanced down at the little girl and his gut twisted. Harry's eyes looked up at him questioningly. 'Oh my god, is that little Megan?'

Clarissa beamed. 'Yes, it is. Not so little now.'

'I'm going to school soon,' Megan said importantly.

'Wow,' said John. Harry had showed him photos, but the

child in them had not been much older than his boy was. It made him realise just how much time had passed. And it reminded him of his promise to visit Harry. Okay, so Harry hadn't come back, but John had still copped out. He should have visited.

'Darling, who is it?' said Beth, coming to the door.

'Beth, this is Harry's wife, Clarissa.'

'Oh!' said Beth. 'Please, Clarissa, won't you come in?'

'Yes, sorry. I'm still in a bit of shock,' said John. 'Come in.'

'Thank you,' said Clarissa as she entered the house with her daughter.

John shut the door and led them to the lounge. 'Please, grab a seat.'

Beth dropped Harry into John's arms as she said, 'I'll put the kettle on. Tea? And some cordial for your daughter?'

'Thank you, that would be lovely. Yes, Megan likes cordial.'

Beth left and John bounced his squirming boy on his knee.

'Mummy, can I hold the baby?' asked Megan.

John smiled. 'This is Harry,' he said. 'He's named after your daddy.'

Clarissa put her hand to her mouth as her lips trembled. She looked away and blinked back tears.

John tried to focus on the kids to stop his own tears. 'If I put Harry on the floor then you can play with him, if you like. Just watch your hair, he likes to grab.'

After he put Harry down he sat next to Clarissa and put his hand briefly on her knee. 'I'm so sorry about Harry,' he whispered.

Clarissa nodded and pulled out a hanky from her handbag. 'I'm sorry. It's been a while since his death, obviously, but every now and then it gets me again.' She dabbed at her eyes. 'All Harry's letters were full of stories of you, Macca and Judy.'

John nodded. 'Yep, mine were the same. Harry was amazing – he really took me under his wing. We talked for hours on end about the farms we had.'

'After his death we had to sell the farm,' said Clarissa sadly. 'I live in the city with my parents now. Then when I saw the birth notice for you and Beth I had to visit. I hope you don't mind me turning up like this.'

'Not at all. I've been wanting to see you, but with the baby and all . . .' John shrugged.

'I understand. It can be busy. Harry was great with Megan. She doesn't even remember him, but we have plenty of photos to help.'

'I have some too that I've been meaning to copy for you. Would you like to see them?'

Beth walked in carrying a tray with the teapot and cups.

Clarissa nodded and smiled. 'That would be lovely. Thank you, John.'

He stood up. 'I'll be back.'

He went into the spare room, where his army trunk was. He pulled out the photos he'd taken and paused as he looked over the contents of the trunk. It had been a long time since he'd opened this. Had he opened it at all since getting home?

He shut the trunk and opened one of the packets of photos. The first one he pulled out was his favourite. Judy had taken it for them: John and Harry, side by side. It was only a few months in, and already they were great mates. He felt something rattle inside his chest, as if something was dislodging, breaking free. Lifting the lid of his trunk, he put the photo back. He couldn't share that one. Ever.

John took the packet out to the lounge and went through the rest of the photos one by one, explaining them to Clarissa and Beth. The memories flooded back.

After two rounds of tea and with Harry crying for his dinner, Clarissa stood up. 'I should get going. I've kept you all long enough.'

'Thank you for coming by, Clarissa. It was lovely to meet you,' said Beth. 'Megan is just adorable and so well-mannered. You've done a great job.'

The women hugged like old friends. John also hugged Clarissa goodbye and found her grasp long and tight.

'I'll make sure I send copies of those photos to you,' he said.

'Thank you, John. I . . .' She paused. 'I know Harry died on a mission, killed by the VC.' He nodded. 'Were you there?' she asked.

Beth watched carefully. John hadn't told her much about Harry's death. He hadn't ever wanted to speak of it, but the pleading in Clarissa's eyes was too much to handle. He knew she needed to know. 'I was there. I tried to save him. I killed the man who got him.' John looked down as he watched Beth raise her hand to her mouth. Clarissa stood completely still. For Harry's sake, he found the courage he needed. 'He died in my arms. I was there until the end. It was quick. He tried to speak but I couldn't hear him. I'm sure he would have been talking about you both.'

'Thank you. Thank you. You've told me more than anyone,

and it means a lot to me, John. I will always be grateful.' Clarissa gave him a long look, filled with meaning, took her daughter's hand and walked out.

The moment the door shut John felt his exhaustion set in and a headache loom.

'John, are you okay? Do you want to talk about it?' Beth had Harry in her arms but she reached out to him, touching his shoulder.

'I'll be fine,' he said. 'I've done enough talking for now.' He scooped up all the photos to put them away but they blurred in front of his eyes and he dropped them back on the table. 'I might go down to the pub for a beer, love. Will you be all right with Harry?'

Beth held a wriggling Harry tightly and pressed her lips together. 'Are you sure? I can make your dinner soon?'

'I just need some time out to think, Beth. It's okay. I can grab something at the pub, don't worry about dinner for me.' He stepped towards his wife and kissed her forehead.

'Okay. I love you,' she said worriedly.

'I love you too. See you soon.'

Chapter 34

JOHN walked the four blocks to the local pub. He hadn't been often, thanks to young Harry – and the fact that he felt like the locals all stared at him as though he was some kind of murderer. Some would leave the bar entirely, while others just moved away. He wasn't stupid, he could tell things had changed. But not all of them were like that. Usually he could find a few blokes to drink with.

Today he just needed a drink and some quiet time. He'd be happy if they all left him alone. Actually, he was counting on it.

He pushed open the pub door and walked into the smell of alcohol. He followed the dark-red-and-brown patterned carpet up to the lino of the front bar. John sat on a wooden stool. 'Can I get a scotch, please?' he said to the bartender.

The bloke nodded and poured him a scotch on the rocks. He took his money without a word.

As John brought the glass to his lips his hand shook, making the ice clink. He relished the strength of the alcohol and the way it woke up his senses. Meeting Clarissa had been so unexpected and had brought back so much. His mind was flooding with memories of his time in Vietnam, of his mates. He wondered what Macca and Judy were up to now. Maybe he should try to find them – call them, even – and see how they were settling back into normal life. He wished he could do more for Clarissa, and felt bad that he hadn't gone to see her. Harry would have liked him to visit, to make sure she was okay, but he'd kept putting it off, pushing it from his mind. He swallowed the rest of his scotch, feeling awful, thinking of how he'd let Harry down. If it had been John who'd died, Harry would have been there for Beth, he knew that without a doubt.

John tried to swallow the lump that was growing in his throat. He gestured to the bartender again. 'Another, please. Cheers.'

As he slid his money across the bar he noticed two guys at the end of the bar watching him and whispering. John felt anger growing in the pit of his stomach. Harry shouldn't be dead, Clarissa shouldn't be without her husband, Megan should have her father, and the Vets who fought in the war shouldn't be treated like they were butchers. John had spent a long time ignoring the looks, the whispers, the overt snubs, but that didn't mean he was happy about it. Having guys he knew turn their back on him hurt like hell. He felt like a criminal, when all he'd done was follow the law.

The guys at the end of the bar were starting to give him the shits, interfering with his quiet drink as their whispers grew louder.

'Probably liked it, killing the women,' said the skinnier of the two.

'Probably got his rocks off torturing them too,' said his mate, who had a double chin and a big beer gut.

John took a deep breath and sipped his drink. He closed his eyes, trying to let it wash over him.

'Just licensed killers,' the fat guy said louder.

John snapped his head in their direction. 'You got something to say?' His ears were burning and he could feel the anger reaching release point.

Both the guys got up and walked towards him. 'Yeah, maybe we do,' said the fat one. 'But we don't talk to kid murders.'

John put his drink down and stood up. Could he take the two of them? He wasn't that great at fistfighting. 'You have no idea what really went on over there. Until you've walked in my shoes, you should keep your mouth shut,' said John, poking him in his pudgy belly.

The man took a swing at John, who moved but not quickly enough, and the blow caught his chin. All this did was enrage John. He swung back and missed, making the skinny guy laugh as he stood behind his large friend.

'Take it outside, boys,' the bartender said from the other end of the bar.

But it was too late. The pudgy guy punched John in the guts, knocking the wind from his lungs and almost forcing the scotch from his belly.

John jumped at the man, screaming, wrapping his hands around his neck and pushing him backwards. They fell over the skinny guy and all three tumbled down.

The pub's noise grew faint: the bartender's yelling, people

cheering . . . it all faded away as John focused on the man's neck. A familiar sensation coursed through him. Why? Suddenly it wasn't the pudgy guy's face any more – it was a Viet Cong man he was strangling. Then the face was gone and the pudgy guy was back, choking, gripping at Johns hands, fearful. His blue eyes were large and panicked.

Shit.

Just as John loosened his grip and began to pull away, everything went black.

He came to on the floor of the pub, blinking, as the bartender stood over him with a broken bottle in his hand.

'You need to get out of my pub,' said the bartender.

John tried to sit up. It took a few tries. That's when he felt the sting on his cheek. His hand came away red with blood when he touched it.

'Sorry about that. I thought you were killing him,' said the bartender.

'It crossed my mind,' said John. 'But he wasn't the VC. He was just an idiot who doesn't understand.'

The bartender handed him one of his bar towels. 'Here, use this. You might need stitches. Best you get home. The others have racked off. Don't come back here for a while.'

John held the towel to his face and found it covered in blood. He pressed it back on. 'Yeah, righto. Sorry.' John left the pub, a few eyes watching him carefully from afar. He looked down and saw that his shirt was splattered with blood. Beth was going to have a heart attack when she saw this, he thought.

'Oh, Beth,' he mumbled as he staggered home. His head was

light and he felt like he might pass out. How was he going to explain all this?

When she opened the door, standing there with pink curlers in her hair and her nightgown on, she gasped. 'John, what happened?' She dragged him inside and straight into the kitchen to start cleaning him up.

He sat on a kitchen chair while she moved around him, gathering first aid supplies from the cupboard. 'Someone didn't like that I was a Vet,' he said. 'And after today, seeing Clarissa, it was all too much.' Quietly Beth washed his face and cleaned up the cut on his cheek. John shrugged. 'I just lost it, Beth. I've had enough of being the bad guy, putting up with everyone's insults and judgement.'

He couldn't stop speaking. 'But I'm not innocent, Beth. Far from it. I killed men over there. I'm still a killer, and I can't ever change that.' John stared at the blood on his hands as they rested on his knees. Today it was his blood, but he remembered clearly when it was Harry's. 'The day Harry died . . . I killed his killer with my bare hands. Not with a bullet from across a ditch, but with my bare hands. I watched the life drain from his eyes and I wanted him to suffer for what he'd done to Harry. In that moment I wasn't myself, and somehow I don't think I'll ever be my old self again. I've buried the memory deep, trying to forget it, but it's still there. I can't deal with all those feelings again. That VC was just doing his job. He probably had a wife and kids. I don't know any more . . . I thought I was coping okay.' A tear rolled down his face. Beth wiped it away and stuck some butterfly stitches on his wound.

She cupped his face gently. When he looked up he saw tears lining her cheeks.

'I still love you, John. You are still that man to me, although I understand why you're hurting. I wish I could help you, take some of your burden.'

Beth stepped between his legs and pulled him to her. John leant his unhurt cheek against her chest, wrapped his arms around her and clung on like a child. How had he ended up so lucky with Beth?

'I just want it all to go away,' John mumbled.

After a few minutes Beth stepped back and held out her hands for him. 'Let's get you showered and to bed.' She helped him up and led him to the bathroom.

After his shower Beth took him back to their bedroom, past Harry's room, and she tucked him into bed. He was grateful. His mind wasn't functioning, even for the simplest tasks.

They lay in bed facing each other, Beth's arms around him, the patterned sheets encircling them like a cocoon.

He watched her, taking comfort in those blue eyes, and saw she was tired. Her lashes fluttered closed. Meanwhile John was having trouble finding sleep.

'Go to sleep, John. It's okay. I'm here. I love you,' she whispered with her eyes shut.

John kissed her forehead. 'I love you too, my Beth. Thank you.' How she still loved him he would never know. He was profoundly grateful that she wasn't scared of him, even knowing he'd killed someone.

He turned off the bedside light. As he listened to her rhythmic breathing, John felt the fogginess of sleep descend, and soon darkness overcame him.

'Harry?' John called out.

The jungle smelt like moisture and dirt. His heart raced at the familiarity of it.

John moved to peer around the bushy tree. He knew what was about to happen. He could see Harry down near the ground, fighting with the skinny VC. John took in the sight of the blood over Harry's belly. He could smell its metallic tang, and his tongue moved as if he could taste it. This couldn't be happening again, he thought. But there was Harry, his best mate, just how he remembered him: that smile, those eyes. They pleaded to him, Help me. John knew what he had to do.

Launching himself, he landed on the VC, pushing him off Harry and wrapping his hands around his throat. The guy tried to wriggle free, and John felt him scratching at his skin. So John squeezed harder and harder; he had to kill him for Harry. Had to stop him. Yet as the VC fought back a scent hit John's nose – one he recognised, one that didn't belong in a jungle. He felt something scratch him. Hair brushed his hands, tickling like a feather, but the VC had short hair. Suddenly the man stopped moving and everything went black.

No longer could he smell the blood or the jungle. His hands relaxed as he tried to figure out where he was. It was totally dark, and something was on him. He flicked it off and realised it was a sheet. A sheet? He felt around him and found a pillow.

Suddenly he remembered. He was home. It was just a dream!

He rolled over and turned on the bedside light. Then he lay back on his pillow, trying to get his thoughts straight. His heart was racing so hard he wondered for a moment if he was having a heart attack. He turned and saw Beth lying beside him, but something was wrong. Her eyes were open but unblinking. He reached out to touch her shoulder and saw his own arm was scratched and bloody.

With a crack everything became clear.

'Beth!' he yelled. He could see his fingermarks upon her neck, red and purple, and he cried out. 'Beth, talk to me!' he said, shaking her gently. 'I'm sorry, I didn't know it was you. Baby, talk to me.' He checked for a pulse, but couldn't feel anything. He couldn't hear her breathing. He couldn't look at her staring eyes. Instead he started CPR. 'Bethy, please,' he sobbed. 'I'm so sorry.'

He worked for a bit longer then ran for the phone to call the ambulance. He opened the front door, turned on lights and got back to Beth as fast as he could and continued working on her. He had to go by feel as tears blurred his vision. He had no idea how long he was at it before he felt someone pull him away.

'Have a break, mate,' one of the ambos said.

John sank down to the floor, his body weak. He folded his arms against his knees, tears pouring down his face, and watched them try to save his wife. He couldn't understand how or why. He'd hurt his girl, but he hadn't meant to. Was this a nightmare?

An ambulance officer came over to John and knelt down beside him. 'I'm sorry, mate. She's gone,' he said. 'What happened?'

John had started rocking back and forth. No, this wasn't happening, this couldn't be real. Surely he was still dreaming. His Beth? The man repeated his question and John tried to explain. 'I was dreaming about Vietnam. I didn't know. I hurt her. It was me.'

John lost all sense of time passing after that, and didn't know what was going on. There were police who came and took her body away. He was sure he was still dreaming as they carried her from their house, covered in a sheet. How was any of this possible?

At one point an officer came out with a crying Harry in his arms and John burst into tears. He asked if he could hold him. 'I want to say goodbye,' he said. They let him hold Harry, who was reaching out to him, wanting his dad. The child stopped crying the moment he was in John's arms, but John didn't. He hugged Harry tightly. 'I'm so sorry, Harry, I'm so sorry,' he cried. He cried for his son, for his wife and for his mate. How had this happened?

The police wanted to take him to the police station.

'Please call my parents. They'll look after Harry,' he said as they took his son from him. They handcuffed him and he didn't resist – he deserved all the punishment he could get. John was led to the police car that waited out the front of his house, along with his nosy neighbours in dressing gowns, watching the commotion from their front yards. But he didn't notice any of them, didn't care. He was consumed by the loss of his beautiful wife, and life as he knew it.

Chapter 35

'NOW *this* is living,' said Kim, as Charlie put a plate of bacon and eggs down in front of her.

'I owed you a breakfast,' he said, sitting beside her in only his boxers.

Kim couldn't believe this was happening. A part of her still felt sure it would all end in tears. But Charlie had told her the truth, and he wanted to be with her. Kim walked her fingers along his naked chest. 'I could eat you for breakfast,' she said, bending down to kiss his neck.

'Mmm . . . It's nice to be wanted. Makes me realise what I've been missing.' He reached for her hand and gave it a squeeze.

Kim laughed. 'I could say the same thing.'

'Yoo-hoo, Kim? Are you home?' came a loud singsong voice.

'Sure am, Doris, come in,' Kim yelled back. She looked at her watch. It was ten o'clock – they had slept in this morning. It was easy when you had someone lying next to you. Not that they had only been sleeping.

'Hi, love. I just thought I'd pop round and drop off – Oh, hello,' said Doris as she got to the kitchen and saw Charlie. She took in their attire and smiled. She was barefoot, in faded red shorts and a holey black T-shirt, and her hair looked like spun fairy floss.

'Doris, you remember Charlie?'

'Of course. Couldn't forget that handsome face anytime soon.' Doris smiled again and Charlie almost choked on his bacon. She put some containers of what looked like food down on the table.

'Kettle's hot if you'd like a cuppa,' said Kim. Doris wouldn't care what they were wearing. She was never one to judge.

'Thanks, love.' Doris made herself a cup, moving around Kim's kitchen with familiarity, while Kim and Charlie got through their breakfast.

'What's in the containers?' asked Charlie curiously.

'Just a few sweet things I'm sure Kim won't mind sharing with you,' said Doris.

'She's trying to fatten me up,' said Kim in a stage whisper.

Doris sat down with her cuppa. 'A bit of old-fashioned baking won't hurt no one. Look at you, thin as a rake. Someone has to make sure you don't fade away.' Doris glanced at them both and smiled. 'So what have you two young ones got planned for today?'

'Well, I've got a few days off work, and I'm hoping to spend it annoying Kim and trying to track down some more information on Mr Parson,' said Charlie.

'I have farm jobs that always need doing,' said Kim. 'But Matt won't mind if I'm not around.'

'John Parson?' said Doris.

Charlie sprang up. 'You know him?'

'A little bit. Actually, you should really go and see Tom Murphy,' said Doris.

Kim sat up at this news. 'Tom?'

'Yeah. I remember my brother became friends with Tom after Tom's mate John went to war. That's John Parson, the one you're chasing.'

Charlie leant forward. 'Yes, that's the one. Do you know anything else?'

'My brother would have, but he's six feet under. Tom's your best bet. His family's the one that bought the Parson farm all them years ago.'

Kim could see Charlie's eyes light up. Her brain was working overtime. 'To Vietnam? John went to Vietnam?'

'Yep. Think that's why they sold up the farm.'

Kim pushed her empty plate away and leant back in her chair. Her mind was going a mile a minute. Was that photo she'd seen of 'John and Harry' the John who Charlie was chasing? Could his dad be Harry's old mate from the war? She hoped John wasn't dead, but at least this was a lead.

Charlie was looking at her. 'Do you know Tom?'

Kim nodded. 'Yep. Harry works on his farm.'

'Do you reckon we could go see him? Right now?' Charlie stood up, waiting.

'Sure.'

Charlie set off for her room. 'I'll just throw on some clothes.'

Doris raised her eyebrows. 'He's in a bit of a hurry.'

'I'm sorry, Doris, looks like we're off. It's a long story, but I hope we can share it with you soon. If I don't hurry I'm afraid he'll leave without me.'

Doris waved her off with both hands. 'Go, I'll tidy up here before I head to Matt's.'

Kim hugged Doris quickly. 'Thanks. Love ya.'

When she got to her bedroom Charlie was already dressed and tossed her jeans to her.

'I'll be in the car,' he said as he passed.

Half an hour later Charlie was driving towards Tom's place. He was a mixture of nerves, excitement and fear. He gripped the steering wheel as hard as if he was riding a bucking bronco.

'I can see Tom's ute at the shed. Head there,' directed Kim.

He glanced her way. She was dressed but barefoot. He hadn't really given her much time to get ready, but this was the biggest lead he'd had so far. Right now he was actually driving onto land that had belonged to the Parsons. His possible blood relations. That was just mind-blowing. He shook his head in amazement.

'You okay? You haven't said much.'

'I'm – I don't know. Excited, scared, jumping out of my skin. I just hope Tom has some information. What if he knows where John lives? Do you think he'd know about me? Wow.'

'Guess we're about to find out,' Kim said as she reached across and squeezed his hand.

They got out of the ute and met Tom, who'd just crawled back out from the middle of the bar he was getting ready for seeding.

'Hi, Kim,' he said. 'To what do I owe the pleasure?'

'Hey, Tom. We're hoping to pick your brain. This is Charlie, m-my – boyfriend,' she said. Charlie beamed.

The men shook hands. 'Do you want a cuppa?' asked Tom. 'I've got some Tim Tams hidden up the back,' he said, pointing to his shed. 'Let's get stuck in before Marie spots us. She can detect sugar a mile off, that woman. I had chia porridge for breakfast, can you believe?'

'You are looking leaner, Tom, and healthier,' said Kim.

'Yeah, I shouldn't complain. I do feel great. I can actually move about now and my joints don't ache as much. I just miss me sweets. A treat every now and then can't hurt, I reckon.'

Charlie shot Kim a look that said 'can we stop talking about food and get to the point?'

'Actually, Tom, we don't want to take up too much of your time. We'll pass on the cuppa, if that's okay,' said Kim.

Charlie's nerves and excitement ebbed and flowed, washing over him again just when he thought they'd receded.

'All right. So, how can I help you?' Tom asked curiously.

Kim looked at Charlie and he nodded to her to continue. She knew Tom, and it would be better coming from someone he trusted.

'Doris said that you might know a bit about John Parson – that you and him were mates back in the day?' asked Kim.

Charlie watched Tom's eyebrows shoot up.

'Wow, that's a name I haven't heard in a long time.' They stood quietly as they waited for him to continue. Tom sat back against the metal bar he'd been working on. 'We were mates, that's right. He left when he was just twenty to do his national service and his dad sold the farm to my dad.'

'This farm?' asked Kim, gesturing around them.

'Yes.' Tom cleared his throat. 'Um, the rest of the Parson farm is down where Harry lives. He's in the old homestead.'

'Oh, right. Where is Harry, by the way?' Kim asked, glancing around.

'He's getting the tractor going. Been parked up in the shed and the battery went flat. We're just trying to get ready for seeding. We're running a bit behind, what with fitting all these coulters onto the seeder bar. I just hope they get through the melons.'

'I hear you. We'll be doing the same thing next week.'

Charlie couldn't take the small talk any more. 'What else do you know about John? What happened to him?' he asked.

Tom frowned. 'Are you new to town, Charlie? I haven't seen you around before.'

'Yeah, just moved to town. I'm working at Elders Insurance.'

'Oh, righto.' Tom nodded. Charlie got the feeling he was avoiding his questions.

'Doris said John went to Vietnam. Did he die over there?' Kim asked, trying again.

Tom rubbed his face with his hand. 'Why do you want to know about John? That's all a long time ago. Not something I wish to talk about. He was a great mate, but after Nam . . .' Tom shrugged.

'I'm looking for him,' said Charlie. 'For family reasons.'

'Look, he had a rough time in Nam, came back suffering post-traumatic stress disorder, which landed him in jail. That's about all I can tell you.'

'Please, I'd be grateful for anything else you know. I need to find him if he's still alive,' said Charlie. Then he decided to bite the bullet. What did he have to lose? 'Tom, I think he's my father.'

Tom looked up at Charlie, his face white. 'Jesus, that I wasn't expecting,' he said quietly. Tom studied Charlie for a while and then finally spoke. 'Look, I feel it's not my place to tell you much more. It's a messy situation. I think the only person who can help you, who knows what really went on, is Harry. He went to war with John.' Tom glanced to the ground and kicked at a small rock.

Kim pulled on Charlie's arm and he could see she was desperate to say something but didn't.

'Do you mind if we head off now to see Harry?' asked Charlie.

Tom shook his head. 'Nah, mate, that's okay. Just go easy on him, all right?'

'Will do.'

The look on Tom's face was strange. Charlie wondered how he was coping, seeing his old friend's kid. Maybe it was a shock to him too? Could Tom see any family resemblance?

Kim and Charlie got back in the ute and drove down to the old tractor, but Harry wasn't there. It was almost lunchtime, though, and Harry had probably headed back for something to eat. They drove to Harry's place.

'Charlie,' said Kim as they drove. 'When I stayed at Harry's that time, I came across a photo of two guys in Vietnam. On the back was written "Harry and John".'

Charlie glanced at her, listening. He didn't think he could get his mouth to work at this moment. It was as dry as a salt lake.

'I didn't even think about the connection until now. Harry

told me once that his best mate died in Vietnam, so I just want to prepare you for the possibility that John may be dead.'

Charlie nodded again, and felt the heaviness of that word hit him. 'Kim, I've been preparing myself for that since I started out on this journey. I'm trying to approach it all without expectations. I'm just after answers.'

As they reached Harry's house, Charlie could see his ute outside, and his heart started to race. He pulled up at the house and spotted the old man by the verandah, filling up the water bowls for his dogs. This man who Kim had befriended knew John. It felt like they'd been going around in circles. Charlie had been here only yesterday, nervous. Yet today's visit had him anxious for different reasons.

Kim glanced at Charlie as they sat in the car. 'I know you're just after answers, but you're more involved than you think.'

'Yeah, I know. It's hard not to hope. I know I might be gutted by what I learn.'

Kim squeezed his hand. 'Let's go talk to Harry.' They got out of the car.

'Hello, Kim and Charlie, what brings you here again?' said Harry, standing up from the tap. 'Two visits in two days.' He held Molly and stopped her from jumping up on Kim.

'Just a chat, if you have time,' said Kim.

'Sounds serious. What's up?'

They sat on the edge of the verandah, and Charlie gave Kim a nudge.

She nodded, gave him a smile and then turned to Harry. 'We're here to ask you about a bloke called John Parson. Apparently he owned this place once,' said Kim, gesturing to the house.

Harry looked at them blankly, as if he hadn't heard what she'd said. His face was pale under his grey stubble.

'Is he the mate you lost in the war?'

Finally Harry spoke. 'That war took a lot of things, changed men, killed men, sent them crazy.' He shook his head. 'John was one of them.'

Charlie couldn't stop his hands from fidgeting. He clasped them together, holding his breath. Harry knew something, he could tell.

Harry's hands had begun to shake. Kim slid closer to him and held his hands in hers. The touch jolted him and he looked at her strangely. 'Sorry, is this okay?' she asked worriedly.

'It's just . . . I haven't had anyone hold my hand like that in a long, long time. I'd forgotten what it was like,' he said, his voice gravelly as tears welled in his eyes.

Kim's face fell and Charlie could tell just how much she had come to care for Harry. His pain was hers.

'What happened to John? And how did you come to live here, Harry?' she asked softly.

'I had nothing left, and I knew how much John loved this place. He talked about it often during the war. So when I needed to disappear, to recover, this is where I came. Tom owned the farm by then, but he understood and took me in. The war broke me. It broke many of us.' Harry squeezed her fingers, his eyes filled with pain. 'Why do you want to know about John?'

Kim turned to Charlie. He knew it was time to speak up.

'I want to know, Harry. I've been searching for him. I believe John is my father.'

Suddenly Harry drew his hands back and his brown eyes went black, as though metal doors had dropped down. 'No. No good comes from finding John.'

'Why?' said Charlie as Harry got up. He stood up too. 'What's so bad about John?' he asked, reaching for Harry's arm.

Harry started to turn red, a desperate look on his face. Charlie could see emotions building up.

'Because John killed his wife and left their son alone when he went to prison. Can you tell me how knowing that might help his kid?' Harry looked at Charlie. 'If you really believe he's your father, how does that help you?'

Charlie's mouth opened and closed. He almost physically reeled backwards. John had murdered his wife? Jesus.

'Now you see why you're better off not knowing. Stick with the family you have, son. Why ruin that?' Harry was shaking all over.

'Don't you think I deserve the truth, no matter how awful?' said Charlie, whose voice had raised an octave. His heart was racing.

'No. Quite frankly, I think you're better off as you are. John would want that. John doesn't want to be found, and he doesn't want any forgiveness. Just pretend he's dead.'

Harry pulled free of his grip and went inside, shutting his door firmly. Kim turned to Charlie, and they gazed at each other, open-mouthed.

'What the hell?' said Charlie. Then he thought about what Harry had said, and he smiled at Kim. 'He just told me John's alive!'

Chapter 36

'OH my god, you're right.' Kim shook her head. Tension lingered in the air. 'Charlie, I'm sorry. I wasn't sure how Harry would handle all this war talk. I understand it's hard for you too, but I'm conscious of his PTSD.' Kim could feel the thudding of her heart so strongly she felt faint. Her stomach was churning. 'How are you feeling?'

'Feeling? Shit, I don't know where to begin! Happy, sad, angry, hurt, relieved, exhausted.' Charlie put his hands on his hips and drew a breath. 'Did he really say that John had killed his wife? Am I their son? Does that mean that neither of my parents are my biological parents?' Charlie sat back down on the verandah, his face pale. 'I hoped that Mum had just had an affair but this . . . this is way more than I'd imagined.' Charlie's laugh was strained.

'Oh, Charlie, I'm so sorry.' Kim sat beside him and held him in her arms. 'I can't imagine what you're feeling right now.'

'Sometimes I wish I'd never found that card, and then other

times I've been so excited to think I might have family out there. And now my real father might be alive, but he's a murderer. I just . . . I don't know how to feel.' His shoulders dropped and he sagged against her.

Kim thought over his words. John was alive. Things started to coalesce in her mind: Marie saying Harry was dangerous, Harry living here on the Parson farm, Harry having lost his best mate in the war. Kim had assumed that mate was John, but if John had died in the war, how could he have killed his wife? Things just weren't adding up.

'Let's go,' she said suddenly.

'Go where?' said Charlie, as Kim pulled him up.

She grabbed his hand and led him to Harry's back door, which she opened without knocking.

Harry was sitting on the edge of his lounge chair, his shoulders hunched and head down. He stood up, startled. 'What?'

Kim pulled Charlie forward. 'Charlie, tell Harry your full name.'

'Why?'

'Just do it. What's on your birth certificate?' she asked him.

'Harrison Charles Macnamara,' said Charlie

The moment the words left Charlie's lips, Harry clutched his chest and drew in a jagged breath.

Clearly the name meant something to Harry. She knew she was on the right track.

Harry slowly tilted his head towards Charlie. 'What makes you think you're John's boy, anyway?' he said shakily.

'When my mum, Rachel, passed away, we found a card in her

papers addressed to me. It was a seventh birthday card from my dad. Only thing is, my dad wasn't J Parson, which was the name on the envelope. Since that time I've been searching for the truth.'

Kim watched as Harry squinted at Charlie, his mouth contorted. She couldn't tell if it was in agony or fear. Both men gazed at each other and then tears began to run down Harry's cheeks.

Kim knew in that moment, as Harry gazed at Charlie, that Harry was seeing his child for the first time in many years. 'He's your son, isn't he? You can tell,' she cried, tears welling up. 'You're really John, aren't you, Harry?'

'What?' said Charlie, glancing between the two of them.

Kim turned to him and nodded, her eyes shining. 'I just had a feeling. I knew if I pushed a little I'd be able to tell. I'm sorry,' she added.

Charlie turned to Harry and whispered, 'Is it true? Are you John Parson? Are you my real dad?' Kim felt his body tremble beside her. His hand grew clammy in hers as she held it tightly.

Charlie moved and sank down on the couch beside Harry, Harry's eyes on his face.

'Those eyes,' Harry choked out. 'You have your mother's eyes. I thought I'd never see them again.' He took one last look at Charlie before covering his face with his hands and beginning to sob.

'Wow.' Kim didn't know what else to say. 'I'll get you some water, Harry,' she said. Or was it John now?

Charlie stared at Harry while Kim went into the kitchen and got Harry some water, and grabbed the box of tissues off the fridge on her way past.

'Here.' She put the water and tissues on the coffee table beside Harry's chair and then sat down next to Charlie on the couch.

Harry grabbed a handful of tissues and tried to clean himself up, sobs still escaping. Then he had a sip of water and nearly spilt most of it as his shaking hands tried to control the glass.

'When you're ready, I'd like to know about my real family,' said Charlie.

Harry sniffed back the last of his tears and said nothing for a moment. Then, slowly, he nodded. 'Your family is your real family,' he said.

Charlie frowned. 'What do you mean? Doesn't all this mean that Rachel and Robert adopted me?'

'They did adopt you, but that doesn't mean they're not family. Your biological mother's name was Beth Fairchild.'

Charlie's eyes widened in recognition.

'Yes,' said Harry, nodding. 'Your mum was Rachel Fairchild before she got married. She was Beth's sister, and she took you in after . . .' Harry couldn't finish his sentence. After a moment he asked, 'Did Rachel ever mention Beth?'

Charlie nodded. His eyes were still wide. 'Yes. She said she died before I was born. Car crash.'

'Oh, I'm sorry,' said Harry, his voice cracking again. 'I wish it was that simple. Looking at you now, I can see you need the truth . . . but what I'm about to tell you may make you hate me. I wouldn't be surprised if you never wanted to see me again.' He paused, mopped at his eyes and took a sip of water.

Kim felt torn. Both these men were hurting, and both had special places in her heart.

Charlie let the old man gather his thoughts, waiting patiently. Eventually Harry spoke.

'I sent that card after I got out of prison. It was silly, but I guess I thought that with my freedom came a chance to get to know you again. But Rachel didn't want that. She'd raised you as her own and didn't want me to interfere. I'd given up all rights when I – I killed Beth,' he said, struggling over the words. 'I don't think Rachel ever forgave me. I will never forgive myself either.'

Charlie reached for Kim's hand, and his expression seemed lighter. 'So all these years my Aunty Beth was really my mum, and Rachel was in fact my aunty. Which makes my sister my cousin?'

Kim nodded. 'They're still your family,' she said, knowing how much this meant to him.

'The wattle. Of course,' said Charlie, his eyes glowing with amazement. 'My mum – I mean, Rachel – had a wattle tree in the yard of her house. It was special to her.'

'Yes, Beth loved them. She planted most of these ones from seeds she'd collected. After I got out of prison I came back here to the old farm, the only place I truly felt I belonged, and where Beth and I had dreamt of our future. Some days I feel as if she's here with me,' said Harry as tears filled his eyes again. He dabbed at them with the screwed-up tissues in his hand.

'Can I ask what happened to Beth? Do you mind?' asked Charlie. 'I'd really like to know.'

'Do you need more time, Harry? I know how hard this must be for you,' said Kim quickly. She was scared of what all these memories might provoke for her friend.

'I'm okay, lass. Charlie needs the truth, and after everything that's happened it's the least I can do for him. Actually, Kim, my old war trunk's in the spare room, under the bed. Could you please bring it here?'

Kim got up and touched his shoulder. 'Sure thing.'

She was soon back with the trunk, which she put down in front of Harry. He opened it and pulled out a photo, passing it to Charlie. Straightening his shoulders and with a deep breath, he began. 'It all started in Vietnam when I lost my best mate, Harrison Johnston, who was killed by the VC. And I killed the bloke who got him, with my own hands. Strangled him to death. I didn't realise then just how much that affected me. I buried the emotions, served out my time and headed home to Beth. Soon your mum and I had you, and it was her idea to name you Harrison Charles, after my mate Harry and her father Charles.'

'Yes, my pop,' said Charlie. 'Rachel said that's where my name came from. Pop died when I was twelve.' Charlie smiled shakily at the pieces falling into place.

Harry smiled in return, and continued. 'Life was going okay. I was trying to settle back in, which was made harder by the reception I got from some people. Vets weren't well-regarded in those days. I didn't like to leave the house much. And then one day Harry's wife, Clarissa, showed up with his daughter. She wanted to know how he'd died, of course, and we went through my war photos. That set off everything I'd been trying to repress. I went to the pub for a drink that night, and some guys picked on me for my war service. Anyway, we got into a fight, which is how I got this,' he said, pointing to his scar. 'But I'd tried strangling the fellow, and that stirred up my memories of the VC I'd killed. To cut a long story short, that night I had a nightmare. I relived Harry's death as if it was real, and I fought the VC again. Only when I woke up, I found I'd been fighting Beth,' he said, his voice almost a whisper.

'Do you need a break?' Kim asked, sensing his battle to keep himself together.

'No.' He took a deep breath and continued. 'I tried to save her, but she couldn't be revived. I couldn't believe what I'd done. I ended up in prison for manslaughter, and you went to live with Beth's sister. I was happy to suffer in prison, to pay for what I'd done, and I knew you were safe with Rachel. It wasn't until a few years down the track that it became known that Vets were suffering from the war, and we finally got a name for our condition: post-traumatic stress disorder. I worked with a prison counsellor who realised that's what I had, and, knowing that, it was a little easier to come to terms with what I'd done . . . but it didn't excuse it. Even though my sentence was reduced because of the PTSD and my good behaviour, to me it was still a life sentence. I felt like ending my life many times, but I knew that would be the coward's way out. I felt I deserved to live so I could suffer longer.'

Kim wiped away her tears, before reaching over and putting her hand on Harry's leg. 'Oh, Harry, you can't punish yourself forever. I know you didn't mean to do it.' One moment had changed his life forever, and he'd paid a high price.

'What prompted you to send the birthday card?' asked Charlie.

'As I said, I'd just got out of prison. I wanted to let you know just how much I thought about you. I called one time and spoke to Rach, to see how you were, and after that she made me promise to leave you alone. She was right. You didn't need to know, it would have only confused you. But I'm bloody glad she kept that card, because seeing you today is a miracle. I feel as if Beth is in this room with us. She lives so strongly in you.' He smiled, his eyes filled with emotion.

Kim reached for a tissue at the same time as Charlie, both of them wiping away tears.

'Can you tell me about yourself? About your life?' asked Harry.

Charlie nodded and gave Harry a quick summary.

Harry nodded as he listened. 'Your mum, Beth . . . she was so different to Rach. She loved it out here on the farm. We lived in this house for a while before we sold up when I went to war. She was a hard-working woman, Beth – much like Kim here. I think that's why I've loved your company so much, Kim. You remind me of Beth. You have her strength and independence.'

'Must be why I like Kim myself,' said Charlie, putting his arm around her. 'And it explains why I feel so at home out here in the country. I didn't expect any of this when I came to Lake Grace. I certainly didn't expect that I'd find you. I hoped to learn some details, maybe find a grave, but not find the man himself.'

'It's been a shock to my system.' Harry did look worn-out. 'Have you got time to hang around for a bit? There's some stuff I can show you.'

'Yes, sure,' Charlie replied, after glancing at Kim.

Harry pointed to the war photo. 'That's the bloke you were named after, and the guy whose name I took. I was worried people would put two and two together if I came back to this area as John. So I called myself Harry, and Tom kept my secret. He's been a good mate since we were little. I owe him a lot.'

'I've never been called Harry, or Harrison, even though it's on my birth certificate,' said Charlie. 'I didn't even know Harrison was my first name until recently. Should we start calling you John, or have you been Harry for too long?'

Harry shrugged. 'Maybe it's time to go back to John, to stop pretending. I am John, and I do have a past I'm not proud of. To be honest, I think having you call me John would make me very happy.' He bent over and pulled out from the trunk a little blanket and some tractor toys. 'These were yours too.' He then pulled out some photos of John, Beth and baby Harry on the lawn of their house in Perth. His eyes glistened with fresh tears as he gazed at the photos.

'Look, baby photos of you,' Kim said. She empathised so deeply with Harry – or John, as she knew she would now call him. She knew he would probably punish himself forever for what he had done. She could tell he'd loved Beth deeply, which only made the circumstances more bittersweet. Who could have imagined that when she'd met John on that stormy night, it would lead to a connection to the man beside her, the man she'd grown to love?

'And these are letters that I wrote to Beth, and ones of hers I kept. Neither of us could part with them. Now they're yours. I hope they give you some insight into how amazing your mother was. And just how much I loved her.' John put them back in the trunk. 'This whole trunk is for you.'

Charlie nodded as he gazed at the trunk and its treasure trove of history. Kim smiled at Charlie. She could tell he'd found out more than he'd ever dreamt.

'Do you mind if I come out here sometimes to visit, John?' asked Charlie as he tried out the new name.

'I would like that very much,' said John. His lips twisted together as he tried to hold back a fresh round of sobs, but the tears fell thick and fast again. Only this time they were happy ones.

It was much later when John got up to call Tom and let him know what was happening. He went to the office, giving Charlie a moment alone with Kim. 'Poor guy's probably wondering if we're all okay and what happened to the tractor.'

'How are you coping with all this?' she asked him, resting her hand on his leg.

'Better than he is,' Charlie said, with a warm smile. 'I just feel relieved, I think, to know that Mum, Dad and Sarah are still my real family. And now I have a dad again. I really want to get to know him.'

'He's a good bloke. He's done his time and deserves some happiness with you,' said Kim.

'I can tell how much he loved his wife. I can't imagine what he went through back then. I can't hold what he did against him.'

'Does this mean you'll be sticking around here?' she asked. She hoped her voice didn't give away her hope.

'It does. But not because of him. I could drive back anytime to visit. It's you I want to stay here for.' Charlie reached out, touching her cheek softly. 'I can't handle the thought of being apart from you. I'm crazy in love with you. Maybe it's too soon, but I can't help the way I feel. You're the most amazing woman I've ever met. Could you ever love an old guy like me?'

Kim melted as his dimples appeared. She stroked the silver strands in his hair and smiled. 'I don't know,' she said with a teasing smile. 'Depends on how well he kisses.'

He leant over and kissed her softly, with so much passion and tenderness that she forgot where she was.

An hour later, Kim sat on John's verandah with all the dogs at her feet, watching John and Charlie walking together through the front paddock. The sun was bright and bounced off the tall dead grass left over from the fast-fading summer. At her feet was a carpet of green that had sprung up from the rain. Her heart felt full, her eyes were sore from crying, but she was unbelievably happy. A father and son were reunited.

Epilogue

KIM wrapped her arms around Charlie. There was a chill in the air, but that wasn't what motivated her. 'Are you okay?' she asked.

They stood in the cemetery in Perth on a bleak, overcast day. Somehow the grey of the headstones dotted around them matched the sky, but in between there were bursts of colour from the beautiful flower beds and the dark green grass that covered the ground. It was quiet except for the faint sound of the breeze whistling through the large old trees that made this place seem like an island in the city. The pines acted as a sound wall against the traffic and the outside world.

Charlie stood strong beside her, wearing a black beanie and a leather jacket, and even in the sombre setting Kim couldn't help but notice how sexy he looked. Kim watched him closely, waiting for his answer.

'Yeah. I think it's better to wait here,' he said. 'He needs to do this on his own.'

From the next row of headstones across, they watched as a man in an overcoat stepped towards his wife's grave. John paused when he found it, his hand going to his mouth. He knelt down beside the grave and placed bright-yellow flowers by her rectangular headstone. From where they stood they could see his shoulders begin to shake. The picture before them was harrowing but poignant, an image of loss that you might find hanging in a gallery. Kim clung to Charlie as she watched John mourn his wife. Her heart ached for the pain she knew he was in. Finally he could say a proper goodbye.

A cold breeze drifted across the cemetery, bringing with it a mournful sound that could only come from somewhere deep. It sent chills up her spine.

'I love you so much that I think I can understand a little of how he feels,' said Kim. She gazed intently at Charlie. 'You're my world, you know that?'

Charlie kissed her forehead. 'You're my world too, Kim. Thanks for coming along with us.' He held her hand and walked her towards the pine love seat that was nestled away near a flower garden bed.

'It's really pretty here. A nice place to rest,' she said as they sat down. 'I'm glad to be here with you both. I'm glad you brought him here. I think he needed this.'

'I know. Can you imagine losing the one you love and not having the chance to say goodbye?' Charlie blinked back tears and she saw his Adam's apple bob up and down as he swallowed his emotion. 'Life is short. I want to be happy in the time I have left.'

'Me too,' she said, squeezing him tightly.

He held her chin in his hand, brushing her lips with his thumb. The look he gave her warmed her soul. It was one she'd never seen on any other man and it was why she knew that what she had with Charlie was special. He truly loved her and there wasn't a bone in her body that doubted it. 'Do you know how much I love you?' she said softy.

'Nowhere near as much as I love you,' he said with a wink.

Charlie's eyes changed to a deeper shade of blue as his hand now caressed her face. He took a deep breath and held it for a long time. Just as she was starting to worry about what was on his mind, his words flew out in a rush.

'Kim, you're the love of my life. We don't know what the future may bring but I want to spend whatever time we have left together. Will you marry me?'

Kim raised her eyebrows. She'd not been expecting that and yet it didn't surprise her. It was exactly how she felt too.

'When I'm divorced properly, of course.' He smiled cheekily, letting go of her chin and reaching into his pocket. He pulled out a ring. 'This might not be the place . . . but I couldn't wait any longer.' He paused and cleared his throat but the tears formed in his eyes. 'Seeing John . . .'

Kim reached for his hand and gave it a squeeze. 'I know. I understand.' Kim felt hot tears roll down her cold cheek as she smiled. 'I'd love to be your wife, Charlie.'

He grinned through his own tears and slipped the large solitaire diamond onto her finger.

'It's so beautiful.' Kim loved the simplicity of it. It was her to a tee. 'So does this mean you'll finally move in with me?' she asked. She'd been trying to get him to move out to the farm with her. Well, he did stay over a lot – in a way they already lived together. 'I want the farm to be your home too.'

'You don't have to sell it, Kim. I knew marrying you would mean marrying the farm as well and I'd never ask you to give that up. Never. Yes, I think it's time I moved in properly.'

Kim knew now he'd be settling in for good. The thought of it made her grin uncontrollably.

'I can't wait to tell Loz,' she said. 'Her first question will be *When's the date?* followed by *When will you have kids?*'

Charlie raised an eyebrow. 'I was thinking of starting as soon as possible. I'm not getting any younger, you know.'

Kim couldn't help but brush the stubble along his cheek. The patches of grey fascinated her, and on Charlie they made him appear wiser and sexier. She loved everything about this bloke. 'I'll keep you young,' she said with a wink. Kim glanced at her ring again in awe. She'd never thought this day would come. 'Does your sister know?' she asked.

'Yes, so expect to be mobbed by her and Laura when we get back to her place.' Charlie glanced across the lawn to John. 'Dad knows too. He loves you almost as much as I do.'

Kim felt the waterworks start to build. 'I love hearing you call him Dad, and I love the way it makes his eyes sparkle when he hears it too.' Her cheeks felt numb with cold but the rest of her body was burning.

'Wait until you start calling him Dad,' said Charlie with a smile. After a deep breath he said, 'When I came to Lake Grace I felt as if I had lost a family and I didn't know who I was. Truth is, I was still me. And I ended up finding a much bigger family. I also found a community, and now I have a relationship with my real father. It's funny how life turns out.'

'You also found a wife,' said Kim.

'That I did.'

Then he kissed her as if there was no tomorrow.

ACKNOWLEDGEMENTS

I can't quite remember how this story came to me. Maybe it was after seeing veterans' names listed on local war memorials or maybe it was just my knowing local men who had been to Vietnam, but I felt compelled to write about it. I didn't know much about the Vietnam War, most of what I knew came from *Tour of Duty*, but embarking on this journey was an eye-opener.

Firstly I want to say that I've tried to write about Vietnam as truthfully as I can. I have woven facts into the work but I have manipulated certain events and happenings to suit my story. For example, I have used the actual names of battalion operations and regiments, but they may not fit with the times and dates cited. I've tried to write an engaging story while conveying the war realistically. I couldn't have done this without lots of research. And it was quite shocking to learn that many soldiers came back from the war with PTSD, which was only officially recognised as a diagnosis in 1980. This revelation played a big part in how *The Family Secret* turned out.

A huge thank you must go to Ned Dixon and Bob Eddington, two Vietnam Vets who gave up their time to talk to me. I was truly honoured to hear about their experiences, as they have helped bring my book to life. I've blended the two men's stories, which I hope I've done justice, and created a few myself. Thanks Ned and Bob, I couldn't have done it without your help.

As with every book, there are many to thank. To the people who are out there pimping my books, love your work! To friends like Lea, Jacinta and Jeni, and to pretty much the whole town of Pingaring – I do live in the best place! – thanks for the support. Then there is my extended family: my cousins, aunties, uncles, sisters, brothers, parents. I'm probably biased but I do have the best family too. You guys are always there if I need, even if it's just to keep me company on a relaxing break in Bremer. (Thanks Julene and Jas!) Our recent Christmas family reunion is one I'll never forget!

To my bro and sis-in-law, Chad and Mel, thanks for letting us use your place like a hotel. We are loving the regular catch-ups! To my parents, thanks for your help – for reading my work, for listening to my ideas and helping with the kids. You name it, you guys are always there. And to my own family, hubby and the kids, thanks for putting up with my 'computer time' and my blank looks when I'm off creating stories in my mind. Love you all heaps.

My Penguin family. Thank you Ali as always for doing such a wonderful job to make my words shine. You're the best. Thanks also to Lou, to Maria, publicist extraordinaire, to Fay, Clem, Julia, Kim and anyone I may have missed who has helped me over the years. We've been on a long journey together since I received that amazing first email from you, Ali, in August 2008.

To the RRR ladies, thank you for inspiring Kim and for inspiring me. I'm truly honoured to rub shoulders with such amazing ladies. We are all like Kim, fighting to preserve, improve and support our regions. To my readers, if you haven't already, check out rrr.wa.gov.au and see what we are about. Also have a look at campkulin.com.au. Tanya Dupagne and the team at Camp Kulin do an amazing job! Thanks for your help, Tanya.

I have some great author buddies who are always there to help out, you all know who you are. (Pretty much most of the RWA girls!) Special mentions to Cathryn, Margareta and Rach. Especially you, Rachael Johns. Not only are you a great sounding board, idea helper, friend and tour mate, but you also offer up your home whenever I visit the city. I treasure our friendship.

Massive hugs to all the readers who have come along on this journey with me and who take time out to send emails or comment on Facebook about my stories. Your thirst for the next book keeps me coming back to write more.

ALSO BY FIONA PALMER

The Saddler Boys

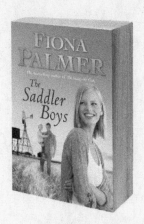

'This is a book about rural Australia, love gained and lost, and fighting for what you believe in. But, unlike many books in the same genre, The Saddler Boys is subtly about so much more.'
THE WEEKLY TIMES

Schoolteacher Natalie has always been a city girl. So when she takes up a posting at a tiny school in remote Western Australia, it proves quite the culture shock. But she is soon welcomed by the inquisitive locals, particularly young student Billy and his intriguing single father, Drew.

As Nat's school comes under threat of closure, and Billy's estranged mother turns up out of the blue, Nat finds herself fighting for the township and battling with her heart. Torn between her society life in Perth and the rural community that needs her, Nat must risk losing it all to find out what she's really made of – and where she truly belongs.

'Palmer's passion for the land bleeds into the story, and her scenes are vivid and genuine, just as her characters are.'
BOOK'D OUT

'Fiona Palmer has well and truly earned her place as a leading writer of one of Australia's much-loved genres.'
COUNTRYMAN

The Sunnyvale Girls

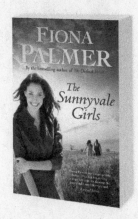

Three generations of Stewart women share a deep connection to their family farm, but a secret from the past threatens to tear them apart.

Widowed matriarch Maggie remembers a time when the Italian prisoners of war came to work on their land, changing her heart and her home forever. Single mum Toni has been tied to the place for as long as she can recall, although farming was never her dream. And Flick is as passionate about the farm as a girl could be, despite the limited opportunities for love.

When a letter from 1946 is unearthed in an old cottage on the property, the Sunnyvale girls find themselves on a journey into their own hearts and across the world to Italy. Their quest to solve a mystery leads to incredible discoveries about each other, and about themselves.

The
Family
Farm

Isabelle Simpson longs to take over the family farm, but her ailing father won't give her a chance. Their stand-off threatens to tear the family apart. Handsome neighbour Will Timmins holds the secret to building bridges between them, if Izzy can forgive him his past.

Izzy is forced to make a tough decision – sacrifice an exciting new romance or relinquish her lifelong dream? But then unexpected tragedy falls on the farm, and Izzy is thrown the greatest challenge of all.

As she gathers with family and friends by the shade of the gum-tree tavern, confessions are made, long-held secrets are revealed and hearts are set free.

'A good old-fashioned love story.'
SUNDAY MAIL BRISBANE

'A heartwarming romance about finding true love
and following your dreams.'
FEMAIL.COM.AU